"You're right, you k

"About what?" she asked, deigning to turn around and face him.

"You're not in danger tonight." He hesitated, and she moved another step. "But don't become complacent. Danger can come from many directions."

He saw only the bottom half of her now as she moved on. And then her feet touched the seventh step, for he'd been unconsciously counting as she climbed. She was unmoving, and he waited.

"I think the biggest danger is not from you, Nicholas, but from within *me*." One foot moved and then lowered again to settle beside the other. "I fear I'll make a fool of myself one of these days if I don't walk away from you."

"But not tonight?" he asked, so quietly he wondered if she had heard him.

Her feet shifted, then moved upward, her voice trailing behind her.

"No, not tonight."

Reading, writing and research—**Carolyn Davidson**'s life in three simple words. At least that area of her life having to do with her career as a historical romance author. The rest of her time is divided among husband, family and travel—her husband, of course, holding top priority in her busy schedule. Then there is their church and the church choir in which they participate. Their sons and daughters, along with assorted spouses, are spread across the eastern half of America, together with numerous grandchildren. Carolyn welcomes mail at her post office box, PO Box 2757, Goose Creek, SC 29445, USA.

Recent titles by the same author:

THE FOREVER MAN
THE MIDWIFE
THE BACHELOR TAX
TANNER STAKES HIS CLAIM
THE WEDDING PROMISE
MAGGIE'S BEAU
A MARRIAGE BY CHANCE
THE TEXAN

TEMPTING
A TEXAN

Carolyn Davidson

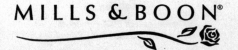

All the characters in this book have no existence outside the imagination of the author, and have no relation whatsoever to anyone bearing the same name or names. They are not even distantly inspired by any individual known or unknown to the author, and all the incidents are pure invention.

First published in Great Britain 2005
Harlequin Mills & Boon Limited,
Eton House, 18-24 Paradise Road, Richmond, Surrey TW9 1SR

© Carolyn Davidson 2003

ISBN 0 263 84386 6

Set in Times Roman 10½ on 11½ pt.
04-0905-86388

Printed and bound in Spain
by Litografia Rosés S.A., Barcelona

All the characters in this book have no existence

TEMPTING
A TEXAN

Chapter One

Collins Creek, Texas, April, 1897

"I don't have a sister," Nicholas muttered beneath his breath, reading for the third time a scribbled message carried into his office only moments before.

"It seems you do," the sheriff said, grinning widely. He stood in the doorway, the messenger of tidings ill-received; and if the smile he wore was any indication, seeing Nicholas Garvey at a loss was well worth the time he'd spent delivering the message.

"Are you sure Henry got this right?" Nicholas asked, his mouth taut as he lifted the lined paper for the sheriff's scrutiny. "Were you there when it came over the wire?"

"Sure was," Cleary answered. "That's why I offered to deliver it by hand. I figured it was important when Henry sputtered out the words and then tried to cover up his scribbles when I looked over his shoulder." He moved to a chair in front of the wide, mahogany desk. One booted foot lifted and rested against his other knee as he removed his hat and appeared to settle in.

"Did you read the whole thing?" Nicholas asked, sinking into his own chair, a scowl creasing his forehead.

"Nope. Only got as far as the words…" He looked up at the ceiling, his thought processes obviously in good order as he spoke. "Let's see. It said something about you being named a guardian of your sister's child. A girl, I think."

"There's been a mix-up somewhere," Nicholas growled with a ferocity that matched his dark, angry visage. "I've never had a sister."

"Somebody back East doesn't agree with you," Cleary said mildly.

"Well, they can just look elsewhere for a dumping ground," Nicholas said harshly. "I don't know what this lawyer expects of me, but raising a child is not on my schedule."

"You seem to be quite taken with your godson," Cleary said, his index finger following the crease in his hat brim. He looked up, his initial reaction to the message apparently diluted by Nicholas's somber behavior.

"That's different, and you know it. I won't be saddled with a child purported to be my niece, when I know good and well that my background doesn't include her mother."

Cleary stood up, a lengthy procedure, adjusting his gun belt and glancing toward the open door. "I don't suppose…" He hesitated, frowning.

"What?" Nicholas rose from the depths of his leather chair, discarding the wrinkled message on his desktop. Hands widespread on his blotter, he leaned forward. "You know a little about the law, Cleary. Is there anything I can do to put a crimp in this?"

"Is the child on her way here?" Cleary's innocent expression denied the knowledge he'd gained by reading the message, and Nicholas felt the urge to grind his teeth in frustration.

"You know damn well she is." He glanced down at the scribbled note. "Accompanied by a companion, is what it says here."

"Who sent it?" Cleary asked.

"A law firm. Under orders from the court. According to this, the child is alone in the world."

"Well," Cleary drawled quietly. "You oughta make a good pair, then. I've never heard you mention any family."

"That's because I don't have one." Frustration emphasized every word as Nicholas repeated his original statement. "Where the hell somebody got the idea of sticking me with a five-year-old is beyond me. I've got other fish to fry."

"This wouldn't have anything to do with Patience Filmore, would it?"

Nicholas looked up, suddenly feeling defensive. "I've spent some time with her."

"Planning marriage?"

"Not yet. But it's a definite possibility." And yet, his instincts were even now pushing that reasoning to the back burner. At least until this matter was cleared up.

"You want to send back a reply?" The lawman motioned to the crumpled message, lifted an eyebrow and waited.

"And what good would that do? According to this, my visitors will arrive any day now."

From the doorway a young man, his hair slicked back with pomade, his shirt starched to within an inch of its life, cleared his throat. "Sir. Mr. Garvey."

"Yes." The single syllable held the force of a bullet and the clerk winced.

"You have a visitor, sir. A young lady, accompanied by a child, sir."

"Well…sh—" A hissing sound died upon leaving his lips as Nicholas turned again to Cleary. "I don't believe it. How could she have gotten here so soon?" He snatched up the message, smoothing it across his wide palm. "Has the morning train arrived already?"

"Yep. Pretty near two hours ago." Cleary turned back and settled once more in the chair he'd vacated. "Maybe I'll stick around for a while, after all."

Nicholas nodded wearily at the clerk. "Show her in." And then he turned to Cleary, his eyes narrowing in an unmistakable warning. "Not a word from you."

A look of solemn promise was obliterated by the glittering humor in the sheriff's eyes as he watched his friend stride to the doorway. And then, as if the woman who appeared just beyond the threshold had the ability to change his demeanor, the sheriff stood as she spoke to the banker, her accent soft and genteel.

"I'm Carlinda Donnelly," she said, extending a hand. "I've brought your niece to you, Mr. Garvey."

Nicholas felt helpless anger engulf him as the russet-haired female waited for the courtesy of his palm to meet hers. At his obvious reluctance to offer her the simple gesture, her stilted smile faltered, and as he watched, her hand fell to her side. It was snatched up by a tiny female creature whose eyes widened in dismay as she gazed at him.

Eyes the exact color of blue he'd observed in his mirror every morning of his life. Her dark hair hung in curls past her shoulders, and her petite form was garbed in a dainty flowered dress that met the tops of high-buttoned shoes. The delicate rosebud mouth trembled as she spoke.

"Are you my uncle?" she asked timidly. And then she looked up at the woman beside her, her whisper loud in the silence as she confided her fear. "I don't think he likes me," she said, her eyes filling with tears.

Nicholas cleared his throat. "I don't know if I'm your uncle or not," he admitted after a moment. "If I am, it's news to me. I'd have sworn up until ten minutes ago that I was alone in the world." He squatted before the child, his sharp gaze taking in the long lashes, the wide brow, and finally, the small beauty mark beside her mouth. Without thinking, his hand rose to touch an identical brown speck beside his upper lip.

"It isn't a matter of not liking you," he said quietly, unable to be cruel to an innocent child. "It's just that I can't imagine who decided you were my responsibility."

"A judge in New York City," the woman said quietly. "Her mother and father were in an accident while traveling in Europe. A fatal accident. She became a ward of the court until your whereabouts were discovered. I'd been caring for her in their absence, and I've been hired now by her father's estate to bring her to you. Another party is vying for her custody, but the judge decided in your favor."

He needn't have given me his blessing. Nicholas scowled at the thought.

Miss Donnelly retrieved a package from beneath her left arm and placed it on his desk. "This is the result of the court hearing, and includes a copy of the will. I'm sure you'll find everything you need in here."

He glanced down at the envelope, then at the child, his gaze caught by the turmoil in her face. "May I ask for an introduction?"

Carlinda Donnelly nodded quickly. "Of course. This is Amanda."

As if hearing her name spoken aloud was a signal, the child extended her dainty fist, uncurling the fingers as she offered it to the man before her. "I'm pleased to meet you, sir," she whispered, obviously well mannered and primed for this introduction.

Nicholas took the fingers in his, looking down at the hand that was resting like a small bird in his palm. "Hello, Amanda," he said politely, then glanced up at the woman beside him. "Miss Donnelly—" He broke off abruptly, as words failed him. What did a man say to a woman who had just invaded his life, whose courteous gestures he had scorned, and who waited now for his reaction to her presence?

He glanced aside at Cleary and noted the subtle shake of the man's head and slight lift of shoulders. No help there. In fact, it looked obvious to him that the sheriff was about to make an exit, standing and brushing the brim of his hat.

"I believe my wife's holding dinner for me," Cleary said, smiling blandly at the visitors and waiting for the doorway to clear.

"I'm in your way," Carlinda said. "I'm so sorry." Stepping back, she allowed him to pass, almost swaying on her feet. She looked confused, travel-weary and disheartened, Nicholas decided. None of this was her fault, and yet he found her a ready target for his anger as he watched Cleary stride toward the front of the bank.

"I'm not certain what I'm expected to do, Miss Donnelly," Nicholas said abruptly. "I haven't the proper facilities to care for a child."

"Are you married?" she asked quietly.

He shook his head. "Certainly not. I'm a businessman, and marriage is not in my immediate future. Right now, I see no need for a woman in my home."

She flinched at his words. "You don't *like* women?" she asked, flicking a look of conjecture in his direction. "I mean—" Her mouth thinned as if she regretted the inference her words suggested.

"I like women just fine. In their proper place," he retorted.

"And that is…"

Her hesitance was deliberate. He knew it from his depths, and even as he bristled at her words, he silently saluted her bravery at defying him. "Wherever I decree they are the most useful," he said smoothly, watching as a red tide washed upward from her throat to cover her cheeks. Beneath her bonnet, her hair was a deep shade of auburn, caught up in a heavy, somewhat untidy knot at her nape. Several curling strands touched her forehead, softening the brown eyes that glared in his direction.

"I see," she said harshly, although he very much doubted that she was nearly as sophisticated as she would like him to believe. "Well, perhaps you'll have to seek out someone to help you in your care of Amanda," Miss Donnelly suggested. "I'm only the person hired to deliver her into your hands, sir. I suppose there's no reason not to be on the early train tomorrow morning, back to Saint Louis and then on to New York."

She's bluffing. The thought pleased him. "I don't think that's an option," he replied smoothly. "You can't leave me here with a child and sashay off without a by-your-leave. It would be grossly unfair to—" he looked down at the little girl, and then continued with a cool smile "—to the child."

Her eyes narrowed, and her chin lifted defensively. "I beg your humble pardon, Mr. Garvey, but I can do anything I please. I am not a servant in your employ."

"That's true enough, but this is a small town, ma'am. You might find it difficult to board the morning train, should I decide to say otherwise."

"You'd keep me here against my will?" Her blush faded quickly, leaving her pale beneath a naturally creamy complexion. Her lips were compressed, their fullness narrowed by the gesture, and he caught sight of a glimpse of panic in her brown eyes.

"No, of course I wouldn't. I didn't mean to say that," Nicholas answered quietly. He glanced down at Amanda, whose eyes were glued on his face. Sparing her a quick smile, he directed his attention to the young woman before him. It might be time to backtrack and let her off the hook. "Let's rethink this a bit. I'll make it worth your while to stay. This whole thing needs to be sorted out."

"And where would you suggest I live while I'm at your beck and call?" she asked. Her jaw was taut and he sensed a quality of brittleness in her demeanor, as if she might shatter into a thousand pieces should she loosen her grip on the situation enveloping her.

It would not do for the woman to lose control, here in the bank where he prided himself on his immaculate reputation. He reached for her, grasping her wrist and drawing her into his office. Reaching behind her, he closed the door. A hum of voices reached him and he winced, aware that several customers had been privy to the low, murmured argument he'd allowed himself to be involved in.

She reacted to his maneuvers, tugging at his hold as he led her from the door to a chair across the room. "Please release me, sir," she said sharply. Beside her, Amanda caught her breath in a sob; and Miss Donnelly looked down, her face reflecting the sadness the child expressed.

Nicholas felt a tide of confusion sweep over his entire being. Always in control, priding himself on his grasp of business and aware of the enormity of his influence, he'd never felt so totally at sea in his entire career. His early years were another story. But in the past twenty years, he'd come a long way from the young man who'd dug through the refuse in alleyways for food.

Befriended at fifteen by a man whose life he'd saved during a nighttime robbery attempt, he'd been sent to school, then on to a university. His boyish rescue of the wealthy stranger, who, beset by thieves, had taken the scrawny youth home with him, led to a future he'd never in his wildest dreams thought to hold within his grasp.

His upward climb in the financial market, bulwarked by the tidy fortune left to him by his childless benefactor, had led Nicholas here. Here to Collins Creek, a small town north of Dallas, where he was known only as the owner of the town's bank. A situation he'd chosen, where peace and security were his for the asking. Where he was considered to be, over the past two years, the town's most successful citizen, and given the friendship of the simple folk surrounding him. His past was just that, those years behind him as he sought the tranquillity available in this small town.

Now, in barely thirty minutes' time, he was swept back to that life in the city by the appearance of a young woman and her charge, a child alleged to be his niece. Miss Donnelly was dressed in a simple gown, yet wore the look of a woman from New York. That distinctive air of refinement clung to her, and her voice was overlaid with a soft, cultured accent she did not attempt to conceal.

Yet, there was no guarantee she was what she appeared to be. He'd learned early on not to take people at face value, and years of living had not eased the pain of experience. She faced him with pride and anger at war within her, her expressive face reflecting the turmoil of the situation in which she found herself.

Crouching beside Amanda, only the crown of the woman's hat was visible to his discerning eye. It was circled by a narrow band of grosgrain ribbon, simple, yet stylish, and beneath its brim, he sensed her smile was warm as she spoke to the child.

"It's all right, Amanda," she said quietly, the soothing syllables having an immediate effect.

"Where will we go, Linnie?"

Linnie? Nicholas felt a warmth expand within his chest as the child spoke the name she'd chosen for her nurse. And he inhaled sharply as he considered his harshness. "You'll go to my home," he said, dropping to one knee, the better to look squarely at the little girl. No matter the woman's mission here, the child deserved decent treatment.

Yet Amanda appeared not to welcome his offer. "You

don't like us," she said firmly. "And I don't think I like you, either. You're not a nice man."

"That's not polite," Miss Donnelly stated matter-of-factly, holding Amanda's hand tightly. And then she turned her head to look directly at Nicholas. "I'm sure there will be room at the hotel for us. We wouldn't want to inconvenience you. I'll keep Amanda for the night and talk to her about the situation. I can't force the issue with her."

Nicholas grasped the woman's elbow and assisted her to her feet, rising to look down into her dark eyes. "I have a comfortable home just down the street," he said politely. "My housekeeper will be happy to settle you in. In fact, we'll leave now and I'll see to it myself. Amanda will be more comfortable there than in a hotel. You and I will talk this evening, Miss Donnelly."

She attempted to withdraw from his hold and his fingers only tightened, putting force behind his statement. "There isn't room to argue the point," he told her flatly. "The child must be weary, and I think you're ready for a chance to sit and relax, yourself." He reached toward the rack by the door, snatching his wide-brimmed hat from a hook, then ushered her from his office.

"I'm going home for a while, Thomas," he said to his clerk. "I'll return soon. In the meantime, send someone to the train station to collect Miss Donnelly's things. And those of the child. Have them delivered to my house."

The wide-eyed young man nodded, his gaze enquiring as he shot a sidelong glance at Nicholas's visitors. "Yes, sir, Mr. Garvey. I'll handle things."

The door opened onto a wide, wooden sidewalk, and Nicholas offered his arm, turning to the right. To her credit, Miss Donnelly accepted his gesture, and he looked down to see her narrow fingers ease past the crook of his elbow to rest on his forearm. A warmth settled into his flesh where that elegant hand rested, and his eyes sought her face, intrigued by the rush of heat that coursed throughout his body.

Her face averted, she seemed to be concentrating on the child who walked nicely on her other side, who, even as he watched, lifted a tiny hand to cover a yawn. He was right, he decided. These two females needed a place to rest, a cool, clean refuge in which to recuperate from their travels. He could think of no other place more fitting than his own home. He'd spend the rest of the day deciding his next move.

Thus far she'd accomplished her purpose, although living in Nicholas Garvey's home had been more her goal for Amanda than for herself. Irene had wanted her brother to have his niece, and if being under his roof would accomplish that purpose, Carlinda would stay as long as necessary. She recalled her threat to leave and shook her head. He'd upset her and she'd responded with haste, and now she'd be the one to backtrack.

Her only hindrance in staying here until Amanda was well settled was the appeal of the man himself to her female person. Handsome didn't begin to describe him, and autocratic didn't start to pay just due to his confident aura.

She looked around the comfortable room she'd been assigned and released a deep breath. The house was large, two-storied and surrounded on the front and two sides by a wide veranda. Sitting over a hundred feet from the sidewalk, it was situated behind a tall fence built of wood, painted white and woven in an intricate pattern, with a wide gate and arbor at its center.

Her surroundings were cool and comfortable, with fine carpets and gracefully hung draperies at the windows. She'd noted comfortable couches and gleaming wooden tables filling the parlor, visible from the central foyer, where a dining room flanked it on the opposite side of the wide hallway.

As she'd climbed one side of the two-pronged staircase to the second floor, she'd looked back to see her elegantly clad host watching her progress from below. His lifted hand offered a salute, and then he'd turned to depart through the front door.

Katie, the woman who kept this place immaculate, had given Carlinda a searching glance as she opened the bedroom door and ushered her inside. "I've already put the wee one in the room next door," she said. "Tucked her in nicely, and barely had her shoes and dress off before she curled up and closed her eyes."

That was one mark in the woman's favor, Carlinda decided. Treating Amanda kindly gave the housekeeper points. It bode well for the child's future.

Now, Carlinda walked to the double windows overlooking the front yard and the street, easing aside the white curtain, the better to search the sidewalk below. He was there, walking briskly, crossing the street almost a hundred yards away. His stride was long, his back straight, his hat at a jaunty angle atop dark hair.

She'd noticed his eyes first, that brilliant blue that proclaimed him as Black Irish. The same blue that had been replicated in the small face of the child she'd brought to him. He was wary. Of that there was no doubt. And well he might be. Nicholas Garvey was a man with secrets, a man with a fortune at his fingertips, and a past that didn't lend itself to investigation. She'd known all of that. But she hadn't expected the effect of dark hair and blue eyes, and the flash of white teeth as he spoke and smiled.

She knew of his past, had heard his sister's whispered words of confession before she left Amanda behind as she'd set out on the final journey of her life. That she'd been able to furnish the court with a sealed document identifying Nicholas Garvey as the child's only living relative had been fortuitous for Amanda's well-being.

Irene knew about her brother, knew of his success, and was shamed by her father's series of affairs, one of which had produced Nicholas. Before her marriage to the man who'd given her child a name, she had refused to call on Nicholas for help. But after Irene's death, Carlinda determined to make the rich financier aware of his sister's life and death, and place him under obligation to the child left behind by her mother's tragic end.

"I'm doing my best, Irene," she whispered, tracing a line in the wavy glass before her. "He'll never know, not from me anyway, about Amanda's beginnings." Her sigh was deep, her eyes filling with tears as she turned away from the window. Unless she had overplayed her hand, Nicholas Garvey would do his best to persuade her to remain here in his home, at least until Amanda was settled in and made a part of the household. And she would be wise not to protest too much.

There was nothing left for her in New York City.

She awoke late in the afternoon in the big bed, its comfortable mattress forming to her slender body, and for a moment she looked around her in confusion. And then her memory kicked in and she recalled the long climb up the staircase, remembered looking back at the dark-clad figure watching her from below. He wore the look of a worthy opponent, and she girded herself for whatever he might say or do. Swinging her feet to the floor she looked around, searching the room for her dress.

She'd unbuttoned it and placed it on a chair before crawling beneath the sheet on the wide bed. Now it hung over a rack near the wardrobe, freshly pressed by an unknown hand wielding an iron. No doubt that of the housekeeper. Katie by name, she recalled.

From the hallway beyond the closed door, she heard a

tinkling laugh, almost a giggle, and recognized the voice immediately. Amanda at her best, cheerful and lighthearted.

Overlaying the child's tones, a deeper, masculine tone prevailed, and Carlinda hurriedly slid the dress over her head, aware of Nicholas Garvey's presence just a few feet away. Even as she buttoned the small, black fastenings on her bodice, she heard the single rap of a knuckle on the wooden panel.

"Yes, I'm coming," she said, hastening across the room to turn the handle. It swung wide and she looked up into the dark, masculine features of the man she'd traveled halfway across the country to find. "I'm sorry. I only planned to rest for a bit, and I'm afraid I slept longer than I thought."

"That's not a problem, Miss Donnelly," he said nicely, his gaze sliding down the length of her. "We came to rouse you, since Katie announced that supper was served, and Amanda thought you were likely hungry. She tells me you didn't eat much today."

Carlinda flushed deeply. The child saw more than she should, and this morning had been a hodgepodge of activity, arriving in Collins Creek, pausing only at the hotel for breakfast before they sought out the bank. Unable to eat the meal she'd ordered, her stomach protesting as she planned her approach to Nicholas, Carlinda had only watched and encouraged Amanda's halfhearted attempts to get through the plate of eggs and sausage before her.

"I wasn't hungry," she said now. "The journey was tiring, and I fear I'd lost my appetite."

"Well, you'd do well to locate it now. Katie has outdone herself. We don't often have company," he said, taking up Amanda's hand in his and leading the way to the double staircase.

"Mr. Garvey has two sets of steps and two bannisters," Amanda announced gleefully. "And lots of bedrooms."

With her free hand, she tugged at Carlinda's skirt, and her whispered words were an easily heard suggestion. "I'll bet he's got plenty of room for us to stay here."

"Yes, I have," he said, unabashed at listening to her murmured suggestion.

"I had the impression we weren't as welcome as the flowers in spring," Carlinda said, her forced smile for the child's benefit apparently not lost on Nicholas.

He shrugged nonchalantly. "We'll have to take this one step at a time. Right now, I think it would be unforgivable to keep Katie waiting. She likes to serve her meals hot."

Carlinda's feet were silent against the carpeted stairs and she slowed her pace, the better to observe the first floor below. Besides the parlor and dining room, two other doors led from the wide foyer, both of them open. As she moved downward, a desk was visible inside one room, probably Nicholas's private retreat, she decided. The other appeared to be a small sitting room, a woman's room by the looks of things. She was entranced by a glimpse of a delicately constructed sofa and chair, and late-afternoon sunshine pouring through a window.

"You have a lovely home." The compliment was sincere, probably the first entirely honest thing she'd said or done today, she thought. And felt a pang of guilt as she considered her omission of all the facts.

"Thank you," he answered gravely, although a smile flashed as he met her gaze. "I don't often have an opportunity to offer my hospitality. I was amiss in not extending a welcome to you and Amanda when we first met today. I fear my thoughts were in a state of flux, and my mind did not function as well as it should have."

"You were presented with a done deal, as they say, Mr. Garvey. I can't blame you for being taken unaware and being less than welcoming."

"Nonetheless," he said with a shrug, and she looked up

to catch a glimpse of heat in the depths of his blue eyes, a quickly masked impression. He'd looked at her as a man might who sought the interest of an available woman. For just a moment, she'd felt the warmth of masculine interest, and she stiffened against the lure of such a thing being cast in her direction.

Perhaps staying in this house was not a good beginning. He might think she was obtainable, a woman of loose virtue, should she agree too quickly to his hospitality. And yet, she could not in good conscience leave Amanda here without her. "We don't want to put you to any trouble," she murmured, reaching the bottom of the staircase. "I'm certain the hotel would do very well for us." She looked up at him. "At least until you have an opportunity to check out the facts of this matter."

"I won't hear of it." His tones were clipped, bringing an abrupt end to the discussion and she subsided, unwilling to argue in front of Amanda. As though he understood her position and agreed, he nodded at the open door of his study. "After supper, perhaps you'll join me in here and we'll discuss this at greater length."

Carlinda nodded, and stepped up her pace to the dining room, where a long table was set with three places and, at one end, a tureen of soup sent up a steam of fragrance. She was seated with a courtly gesture, and she opened the linen napkin beside her plate, aware of Amanda's copycat gesture as the child followed her example.

Nicholas served the soup, waving Katie's offer of help aside as the woman brought a plate of fresh bread from the kitchen. It was delicious, a clear broth with traces of rice and bits of chicken adding flavor, providing a light beginning to the meal. It was followed by a roast, again served by Nicholas, who stood before his chair and offered thin slices of the meat to his guests. Small potatoes, cooked with the skins intact, were accompanied by whole green beans, redolent with the scent of bacon and onions.

It was a filling repast, and when Katie brought forth a tart for each of them, Carlinda was tempted to refuse. And then she caught sight of the dark, thick juice of purple berries that spread before the force of Nicholas's fork as he cut into the dainty bit of pastry.

"I shouldn't," she sighed, even as she watched the tiny wisps of steam rise from the delicacy.

"It's a specialty of Katie's," Nicholas said, coaxing her with a smile. "She'll be insulted if you refuse a bite."

"I fear I'll eat the whole thing," Carlinda said, tasting carefully of the hot offering. "Don't burn your mouth," she warned Amanda.

"I've got cream to put over it, if you like," Katie said from the kitchen doorway, then approached with a small pitcher of golden liquid as Amanda nodded her agreement. "It tastes good this way," she told the child, pouring a generous amount.

"I'll take some, too," Nicholas said, offering his dish.

"And you, miss?" Katie asked.

"If it tastes better that way, I suppose I should join the group," Carlinda agreed.

The meal was long, Nicholas asking Amanda about the trip, skirting the topic of her parents and offering small glimpses of his life in this small Texas town. He delivered an occasional aside to Carlinda, but his attention was focused on the child who sat at his right hand.

The resemblance between the two of them was obvious to anyone who cared to look, Carlinda decided. Even Katie glanced back and forth between the man and the young girl who absorbed his interest, and before the end of the meal, she had shot a look of understanding at the other woman.

Nicholas pushed away from the table finally. "I believe

I've eaten more than my share, Katie,'' he said, watching as she cleared the plate from before him.

"You don't usually eat enough," she snipped. "About time you sat down and did my cooking justice."

"Yes, ma'am," he said obligingly, looking suitably chagrined. And then he rose and spoke kindly to Amanda. "Would you like to sit on the porch for a while?" he asked. "Or perhaps look at the stereopticon in the parlor?"

"Stere—" Amanda halted halfway through the word, obviously puzzled at its meaning.

"A stereopticon is something you hold up to your eyes and then look at pictures with," he said. "I have a whole box of prints you can see." He took her by the hand and led her from the room, sending an apologetic look in Carlinda's direction.

"In the parlor?" Amanda asked brightly, doublestepping to keep up with his long strides. "What kind of pictures do you have?"

"Some of Rome or Venice or even London," he said. "And lots of New York City and other places here in America."

"I've already been to New York," the child told him flatly. "I'd rather see somewhere else."

"How about Niagara Falls?" he asked. "Or maybe ships on the ocean?"

"Let's steer clear of P-a-r-i-s," Carlinda said quickly, spelling the city's name in a rush of letters, lest Amanda get the drift of the word she attempted to avoid speaking.

"Is there some reason for that?" he asked in a muted tone as he stepped to a bookcase where the instrument lay. Amanda settled herself on a sofa, smoothing her dress over her legs with a practiced hand, anticipation alive in her blue eyes. He glanced back at her, and Carlinda detected a softening in his eyes, those eyes so like the child's.

"The accident took place in Paris," she murmured. "I

try not to mention it. She was quite traumatized for days after we heard the news.''

''I wasn't aware you knew her mother. You were with Amanda, even back then?''

Carlinda hesitated, then nodded briefly. ''Shall we light a lamp, so she can see these better?'' she asked, changing the subject deftly.

Yet, even as he acceded to her suggestion, she was aware that the issue would be raised again. And she prepared herself for a battery of questions.

Chapter Two

Nicholas's study was a reflection of the man, the fittings surrounding him luxurious, yet masculine. An enormous desk, its surface glowing with the sheen of polished mahogany, took her gaze as Carlinda walked over the threshold. Sitting behind it, leaning back in his chair, Nicholas resembled a king surveying his domain, judging his subject as she entered the throne room. She suppressed a smile at the thought, concentrating instead on the man himself. His hands were tanned, his fingers long, and laced together in a casual display of patience as he glanced up at her.

"Is the child asleep?" His voice appealed to her, she found as he spoke his query. It matched the man. Deep and cultured, yet with a strength beneath its resonant tone, it gave warning that he was not a man to be underestimated.

"Amanda?" She spoke the name as a query, her reprimand subtle, and Nicholas frowned. "Such a pretty name, don't you think?" Carlinda asked, and then sighed, relenting. "Yes, she was tired." *And so am I.* Perhaps this was not a good time to face the man and make her position clear. His next words told her he was aware of her hesitation as a slow smile lit his brilliant blue eyes.

"I'll try to remember from now on to use her name when

I speak of her.'' He waved in the direction of a seating arrangement across from his desk. "I don't plan on interrogating you, Miss Donnelly. Sit down for a moment. I only want to talk.''

A brown armchair lured her and she settled in its depths, seduced by the high back and soft leather surrounding her. Her feet touched the floor, her knees weak as she eyed his ebony hair and tanned features. It wasn't fair that one man should be so endowed with masculine beauty, she thought, masking her admiration with a polite smile.

"I fear I won't be good company, sir. Although my nap was refreshing, I find I need the comfort of a long night's sleep. Perhaps your discussion will wait until another time.'' She watched as his gaze swept her from top to bottom, a very short distance, given her position in the chair. That his eyes hesitated as they touched upon her full bosom and then traveled to where her feet were clad in soft leather was not a surprise. The man did not pretend a lack of interest in face and form, but made his intentions apparent.

"You don't look like a nursemaid, Miss Donnelly,'' he said bluntly, a small smile playing about his lips, as if he would draw a quick retort from her. "I've seen women who looked much as you do while at the opera house in New York City. You're dressed in a conservative manner, as a cultured young lady would be, yet you give the impression of being knowledgeable about life in society.''

"Nevertheless, I am what I am,'' she said quietly. "My looks have nothing to do with my occupation, Mr. Garvey. Women such as myself work in the finest homes in the city.'' She glanced down at her modest, yet decidedly fashionable gown. "Surely I'm not dressed for the opera or a French restaurant, sir. I have references if you feel the need to see them, but I assure you I'm just a simple woman who has accompanied your niece from the East Coast.''

"You may be many things,'' Nicholas said quietly, nodding his head as if he accepted her words as truth, "but you are not a *simple* woman."

She felt her heart flutter as he spoke the words with emphasis, his eyes again touching her face, openly admiring the picture she presented. Aware of his scrutiny, blood rushed through her body, his measured gaze setting in motion a reaction she could not control. Tendrils of that same warmth lent color to her cheeks and she lowered her gaze to her lap.

Then courage took hold and she lifted her lashes to shoot a quick glare in his direction. She sighed at her own small betraying gesture, and smiled, ruing her short temper. "Perhaps not. But I am a weary woman, and unless you have instructions for me, I beg your leave to return to my room."

He looked taken aback, yet rose with a graceful movement "Certainly. I only wanted to spend some time becoming familiar with your relationship to Amanda." His mouth curved, an enticing movement of lips that drew her like a magnet. "May I call you Carlinda? Or is our acquaintance of too short a span to allow such a thing?"

"I probably won't be here long enough for us to become friends, Mr. Garvey." Rising from the chair without revealing her aching back and the sudden stiffness that gripped her knees made her hesitate, and he shot her a calculating look, then stepped quickly around the desk to offer his hand.

"I think you're feeling the effects of travel," he ventured. "Let me escort you up the stairs."

She wasn't certain she could tolerate the warmth of those fingers for any length of time, Carlinda decided. And then his hand moved to settle gently at the small of her back as he turned her toward the door of his study. It was even worse there, sending shards of heat from that place to envelop her entire body in awareness of the tall, masculine creature who was her host.

If she were certain of his trustworthiness, certain he would treat Amanda as he should, she'd be better off leaving. Though where she would go was still in doubt. She bit back a sigh as they crossed the threshold of the study. She'd already decided he was a magician, this elegant banker whose eyes warmed her, whose hand persuaded her without effort into doing as he willed.

So she walked beside him to the staircase, lifting her skirts, climbing to the second floor, her feet moving in unison with his. Beside her, his clothing, and the body beneath the fine wool and linen, exuded a fresh scent, one that blended with a subtle musky aroma, seducing her senses.

He reached to open the door of her room and the hand was gone from her back as he nodded politely in the direction of the bedside table where a pink-shaded lamp glowed, a beacon drawing her to the comfort of cool sheets and soft pillows.

"Have a good night," he said quietly. "I'll see you at breakfast. We eat rather early, I should warn you."

"I'm used to arising when the sun comes up," she told him, moving away across the carpet, then turning to face him. "Is that a connecting door to Amanda's room?" She glanced at the wall where a single door sat ajar. "I didn't pay attention earlier."

Nicholas shook his head. "No. That's a dressing room. I don't have any suites in the house." His smile was apologetic. "I fear you are in the wilds of Texas, ma'am. We don't supply the conveniences of big-city living."

She blushed anew at his words. "I didn't mean to criticize. I just wanted to be able to hear Amanda should she awake in the night."

"Does she have nightmares?" His brow wrinkled in a frown.

"Once in a while. Not during the journey, but then, it

was all new and exciting to her. She dreams of her mother sometimes, and wakes crying.''

''Perhaps you should leave your door open then,'' he suggested. ''Hers is already ajar.'' At her hesitation he grinned, a taunting look enveloping his eyes, crinkling the skin at their outer corners. He leaned against the doorjamb. ''I promise not to intrude on your privacy.''

''Unless the walls are very thick, or soundproof, I'm sure I'll hear her should she cry out,'' she said hurriedly. She glanced at the window and noted the lights of town to the east. Even as she watched, one flickered and disappeared. ''It seems things are settling down all over,'' she said quietly. ''Amanda shouldn't be roused by noise from outdoors.''

''I'll leave you then,'' her host said. ''If you like, I'll open the sash. The fresh air will help you sleep.'' His eyes looked black in the dim light and she inhaled sharply, shaking her head in refusal of his offer.

He gave her a last, long, surveying look. ''Good night then, Miss Donnelly.''

His back was straight, his footsteps silent on the carpet as he turned toward the stairway and she relaxed, stepping to the side of the bed to perch on the mattress. The man's effect on her was without precedent. Never in her twenty-four years had she known instant attraction to a male, unless she counted the tall youth, almost fifteen years older than she, who had lived next door in her growing-up years.

Jack had been her idol, her secret flame until the day he'd married a young lady and settled down to become a husband and father. His attraction for her had become null and void, and she could only ever after look at him as a staid creature with a string of children and a dutiful wife trailing behind as he entered the church on Sunday morning.

And now there was Nicholas Garvey, a man who looked

at her as if he considered the thought of possessing her. She shook her head. What foolishness. The man was a flirt, a consummate ladies' man, and she was a decent-looking female who'd just come into his orbit, offering a moment's distraction.

Yet, there had been a response within her she could not deny. It would behoove her to leave this town as soon as she could assure herself of Amanda's well-being here. She'd spend a bit of time backing away from the bonds formed by the child's bereavement, and then decide where she might go from here.

She rose and slid open a bureau drawer, locating her nightgown. A swift glance at the door reminded her that it stood open and she crossed the room to quietly turn the handle, allowing it to latch. Far enough from the window to allow privacy, she slid from her clothing and into the soft batiste sleeping gown, then folded her underwear and arranged her dress over the back of a convenient chair.

The dressing room drew her, curiosity urging her to open the door fully and peer inside. Empty racks greeted her, with one wall mirrored, reflecting her pale form, her hair glowing in the light from her bedside. He needn't have apologized, she thought. His home held all the comforts of her own in New York. At least the home that had once been hers, where she'd lived with Amanda and her parents.

Tomorrow would be soon enough to unpack the bag someone had delivered from the train station. She looked forward to hanging her few articles of clothing in the vast expanse of that dressing room, perhaps pretending for a while that this was her home.

Turning back to the bed, she folded the coverlet at its foot, then slid between the sheets. Her eyes noted the glass windowpane and she compressed her lips with impatience, aware that it was still closed to the night air. It took only a moment to slide from the comfortable mattress and cross the room to lift the wooden frame. It slid silently upward, and Carlinda dropped to her knees to look down at the lawn below.

A pale shadow caught her eye and she watched as the tall figure of a man walked toward the trees lining the edge of his property. Nicholas Garvey out for an evening stroll, she decided, aware of the long, slow stride that carried him beneath the low-hanging branches.

A flicker of light illuminated his profile as he bent his head to touch a match to his cigar. She hadn't caught the scent of tobacco on him earlier, yet the faint aroma touched her nostrils now, the breeze carrying it upward. A chill of foreboding touched her and she shivered, rising and making her way back to the bed.

He held the scent of danger, and her instincts had seldom been amiss. It would be foolhardy to linger here.

The morning sun was brilliant in the sky, but Nicholas ignored it, his mind caught up with the events of the evening before. She was an enigma, perhaps playing him for a fool with her talk of leaving, then dithering as she seemingly settled into his household. The thought of her departure was not welcome, for Carlinda held an attraction he could not resist, yet resented with his sensible, masculine mindset. She was definitely not the type of woman who would accept for herself what he had in mind.

"Damn. She isn't even beautiful," Nicholas muttered, aware that his steps were heavy, his momentum rapid as he walked toward the bank.

"Who isn't?" Jonathan Cleary's voice shot holes in his concentration as the local lawman stepped to his side and voiced aloud the query Nicholas had known in that split second was coming. He'd caught sight of Cleary just as his voice uttered the exasperated statement, and now he supposed he was doomed to explain the meaning of his claim.

"You know damn well who I'm talking about." Embarrassed not only by his sullen retort, but by his obvious interest in the nursemaid he'd taken to his home, he stopped dead still on the wooden sidewalk and aimed a dark glance at his friend.

Cleary only grinned, further irritating the banker.

"You'll have to admit I'm right," Nicholas said, more quietly as he nodded a good morning in the direction of a passerby.

"That she's not beautiful?" Cleary seemed to consider the matter, and then shook his head. "There's something about her, Nick. Maybe those dark eyes, or the auburn curls. Maybe the creamy look of her complexion, like it would be velvet under your fingertips." He shrugged. "And don't go quoting me to Gussie, you hear? She'd have my neck if she thought I'd looked cross-ways at another woman."

"How could you help it?" Nicholas asked, gloom coating each word. "I don't *need* to be smitten by a stranger. One who won't even be here long enough to form an attachment."

"You're thinking about—"

"Don't even say the words," Nicholas warned him. "I'm not going to dillydally around with a woman here on a short-term basis when I've got an eye on Patience Filmore. I have a notion Miss Donnelly would put demands on a man, when all he's asking for is something temporary. If I marry Patience one day down the road, I'll still be my own person."

Cleary only shook his head and shrugged. "You're right there. You're the least of her concern. Patience is interested in the money you've got in your bank."

Nicholas took affront. "You don't think I'm gentleman enough or handsome enough for the lady?" And yet, he knew that Cleary wasn't too far off the mark. Patience was definitely a lady with an eye to the future. And being the owner of the only bank in town gave him an edge.

"Hell, you can probably talk her into marriage without any trouble at all," Cleary said harshly. "But will you be happy with her?"

"Happy?" Nicholas felt his throat close as he uttered the word. "What does that mean?" And yet he knew. Knew that Cleary and his wife shared a life he found himself observing at times with a sort of awe and envy he'd always thought beneath him. "I'm not a homebody like you, Cleary. I think Patience will suit me just fine."

"Speaking of which…" Cleary lifted a brow and nodded at a woman heading in their direction. "I need to be across the street," he said, tipping his hat at the lady in question before he stepped down from the sidewalk.

"Nicholas." Patience was blessed with abundant dark hair that hung in a series of ringlets from beneath her bonnet. Her blue eyes were wide and fringed with equally dark lashes, and she had an hourglass figure that drew the eye of every man in her vicinity, no matter where she went.

And yet, all Nicholas could see this morning was that there was an enameled look to her, as if she had spent hours perfecting the image she portrayed. His own smile was equally feigned as he offered his arm. She swept to his side, her skirts wrapping around his trouser legs as her slender fingers touched his forearm.

On the other hand, Carlinda had looked a bit frazzled at the breakfast table, her hair curling against her temples and brow, her morning gown a bit wrinkled, having been hauled from her luggage for the occasion. She'd apologized for being late, then spent long moments fixing a plate for her charge before she once more sought his attention.

And in those moments he'd filled his eyes with her soft contours, her rosy cheeks and the hastily pinned-together, russet-hued curls that perched high on her crown, several of them already on a downward slide as she shook her head in response to a query.

"Nicholas?" Patience called his name, her voice curt as she broke into his thoughts. "What in the world are you thinking of?" she asked. "I've been telling you about the party Saturday at the Millers' home, and I do declare, I think you haven't heard a word I've said."

"My mind is on a problem at the bank," he told her, lying without a speck of guilt. The woman had lost her attraction for him, almost overnight, it seemed. And for the life of him, he didn't know how he'd go about shedding her presence from his daily routine, wishing glumly he'd never given her any encouragement.

For the pursuit had been from her direction, he recognized, almost from the first. She'd set her cap for the banker, and been persistent in the chase. And he, idiot that he was, had allowed it. Had, in fact, aided and abetted her in her determination to win his favor. Now she stood before him and he thought how wonderful it would be to hold a magic wand in his hand, just for a moment, so he might wave it over her lush form, sending her back to wherever she'd come from this morning.

Instead, he forced a benign smile to appear. "I have to get to my desk," he said, his words apologetic. "I'll try to find time to call on you later today, Patience."

Her pout had lost its appeal, he decided, as she allowed her rosy lips to form a small moue, and then fluttered her lashes in what he'd once thought was a beguiling manner. Miles removed from the open, honest glare he'd received from the woman in his study only last evening.

His stride was long, as if he could not escape Patience quickly enough, and he crossed the dusty street, heading for the bank where his clerk, Thomas, was sweeping the wide sidewalk before the open door.

''Good morning, Mr. Garvey,'' the young man said cheerfully. ''Beautiful day, don't you think?''

''Depends on your viewpoint,'' Nicholas said with a grunt, his long legs carrying him into the high-ceilinged lobby, leaving behind an employee he knew must be puzzled by his employer's mood. Normally a polite gentleman, the events of the day thus far had not endowed him with hope for the future of this episode he'd managed to entangle himself in. There wasn't a bit of sense in shedding Patience from his existence when he'd be waving goodbye to Carlinda Donnelly in less time than it would take to truly make her acquaintance.

And with that decision attended to, he opened his office door and settled behind his desk. ''Thomas.'' The single word sounded much like the roar of a mountain lion and Nicholas winced, then took a deep breath.

Women. They were at the bottom of almost all the problems he'd faced in his life, in one way or another. And the conundrum facing him today seemed only to prove that fact. It was a good thing that marriage was definitely on the back burner. He was a man who enjoyed his freedom.

She'd been given the grand tour and decreed the house lovely, and, even more important, comfortable. The housekeeper's bright eyes were avid with curiosity and she seemed determined to make Carlinda welcome. ''I'm sure Mr. Nicholas will be home for dinner,'' Katie said cheerfully, her cloth moving rapidly as she dusted the bannister.

Her hair, once flame-red, if Carlinda knew anything about such things, had now settled into a hazy color of grey over auburn. As might her own one day, she thought. A wide smile on Katie's lips sparkled with goodwill and her feet moved smartly as she made her way through the work inherent in keeping such a large home clean and polished to within an inch of its life. Carlinda hovered in her wake, feeling useless with nothing to accomplish.

It seemed a walk was in order, and she pressed a dress from her valise and one for Amanda for the occasion. "Are you certain you don't need any help?" Carlinda asked for the second time, hesitating by the front door. Her charge tugged impatiently at her fingers, but she held back, guilt pushing her into the offer she made.

Katie only shook her head. "No, ma'am. You go on ahead and take the wee one out for a walk. She needs to get some exercise. Young'uns need fresh air and lots of it. Makes them healthy to breathe the morning air, it does."

Reluctantly, Carlinda nodded and opened the heavy door. Leaded glass in long panes almost the length of its frame glittered in the sunlight, and she turned back to admire them as Amanda scampered across the porch.

"I'll just leave it open," Katie said, watching from the threshold. "You go on now and enjoy your stroll."

Amanda was at the gate already, apparently puzzled by the latch, and Carlinda touched it, allowing the spring to stretch and the gate to open. Then she reached her hand for the child to grasp, and was given a dour look in silent reply.

"Young ladies don't run and jump along a public thoroughfare," she reminded Amanda. "We walk properly, without causing the dust to rise and coat our shoes."

"Yes, ma'am," Amanda answered dutifully, and yet it was obvious the little girl longed to run ahead and explore the limits of the small town they'd come to.

Ahead was a square in the center of town, an inviting place Carlinda had taken note of yesterday morning. On either side, east and west, the road stretched for a short distance, with stores and places of business lining its edges, sidewalks forming a neat line in front of the establishments. Women walked from one shop to another, their steps brisk as they performed what seemed a daily ritual, providing for

their families. Two elderly men had staked a claim on a
bench before the hardware store, exchanging greetings with
the ladies who passed by.

In the midst of the square trees grew and three benches
sat, empty in the morning sun. Carlinda wished that one of
them was beneath the shade of a tree. She would surely
freckle, she thought, if she were subjected much longer to
the warmth of the spring sunlight. Sighing, she settled on
a wooden seat, almost in the center of the square, and
watched as Amanda approached another child at her side.

The two little girls talked for a moment, then Amanda
turned, reaching for the girl's hand to bring her along as
she approached her nursemaid. "This is Sally," Amanda
said importantly. "She's going to be my new friend. Her
mama's at the store."

And wasn't it easy for a child to determine the existence
of a friendship so quickly, Carlinda thought wistfully. So
far removed from the adult skirmishes that took place before a friendship could be formed between two women. She
thought of the battle lines that had been drawn the evening
before when she'd gone head to head with the man whose
hospitality she'd accepted. A blush covered her cheeks as
she recalled her quick animosity.

"Hello, Sally," she said, her response to the child au-
tomatic. And then she glanced at Amanda. "Don't go out
of the square," she said quietly. "I'll just sit here and
watch."

The little girls skipped off, then settled under one of the
trees, carefully tugging their skirts to cover short legs,
Amanda looking up for Carlinda's approval. With a smile
and nod, it was bestowed, and the child turned aside. The
murmur of their voices and the soft sound of laughter lulled
her as Carlinda basked beneath the sun's rays. She'd not
lost herself in such a lazy morning in a very long time, and

her eyes closed as she allowed herself to drift in a slumberous state.

A shadow fell over her and she blinked, looking up quickly. Nicholas stood before her, his bulk shading her from the sun and she lifted a hand to her brow as she gazed up at him. "We're enjoying the town square," she said, then blushed anew as he smiled.

"I'm glad to see you out and about. I hope I didn't interrupt your daydreaming, but I wouldn't want you to be sunburned. I see you forgot your bonnet."

Her eyes widened as she lifted her hand higher, as if she'd only now noticed its absence. "So I did. I suppose because I didn't plan on walking this far. Amanda and I were talking and I didn't realize..." Her words trailed off as she took note of his amusement. "You're laughing at me," she said accusingly.

He shook his head. "Indeed, not," he murmured, denying her claim. "I'm enjoying your smile and wishing I had a few hours to sit here with you and share your warmth."

"I'm only borrowing it from the sun," she said. "I'm sure there's enough for both of us." Aware suddenly of her easy acceptance of his presence, she inhaled sharply, unwilling to so quickly bow to his appeal. "On the other hand, perhaps I'd better take Amanda back to the house. It must be nearing dinnertime and Katie may need a hand."

"She's remarkably efficient," he told her, sitting beside her, doffing his hat as he lifted one booted foot to rest it against his other knee. The wide-brimmed hat found a place on the park bench between them, and he looked toward the children.

"Amanda seems to have found a friend." His tone was amused once more.

"Sally." Carlinda spoke the name, and smiled. "She's needed youngsters to play with. Sally's mother is in the general store, and I'm sure the girls are hoping she'll take her time. They seem to be kindred souls. It bodes well for her future, I think.''

"Her future?'' She glanced at him as he lifted a brow and a quizzical expression touched his face. "With me?''

"Certainly. Where else would I mean? She'll need to accustom herself to living in this town, and in your home.''

"This hasn't been worked out to my satisfaction yet,'' he told her, his eyes seeking Amanda once more. "We'll need some time to come to an agreement, I think.''

"Time?'' She refused to look at him, her heart in her throat as she spoke the word that had assumed threatening proportions. "How much time? And what sort of an agreement are you speaking of?''

He scanned her, that lazy, impudent appraisal she'd endured only yesterday. Was it only yesterday she'd met the man? And now his gaze lifted to mesh with hers. "Time? As long as it takes,'' he said quietly. "The agreement we'll discuss another time.''

And then he rose and placed his hat upon his head, nodding as he took his leave. "I'll be home for dinner. Tell Katie to have it ready by one, please.''

Carlinda watched as he walked off. *Strode* was a better word, she decided, admiring his height, the gleam of dark hair touching his collar. He wore his clothing as if it had been tailored to his tall frame, his trousers unpleated and close-fitting against his legs. And the width of shoulders better suited to a lumberjack tested the fabric of his suit coat.

She was besotted. There was no other word for it. The man was beautiful, a word she was certain he would scoff at should it be spoken in his hearing, but she could think of none other to better describe him. A feeling of desolation swept through her as she reflected on the time to come when she must leave this town, the day when she would step on board the train and turn her back on Nicholas Garvey.

She slumped back on the bench and lifted a hand to consult her watch. It hung on a golden chain against the front of her dress and she read the hands through a mist she could not explain. After noon already. She would barely have time to walk home with Amanda and give Nicholas's message to Katie.

Home. The single word rang through her head as though she'd spoken it aloud. It was not her home. Would never be a home for her to live in and enjoy. For Carlinda Donnelly, the future stretched ahead like a long blank road. And only in her dreams could she envision such a thing as the large, white house where Nicholas Garvey hung his hat as a home in which she might dwell.

She rose slowly and looked about for the little girls, aware that she'd almost forgotten their existence for a few moments. They played quietly beneath a tree only yards away, and Carlinda spoke Amanda's name, catching her attention.

"Do we have to leave already?" she asked, her lip drawing down into a pout.

"We'll come back tomorrow," Carlinda promised. "Perhaps Sally can come to visit later today," she offered, willing to use bribery if need be.

Sally's frown brightened and she nodded quickly. "I'll ask my mama," she said, and danced off toward the other side of the park, then turned to walk backward, waving a small hand in a gesture of goodbye as she made her way to the general store.

"Let's walk real quick so we can eat dinner," Amanda urged, fast-stepping as she hastened back toward Nicholas's home. "Then maybe Sally will come to visit."

"We have to wait for Mr. Garvey to come home first before we eat," Carlinda reminded her.

"Maybe he'll hurry," Amanda said, reaching for her nursemaid's hand and skipping by her side. "Sally's mama is shopping, but she'll ask her on the way home."

Nicholas did make haste, it seemed, for barely had they arrived inside the front door and delivered the message when his tall presence came through the front gate.

"Land sakes, here's Mr. Nicholas now," Katie said, bustling down the hallway toward the kitchen. "I'll have the food on in ten minutes," she called back brightly.

"Let's go wash up," Carlinda told her charge, her step light as she climbed the stairs before the man should make his way up the walk and across the porch. For some reason, she felt the need of a few minutes alone, to wash her face and brush her hair into place. To somehow get her thoughts in order before she must once more meet him face-to-face and be assailed by the emotion that filled her.

"You've only known him a day," she told herself firmly, looking into the mirror over her dressing table just minutes later. She'd washed Amanda first, sent her down to the kitchen and gone on to her own room. Now she faced her image, noting the trembling lips, the glittering eyes and the hair that would not be contained neatly, no matter how hard she tried to tame its curls.

"He's only a man, and he probably has women waiting in line to seek his company." She lifted a hand to brush her hair back, then dampened it with a bit of water, hoping against hope it would miraculously behave and turn orderly before her very eyes. It was no use. The ringlets hung against her temple once more, and from the hastily formed bun she'd managed to subdue with an assortment of pins only hours ago, bits and pieces of auburn hair had escaped to curl down, touching her shoulders despite all her urging and pinning it in place.

"I can't do much more," she whispered, stepping back, the better to assess her appearance. Her dress was suitable, neat and clean, and her shoes wore only a bit of dust across the toes, reminding her of the quick walk back from town. She bent to brush at them with her handkerchief and heard a sound from behind her, as a masculine voice muttered a soft word, and then Nicholas distinctly cleared his throat.

"I beg your pardon, ma'am," he said gravely. "I came up to see if you were ready for dinner. I didn't mean to invade your privacy."

She turned quickly, aware that her cheeks were flushed, a condition she seemed to find herself in today, no matter where she was or what she was doing. He'd seen her, watched her bend to brush at her shoes, noted her bottom in the air as she leaned forward. Probably her dress had risen in the back. What if he'd seen her stockings?

She stiffened her spine, resolute in her determination not to be embarrassed any more than she already was, and decided to ignore any what-ifs that flooded her mind.

"Yes, I'm ready," she said quietly, and walked toward him.

Chapter Three

As if he'd never before seen the back of a woman's lower limbs and ankles, Nicholas found himself obsessed over the next days by the vision of Carlinda's slender underpinnings. The remembrance invaded his dreams, haunted his waking hours, even managing to insinuate itself into his thoughts as he discussed a loan with Sam Ferguson two days later.

He felt like an errant schoolboy, and that thought did nothing to elevate his ego. Sam sat across his desk, hat in hand as he enumerated the reasons for needing two hundred dollars. It was a considerable sum, one which should have required Nicholas's full attention, and he bent his mind to the matter.

"We'll take a look at your account here," he said quietly, leafing through the paperwork before him. "I see no reason to deny you the loan, Sam. Your business is thriving. Adding on additional space for feed and supplies makes sense to me." He looked up and smiled at the anxious livery stable owner. "Give me half an hour and things should be in order."

Sam's wide shoulders fit neatly through the doorway Nicholas noted as the man left his office. The papers before him were a blur, but he straightened them and then initialed each of the three pages. "Thomas," he called, aware that his clerk hovered nearby. He held the papers out as the young man appeared in the doorway. "Take care of this for Mr. Ferguson, will you?"

"Certainly, sir." Thomas was efficient, his expression bland, but his eagerness to please was a point in his favor, Nicholas decided. "There is a young lady to see you, sir," he said now, a faint flush apparent as he cut his eyes to the left side of the door.

Patience. He'd lay money his visitor was the very *impatient* Patience. He'd neglected her for the past three days, and he could pinpoint the exact moment his attention had strayed from her. Upon Carlinda's arrival, his suit of Patience Filmore had come to a screeching halt. And stood no chance at all of resuming its previous pace.

Now he sighed beneath his breath. "Send her in, Thomas." Scooping up a stack of papers from his left, he spread them quickly before him and bent his head. Then he looked up as the dark-haired beauty halted before his desk.

"Good morning," he said, coaxing his voice into a welcoming note. "What can I do for you today?"

Her mouth twisted a bit and she hesitated, as if ruing her decision to approach him. "I suppose you can explain why you haven't been at my front door for the past several evenings." Her eyes were suitably lowered, as if she were embarrassed by her own inquiry. Nicholas was not fooled. One thing he'd come to admire about Patience was her forthrightness. If she wanted an answer, she asked for it. This pose of injured pride was just that, a pose, a transparent request for his attention and apology.

"I have company in my home, Patience," he said quietly. "It would be rude of me to abandon Miss Donnelly and my niece to themselves for the evening."

"Ah, yes. I heard rumors that you've discovered a long-lost relative. I would enjoy getting to know your niece,'' she countered.

''Well, I'm only beginning to do that myself,'' he said, lifting a paper from those he'd strewn before him.

Patience allowed her gaze to touch upon the delaying tactic. ''I can see you're very busy,'' she said, and rising, touched her index finger to her cheek. ''I really only dropped by to remind you of the party tomorrow night at the Millers' home. I've told them we would attend.''

Nicholas dropped the paper from his hand and looked up, his gaze ascending the lush figure of the woman before him. ''You shouldn't have done that, Patience. I don't recall agreeing to that.''

Her smile was cool. ''Perhaps not, but we have become something of an item of late. People expect us to arrive at such gatherings together. I'm sure you're aware of that.'' She took small steps, circling the side of his desk and approaching him with her hand outstretched. Long, slender fingers touched the sleeve of his suit coat and she smiled invitingly into his eyes. ''Perhaps I misunderstood your interest in me, Nicholas.''

He felt perspiration break out in a narrow line down his spine, and at the same time he was chilled and angered by the thought of being manipulated in such a way. His gaze dropped to where her hand lay against his arm and, for an instant, he felt her grip tighten, then relax, sliding from its place until her fingers held the strings of her reticule and he was set free from the contact.

''Perhaps you misunderstood, or maybe I was at fault, even premature, in my interest in you, Patience.'' Cruelty was not normally in his nature, but this must be brought to a halt.

He thought he saw genuine surprise in her features as she looked up at him, and then it was masked and her smile became practiced and serene. "Well, we'll see what the future holds, won't we?" she said enigmatically.

And wasn't that the truth? He watched her leave, unimpressed by the same movement of hips he'd found fascinating only a week since. His smile was rueful, remembering again the sight of Carlinda's stocking-clad calves and ankles. Indeed the memory was constantly at the surface of his mind, and he straightened the papers before him with precise movements as he attempted to erase his errant reaction to the woman.

A glance at his pocket watch assured him he would not be amiss in leaving for home. The dinner hour was becoming increasingly important in his everyday scheme of things this week, and he would not insult Katie by making her put the meal on hold while she awaited his appearance at the table.

The walk was short, his pace brisk, and he approached his home with an ear open to Amanda's presence. The child was increasingly vocal; he'd noticed her laughter ringing out even early in the morning, her cheerful voice greeting him from the porch each afternoon when the bank closed and he hastened to make his way from town.

Today, he heard her chanting a singsong rhyme, and slowed his pace, hoping to come upon her unaware. The high hedge at the corner of his lot hid her from his view and he halted there, peering like a voyeur beyond its boundaries to where the child played on the front sidewalk leading to the porch. He'd had cement poured from the street to the house, providing a dry passageway in inclement weather, and Katie had planted flowers on either side of its length.

Amanda stood ten feet or so from the porch, a rope tied to a pillar swinging in a circular motion, while her nursemaid jumped across it in perfect rhythm, her feet moving in time to the chanting song coming from Amanda's lips.

Her skirts caught up in both hands, Carlinda's slender ankles were thoroughly exposed, and then she missed her
step, and the rope tangled around one foot as she came to
a quick halt.

"You did real good," Amanda cried out as Carlinda's
mouth formed a downward turn. "You'll get it yet," the
child said, laughing aloud.

And then Carlinda turned, catching sight of Nicholas at
the end of the walk, one hand on the gate. Her cheeks
burned crimson and her fingers dropped her skirts to press
instead on the rosy skin, covering the embarrassment she
could not conceal.

"Oh! I didn't know you were there," she said, her
breasts lifting as she inhaled deeply. "Amanda was teach-
ing me a new song to—"

He held up a hand, his amusement knowing no bounds
as the woman's usual dignity deserted her. Her hair was
coming down on one side, the curls totally out of control,
and as he watched, one hand thrust itself into the mass of
russet hair and caught it up at the crown of her head. Her
fingers were deft as she rearranged several pins, and he was
fascinated by the process. The sunlight cast a warm glow
upon her head, and the rich, dark tresses seemed lit from
within by glints of gold and tipped by fire.

He wanted her. As he'd never wanted another woman,
he wanted this creature before him. Carlinda. *Linnie. Lin,
perhaps.* And at that thought, he became aware of the taut
formation of his masculinity within the confines of his trousers. His hat provided cover as he swept it from his head
and then held it before him, opening the gate with his other
hand.

Tonight. Tonight he would approach her, speak to her.
She was a mature woman. Perhaps he could offer an arrangement that would benefit them both, and relieve this
urge that kept him from his daily pursuits. He felt young

and impetuous, like a stallion seeking out a mare, or a youth settling upon his first conquest. It would not do. It simply would not do.

"One day, could you teach me how to sing the song, Amanda?" he suggested with a grin, determined to take his attention from the *mature* woman who was swiftly regaining her breath and brushing down her skirts with a quick hand. "We can take turns swinging the rope while your Miss Donnelly jumps it."

Miss Donnelly shook her head, a movement that almost sent her hastily pinned hairdo on its way to disaster once again. "I don't think that's a good idea at all," she said heatedly. "In fact, I fear you are making jokes at my expense, sir."

Nicholas only smiled. And then relented. "Not at all, ma'am. I'm only asking to join in the fun. I haven't seen rope skipping since I was a schoolboy."

"*You* were a schoolboy?" Carlinda asked, doubt alive in the words. "I can't imagine such a thing. I'd have thought you were hatched full-grown. I can't think you ever played marbles or chased after a dog or wrestled with your playmates."

He felt a pang of regret that she had hit the nail so squarely on the head; for indeed, he'd never pursued any of the typical boyish games she listed so readily. But his words covered those memories as he sat down on the porch steps.

"I was just an ordinary—"

"Ordinary?" Her single word doubted his statement. "I think not," she said, judging him, her look grave as she stood before him. "You can't claim that, Mr. Garvey."

Her eyes touched his briefly, then darted to where Amanda stood, jump rope in hand, her small fingers attempting to untie it from the porch pillar. "Let me help you,'' Carlinda said smoothly, as if she had not just peered with soft brown eyes into his past.

Dinner was presented with pride, Katie beaming as she brought forth a platter of sliced ham and bowls of vegetables. Bread still warm from the oven tempted him with its aroma and he looked up at his housekeeper, lifting a brow in question. ''I find your cooking to be improving daily. Are you trying to impress our guests?''

She lifted her chin, a haughty gesture that amused him. ''Certainly not, sir. I always do my best.'' And then her eyes twinkled as she bent to murmur words beneath her breath. ''You're looking mighty fine yourself, Mr. Garvey. Sprucing up for our guests?''

He'd have to see about instilling a bit more respect into her thoroughly Irish demeanor, he thought, ignoring the taunt. Looking up, he met the sober eyes of his young charge, the niece he'd never known. Now she held her plate in both hands, awaiting his attention, and he lifted a slice of ham to rest at one side, then spooned potatoes and creamed corn as she nodded her approval.

''Will you be here this evening?'' Carlinda asked as he attended to her plate in the same manner. She waited patiently as he served her, shaking her head in a small movement as he would have added another helping of greens.

''Yes, I expect to be,'' he said. ''Do you have plans for me?''

''Oh, no. I just thought we might discuss plans for Amanda's future, perhaps put together a timetable for my departure,'' she said quietly.

''You're not leaving, are you?'' Amanda asked, her tone sharp, as if horrified by the very thought of such a thing.

''I must, sometime, I think,'' Carlinda told her softly. ''You know I only traveled here with you to meet your uncle and be sure you were safely in his charge.''

''I thought you would stay,'' Amanda whispered, her

eyes wide, tears threatening to escape past the lower lids. "I thought you liked it here."

Carlinda bit briefly at her lower lip. "I shouldn't have brought this up," she said, and then turned to Amanda. "It won't be right away, not today, or even tomorrow," she explained gently. "We'll talk about it later, sweetie."

"I've got lots of other games we haven't played yet," Amanda said mournfully.

"We'll get to them," Carlinda told her, and then shot a long look at Nicholas, who responded with a lifted brow and a pursing of his lips.

Her intent was obvious. *Say something. Back me up.* And he did neither, only watched and enjoyed her squirming as Amanda plied her with guilt-producing suggestions. By the time the meal was over, the fine line between playing with a knife and using it for a game of mumblety-peg had been explored, and Nicholas had expressed his interest in explaining the more elusive points of the game to them both.

Amanda seemed to have recovered her cheerful demeanor as she spooned up her pudding, and only Carlinda's suggestion of a short rest with a book in hand brought the child's description of tossing jacks on the porch to a halt.

She frowned, pouting just a bit. "Maybe you should read the book to me," she suggested, peering up at her nursemaid coaxingly.

"I could do that," Carlinda said agreeably. "Why don't you ask Katie for a quilt we can place on the grass under the tree in back, and we'll spend an hour in the shade."

Nicholas thought for a moment of the picture those words presented, and rued the fact that he had a business to run. He'd already dallied for almost an hour over a meal that normally would have taken him fifteen minutes to consume, and it was with regret that he stood and announced his departure for the bank.

Katie stood at the door. "Will supper at six be all right?"

she asked, her hands folded at her waist. Her gaze shifted from Nicholas to his guests, and then she smiled. "I take it you'll be here, sir?"

Carlinda eyed him with suspicion. "If you have other plans, Amanda and I are quite capable of making a meal from leftovers. We don't want to interfere with your social life, Mr. Garvey. You and I can talk another day, perhaps tomorrow?"

"I don't have much of a life outside the bank and my study here at home," he said, shooting a warning look at Katie, ignoring the memory of Patience and her assumption of his attendance at the Millers' party tomorrow evening.

That he'd been calling with regularity on Patience over the past weeks was a fact he'd rather not have revealed right now. "I occasionally eat with the sheriff and his family. Other than that, I lead a rather quiet existence."

"Well, don't think you have to entertain Amanda and me," Carlinda told him. "I'm sure a gentleman such as yourself must have friends who expect to have him come calling on occasion."

"If you're referring to *lady* friends, ma'am, I haven't any commitments in that direction."

At Katie's hasty departure from the doorway and into the kitchen, Nicholas relaxed. Not for the world would he allow anything to halt his pursuit of the woman who watched him from her seat at his right. And tonight he would make clear his interest in her. Coax her to stay on for a while.

"I'd like you to tell me all you know about my sister," Nicholas said, his fingers holding firmly to the coffee cup he held. He sat across from her, his demeanor relaxed as he sipped from the steaming cup. He'd chosen to sit on the sofa, and Carlinda moved to perch on an armchair across from him. Now the words he spoke surprised her, and she frowned as she recalled the dossier she'd given him in his office.

"Surely you read the paperwork from the judge in New York," she said. "Certainly it contained proof of your relationship."

He waved a hand dismissively. "I'd rather hear it from you. All I managed to glean from the court record was her name and that of her husband. Irene and Joseph Carmichael, I believe." He leaned forward, the cup held between his palms, his forearms resting on his thighs, and his eyes were clouded by some hidden emotion as he awaited her reply.

"Irene was my friend," Carlinda began, unsure of what she was obliged to tell about the beautiful woman who'd lived in fear of her secrets being revealed. "She married Joseph. I suppose I should mention that she'd also been interested in his partner, Vincent Preston, at one time. But once Joseph came along, she settled on him, and they shared a whirlwind romance."

"Whirlwind?" His inflection was cynical if she read it aright.

"Yes…perhaps a period of two weeks after meeting him, Irene married Joseph."

"And they lived happily ever after?" Beyond cynical, his lifted brow seemed derisive.

"Hardly. For just about six years, as it happens. After Amanda was born, they settled down to the usual married life. Joseph was successful, and his partner was brilliant. Vincent Preston is a man I wouldn't want to cross." *And yet I have.*

"How so?" Nicholas asked, interest lighting his gaze. "Is he a scoundrel? Or just a shrewd businessman?"

Carlinda hesitated, thinking about the tall, almost sinister-appearing gentleman she'd met in the courtroom in New York City. "Harsh, perhaps. Shrewd, certainly. But not a man I'd find it comfortable to spend time with. I think Irene found him frightening. As I did, also.''

Nicholas frowned, as thought he would pursue that bit of information later. ''And what sort of woman was my sister?''

''Kind…beautiful, certainly. A loving mother and a loyal friend.'' It was hard to describe such a creature, Carlinda decided. ''A bit flighty at times, but Joseph was passionately in love with her, and I'm sure she returned his affection.''

Nicholas looked as if he would dismiss her description of their relationship. ''As I said—happily ever after.'' He changed his tone abruptly, speaking briskly as he questioned her further.

''I know Irene was not my mother's child. Am I safe in assuming she was the legal offspring of my father? Of the woman he was married to?''

Carlinda had the grace to be embarrassed at his forthright query. ''You don't make a secret of your beginnings, I assume, Mr. Garvey.''

His shrug was negligible. ''Not when it all happened so long ago. I've long since found that my beginnings were unimportant in the general scheme of things. More important is the man who pulled me from the gutter and sent me on my way to success.''

''Certainly not your father,'' she said flatly. ''From what Irene said, he never acknowledged your birth.''

''She's right. In fact, I'd be hard-pressed to give you his name.''

''You don't know who he is?'' Carlinda felt amazement sweep through her. ''You never sought him out? You truly don't know about the man?''

''He didn't care about me. I saw no reason to enquire as to him or his whereabouts,'' Nicholas explained politely. ''You, my dear lady, are looking at a genuine bastard.''

She refused to allow her embarrassment to show. "I was aware of your status before I arrived here."

"And you spoke to me anyway? Even gave me control over a five-year-old child?" He lifted a brow as he straightened in his chair. "Such courage, my dear. I'd have thought you might protest at my being given custody of Amanda. Are you sure I'm fit for such a responsibility?"

"Whether I am or not, it was what Irene wanted."

"Irene? My *half sister* wanted me to raise her child?"

Carlinda grimaced. "She didn't plan on dying. I think she only named you because her mother is dead, and she has no use for her father. Maybe it was a protest of sorts, though I doubt she ever thought he'd be aware of it." She bowed her head as she thought of the beautiful young woman.

"Designating you as guardian should have been a problematical decision, after all. As I said, Irene and Joseph did not plan on leaving Amanda's fate to a court decision. They fully intended to raise her themselves."

"The best laid plans…et cetera, et cetera," Nicholas said dryly. He deposited his cup on the table in front of him, a long, low structure on which sat the stereopticon he'd left out for Amanda's use.

"I don't know what else you'd like to know about Irene," Carlinda told him. "I was her friend." She shrugged, unwilling to reveal anything more.

"Was she aware of my appearance? The way I look?" His index fingers touched the small spot near his mouth. "I'd considered it coincidence at first that Amanda bears this same birthmark, but I have to admit that we share eye and hair color. My mother was fair, with light-brown hair and gray eyes. I obviously didn't inherit my looks from her."

"I think she'd known for a long time about you, and once, I found her cutting out an article in the newspaper that mentioned your name.'' She hesitated, then looked up into his gaze. ''She had a picture of you and showed it to me, so that I would recognize you if the time ever came that I needed to find you.''

He shot her a look of surprise, his eyes sharp as he probed further. ''Did you work for her long? I confess I'm a little puzzled at your relationship.''

''Yes. I lived in their home and tended to Amanda on occasion. I was your sister's companion before she was married, and Joseph invited me to remain during the months before Amanda's birth.'' She sighed, then leaned back in her chair, remembering. ''I stayed on after that. Sort of a companion and sister combined. I loved Irene, and before long I was totally wrapped up in Amanda and her care.''

''Didn't you have any other life beyond that of being a friend to my sister?'' He sounded unbelieving, his eyes narrowing as he searched her face.

''I'm on the shelf, Mr Garvey. I believe that's the old-fashioned term for being an old maid. And it's a perfectly respectable occupation for a woman like me, that of companion to another woman.''

''You weren't always 'on the shelf,' Carlinda. Surely, there must have been gentlemen in your life.''

She met his gaze, a direct, honest answer to his query on her lips. ''I had nowhere to go after my mother and stepfather moved to Philadelphia.''

''You didn't want to go with them?''

''No, I didn't want to go with them.'' *My stepfather had designs on me.* Wouldn't he love it if she were to offer that as an excuse for staying on in New York? What would he think then of his niece's nursemaid? After all, her own mother had told her she had a vivid imagination. And the woman who had birthed her had made little fuss over Carlinda's refusal to accompany them when they left for Philadelphia.

"So my sister took you in. Where was my father?" As if it pained him to ask the question, he rushed the syllables, his nostrils flaring.

"Off with another one of his women, I suppose. Irene lived in the family home by herself. She's several years older than I, but having a companion makes it acceptable for a woman to live alone."

He watched her, as if weighing her words. And then he leaned forward again. "So you're by yourself, with no attachments? What happened to Joseph Carmichael's house? Was it sold after he and Irene died?"

"I'm certain it's been put on the market by now. No one expects Amanda to return to New York. The house will be sold and the court will handle her funds until you claim them on her behalf."

He made an impatient gesture, as if he were well aware of the legal aspects. "My question is, where will you go, if and when you leave here?" His eyes lit with a glow she began to recognize. He'd looked at her several times with just such an expression, as if the urge to put his hands on her was about to outweigh his good judgement.

"*When* I leave here, I'll make that decision." And it had better be soon, if she knew what was good for her. Although her destination was certainly a puzzle.

"I have another suggestion." His voice was soft, but she didn't make the mistake of thinking he'd relaxed his stance. If anything, he was tense, his jaw taut, his mouth drawn into a thin line, his eyes hooded as if he dare not reveal too much of his thoughts.

She waited, unwilling to invite his response, afraid somewhere deep inside that it would not be palatable to her. She shunned the smile that hovered on her lips as she considered that thought. Perhaps not palatable, but definitely tempting.

"I'm very drawn to you, Carlinda."

Her jaw clenched as she heard the words. It was as she'd thought. An offer from a gentleman—if a bastard could be called such a thing—given to a young woman of limited means, who might be approachable. She'd already had two men toss such a suggestion in her direction, both of whom were surprised at her quick refusal of their proposals. This one would fare no better.

"Don't insult me, Mr. Garvey, or I shall have to leave tonight."

He grinned. "You don't even know what I'm going to say."

"Don't I?" Her heart beat faster as he rose from the couch, and she was suddenly aware of the stillness surrounding the room where they sat. Katie had gone to her quarters behind the kitchen, and Amanda was tucked into bed for the night. One lamp glowed on the table near Carlinda's chair, and outdoors it was dark, with a spring rain falling against the windows.

He stood before her, one hand outstretched. "Come," he said. "Take my hand. I want to show you something."

As if mesmerized, she did as he asked, his palm warm and dry against her cool skin. He drew her fingers through the bend of his elbow and placed them on his forearm, then led her to the door of the parlor. The foyer rose to the second floor, and they stood in the shadows cast by a lamp near the stairway.

"Look around you, Carlinda. This house is empty, save for the presence of my housekeeper and the child sleeping upstairs. Before you came, it was only Katie and me. Now that you're here, even after so short a time, I find I don't want to be alone again." His eyes were warm as he looked down into her face.

"I'd treat you well, Lin," he said, for the first time using the name he'd chosen to give her. "You wouldn't want for anything while you stay with me, and I'd never toss you aside or be unkind should you decide to end our... alliance."

Her heart ached at his words. "You don't need me," she said softly. "You have friends, Nicholas, and surely there are women waiting in line for your attention."

His heat wrapped her in its comforting warmth as he turned her to face him, his hands enclosing her waist, her own rising to touch his chest. She should draw back from him. She knew it, as surely as she knew she was in grave danger with this man.

Not that he would harm her. Not in a physical sense anyway. But the lasting effects of his touch would haunt her for the rest of her life. Yet, she cherished for these few moments the arms that held her, the mouth that claimed hers, and the breath he gave her as she opened her lips to his kiss.

The hair at his nape was like silk, and her fingers slid through the dark length of it, pressing against the clean lines of his skull, embracing the whispers he voiced against her cheek and temple. For now, for just these short minutes snatched from all time, she cherished the man, welcomed his strength and the passion he offered.

And even in her limited experience, she knew it was an offer, not a demand.

Should she so choose, he would take her hand and lead her up the curving staircase to his bed, and there allow her the gift of his body, even as she presented her own into his keeping.

For how long? The words echoed in her mind as temptation ran riot within her. When he tired of her, as surely he must—eventually—would he send her away? And would she be better off than before? The urgency of desire was alive in her blood; unknown and unexplored, it flowed in every vein, and she was inflamed by its presence.

Yet, he did not press her further, only touched her with firm lips and strong hands, his arms encircling her with a promise of more to come, should she choose to accept his loving and the offer of a life here with him.

A life as his mistress.

Her breath caught in her throat and a sob escaped, the sound seeming loud in the silence. Nicholas lifted his head and she met his gaze, her eyes filmed with tears. His smile was singularly sweet, she thought, tilting one corner of his mouth as he accepted her unspoken denial of what he offered.

He bent to press one last kiss against her soft lips, and she responded with a movement of her mouth that held him motionless for a heartbeat.

And then he stepped back from her, bowing his head in acknowledgment of her choice. "I'll light a candle for you, my dear," he said gently. "Mind your step on the stairs." Still holding her gaze, he whispered a soft invitation, his eyes warm with admiration.

"If ever you should change your mind, I'll be waiting. And if you don't—" His shoulders lifted in a gesture reflecting the patience in his gaze. "If you don't, I'll understand."

Chapter Four

New York City, May 1897

Vincent Preston's desk was neat and orderly, and the man sitting behind it appeared every inch the gentleman. Perhaps a stranger might hesitate at that assumption, given the harsh line of his mouth, or the chill light of disdain in his gaze, but in the business community of New York City, he was offered the respect due a successful man.

This morning, he waited for news from far-off. Halfway across the country, in fact. A simple matter he'd considered cut-and-dried only a month ago had now taken on the proportions of a problem he would have to go about solving on his own hook. His time was too valuable to waste, he'd told his lawyers and had, accordingly, expected them to provide him with a solution forthwith.

It had not happened. The child was gone. Whisked away from his grasp, and, to all reports, into the hands of a blood relation, her mother's half brother. He hadn't known Irene had a brother, half or otherwise. The woman had not only robbed him of his child, but made arrangements for his part in the girl's conception to be unknown.

No one else but him knew the circumstances of Irene's

pregnancy. Probably the fool Irene married, he amended. And he'd thought Joseph Carmichael was an astute man, until he'd snatched up Irene and eloped with her, almost without warning. And had, when a daughter was born only eight months later, accepted the child as his own.

Now it went against his grain that a man of his stature should be put in the position of proving that the five-year-old child named Amanda Carmichael belonged to him. To Vincent Preston.

No matter. The girl was of no value to him. But the estate she'd inherited was another matter, consisting of one half of his company, plus a sizeable bank account.

He clenched his fist, and the paper he held crumpled into a ball of linen stationary. He knew the words it held, had read them over again, twice, and then for the third time. Now he waited for the messenger who would deliver an address into his hand.

There must be hundreds of small towns in Texas. But only one of them was the home of Nicholas Garvey.

A home where Vincent Preston's daughter was in residence.

The door of Nicholas's study closed behind her and she leaned back against it, aware of his every movement as he approached. "Mr. Garvey—"

His uplifted hand halted Carlinda's words of address. "Begin again, please," he said quietly. "My name is Nicholas."

Her eyes focused on his throat as she hesitated, and he almost relented as she swallowed and inhaled deeply. But he'd chosen this time to set a precedent, and his hands twitched as he considered touching her chin and lifting it upward, the better to see those dark pupils that examined his collar so intently.

"After the other evening in the foyer, I'd have thought

we were beyond the point of formality, Carlinda.'' He refused to vary his stance, aware that he was purposely intimidating her, crowding her against the door of his study. Yet he was unwilling to allow her room to step aside. Her body vibrated with some emotion he hesitated to name, but was eager to examine.

Whether it be anger or passion, it mattered little. She reacted to him at a basic level, and furious as she might be, she could not control the response he brought forth from her slender body.

''Carlinda?'' He pressed her for an answer, his hand lifting to touch her, hovering an inch above her shoulder, then settling firmly at the nape of her neck. She shivered at the pressure of fingers against her hairline there, ducking her head as if she would dislodge his grip.

''I'm not going away,'' he said softly. ''Just lift your chin and look at me, please.''

''You're a bully, of the very worst kind,'' she said bluntly.

He watched her jaw tense, caught the sound of an indrawn breath she forced through her nostrils, then smiled into her eyes as she met his gaze. ''That's better. Now repeat after me, my dear. *Nicholas.*''

She glared impotently, looking, he thought, like a child being reproved. Her lips pressed more firmly together and then, as if she shared his thought, they twitched at one corner and she was lost, the smile gaining strength as he met it with one of his own.

''You're treating me like a schoolgirl, *Nicholas.*'' She spoke his name, even as she shook her head at his nonsense.

''Sometimes you remind me of one. Now repeat it. One more time,'' he whispered. *''Nicholas.''*

''Don't push it,'' she said flatly. ''I understand the message. And I agree that we have passed beyond the boundaries set by polite society.''

"No one knows but the two of us," he told her quietly. "And we did nothing wrong, Lin."

"That's not my name," she told him, her chin lifting defensively.

"You've been Lin to me since the first time I heard Amanda call you by her pet name."

"She's a child."

"But I'm not." His breath caught and his voice deepened as he answered her sharp retort, and then he released her from his grasp, sliding his hands into his trouser pockets as he stepped away.

"Did you want to talk to me?" he asked nicely, aware that she would not have entered his study without good reason.

"I met the sheriff's wife at the general store yesterday afternoon, and I'd like your permission to invite them for supper one evening."

"I only pay the bills, sweet. Katie runs the house. Whatever day she decrees is fine with me."

She shook her head again as he uttered the teasing words. "I didn't want to impose on you, but I liked Mrs. Cleary, and Amanda was totally smitten with her little boy."

"He's my godson, you know," Nicholas said, recognizing the pride in his own voice. "He's named after me."

"Nicky, I believe his mama said."

Nicholas winced. "Yes, I fear Augusta somewhat ruined my influence in town when she shortened my name in that manner."

"I'll stop by and see her today and issue the invitation, if that's all right with you," Carlinda said. "My thought was to gain some ties for Amanda with your friends. She needs to feel a part of your life." She glanced up at him. "I hope you won't mind my playing hostess."

"Not at all. I was going to suggest such a thing the other night, but things got a bit out of hand and I lost my…"

"Yes," she said quietly as he hesitated. "You did."

"It won't happen again." He thought his voice held a suitably apologetic tone, but her brow winged upward as if she silently doubted his words.

"I'll leave you to your work." Her hand reached behind her for the doorknob and she slipped past the heavy, wooden panel into the hallway.

Nicholas looked at the oak door, minutely examining the molding, the brass fittings, and the handle she'd turned. His fingers touched it as if she might have left some warm trace behind, and then his smile appeared, taunting him with his own foolishness.

The only thing she'd left behind was the faint aroma of wildflowers that seemed to waft from her person. A delicate scent that clung to her clothing and to the woman herself. A scent that haunted him in his dreams.

Perhaps he should go visit Patience. Allow her to put Lin out of his mind. It would take very little encouragement to have the woman in his arms. As angry as she might be, she would no doubt set aside her pique to get her greedy fingers on his assets.

He stalked to the window, brushing aside the lacy curtain to cast his gaze into the side yard. Amanda played on the grass, something held in her hands, and he frowned, leaning closer to the pane to better see what wiggled in her grasp.

A kitten. A tiny, black kitten, all four legs extended, claws at the ready, and Amanda looked around with a frantic cast on her features, as if she sought advice on how to release the scamp without injury to herself.

He lifted the window, leaning out to call her name. "Amanda, look here."

She responded, half turning to face him. "I think he's going to stick me with his fingernails," she said, and then her teeth bit into her bottom lip as she approached the window.

Nicholas swallowed a laugh, and settled for a smile. "Those are claws, sweetheart," he told her. "Bring him to me and I'll help you get out of this pickle."

Amanda walked carefully toward the window, the kitten still squirming as she reached her arms toward the man who seemed to be her only chance of rescue. Nicholas took the wiggling creature and, with quicksilver response, the tiny, needle-sharp claws set themselves into his hands.

"Well, da—" He stifled the curse and brought the kitten to his chest, allowing it to turn and settle its frightened self against his suit coat. The claws left speckles of blood behind and he sighed. Katie would have a fit, muttering to beat the band, he'd warrant, the whole time she worked at removing the blood from the wool fabric.

"Come on in, Amanda," he told the child, "and we'll find a bowl of milk for the kitty. Meet me in the kitchen."

Amanda nodded and smiled, inspecting her own fingers for damage, then ran around the corner of the house toward the back door.

She was in the kitchen when he arrived. He pushed the door open before him. "Katie," he called, looking down at the tiny, black creature who'd laid claim to his chest. "Do we have a bowl of milk for this scamp?"

Looking up from rolling out a pie crust, his housekeeper frowned. "What are you doing with a cat? I thought you didn't like animals around the place."

"It's not a cat," Amanda said quickly, hovering at his side. "It's only a kitten. Just a baby, Katie."

Katie looked down at the little girl, perhaps catching sight of the eagerness of her gaze as she reached out one small finger to touch the tiny, black head. "So it is," she agreed. "And kittens need milk, don't they, darlin'?" She wiped her hands on the enormous apron that covered her from breast to knees and sought out an odd bowl from the pantry. The icebox held a bottle of milk, and Katie poured the bowl half-full, setting it near the door.

"I think he's from a litter born almost two months ago to the folks next door. They've been looking for homes for the lot of them," she murmured as Nicholas deposited the animal beside the offering. "And just look at your hands, will you," she said sternly. "You've allowed that creature to claw you to bits."

"Not quite," he said, disputing her words. "Just a little jab, here and there."

"I'll wash them out for you and put stuff on them," Amanda offered. "Linnie has a box of salve and bottles of medicine in her room. I can fix you right up," she said importantly, obviously quoting her nursemaid as she grasped his hand to lead him from the kitchen.

"Go on along with you," Katie said, turning to the sink to wash her hands before she began work anew on the pie crust. "I'll leave you in good hands, sir. Just do as the little miss tells you and you'll be fine." Her eyes crinkled as Amanda nodded agreeably.

"I'll let you watch the kitty until I get back," she told Katie.

And then he was led through the hallway to the foyer and up the stairs to the first door on the right. Lin's room. Amanda's small fist rapped smartly and, from within, he heard the woman's reply.

"Amanda, is that you? Come in, dear."

Before he could announce his presence, Amanda had turned the knob, and he was presented before Lin's astonished eyes, his hands lifted for inspection as Amanda explained the happenings below stairs.

Amusement ran rife in her indulgent smile as special note was made of each small bit of damage. "I'd say this requires the use of iodine," Lin mused, stepping to the doorway of her dressing room to retrieve a covered, flowered box from the shelf therein.

"Iodine burns." His voice was firm as he issued the statement, attempting to pull his injuries from view.

"Amanda will blow while I apply, won't you, sweetie?"

The child nodded solemnly. "We need to wash his hands first, Linnie. You always tell me that."

"I didn't think," *Linnie* answered, nodding her head. "You're absolutely right." She turned back to smile sweetly at the patient. "Why don't you sit on the chair over by the window?" And then she watched as Amanda used a bit of soap on a washcloth to scrub at the tiny wounds where the blood had already formed small scabs. Industriously, the girl worked at her task, and over her head, he met brown eyes that scanned him anxiously, perhaps apologetically, he thought.

"I'm not badly hurt," he assured her with a grin.

"I know. I was just thinking that I was not kind, or even polite, now that I've spent a few moments considering it. Earlier, I mean."

"You were more mannerly than I," he admitted, wincing as Amanda's scrubbing touched a particularly sore spot.

"I think that's enough soap and water, Amanda."

Lin, for he could no longer think of her as Carlinda once he'd spoken the affectionate shortening of her name, halted the child's ministrations and reached for the box of medicinals. A bottle with skull and crossbones on the label appeared from the depths of the pretty little box, and he eyed it with trepidation.

"I really don't think—" he began and was silenced by a sharp look.

"You don't want to get infection," she reminded him, daubing the iodine on his wounds. Amanda blew softly as he cringed, making a face, the better to impress her with his pain.

"It'll be fine, Uncle Nicholas," she said primly between puffs of air from her pursed lips. "You must be brave."

He nodded, suppressing a smile as he looked down at the two bent heads, their owners tending to his injuries. "*Uncle* Nicholas?" he repeated softly, and was given the benefit of Amanda's immediate attention.

"You're my very own uncle. Linnie said so, and Katie told me I could call you Uncle Nicholas if I wanted to." She took a deep breath, her statement having been a mouthful, and then looked up at him anxiously. "You don't mind, do you?"

Nicholas cleared his throat, a thickening there causing him a problem as he spoke. "No, I don't mind at all, sweetheart. I kind of like it. No one's ever called me that before now." These two females had come to be of major importance in his life in less than a week's time. He tested the waters now with Amanda, reaching out to touch her cheek with his index finger. She smiled widely and shot a look of triumph at her nursemaid.

The thought of spending time with Patience was gone, obliterated as if it had never been. If he had to take long walks to exercise his nagging needs into oblivion, he would do just that. But using one woman to assuage the pain of another's refusal was beneath him.

And certainly, all hope was not yet lost.

He knew, knew it with a certainty he could not explain, that Lin would come to him.

Not tonight. Of that he *was* sure. But sometime, when the passion in her eyes became a desire she could not deny, she would come to him. It was worth the wait. He'd learn to savor the moment, and not to rush his fences. And if those two homilies were somehow not suited to the occasion, it was all right. The end result would be the same.

She would be his.

Augusta Cleary was a vibrantly beautiful woman, yet Lin, a name she realized she had accepted once Nicholas had blessed her with it, was not made to feel any less than attractive in her own right. The men shared their attention between the ladies, and even Nicky, who by all rights should have been in bed at this hour, claimed his own bit of admiration.

"He's a scamp," Augusta said in an aside to her hostess as they watched the pair of gentlemen playing on the parlor floor with the little boy. Just past twelve months in age, he was gloriously beautiful, with his mother's golden hair and his father's dark eyes, a contrast that would no doubt hold him in good stead with the ladies one day, Lin decided. And then said as much.

"Well, he has me totally at his mercy," Augusta told her with a rueful laugh. "And Jonathan spoils him dreadfully."

"Jonathan? I've only heard Nicholas speak of him as Cleary," Lin said.

"He prefers it." Augusta's mouth softened as she shed her gaze on the three male figures, wrestling together on the carpet. "But his name is Jonathan, though when I find occasion to use his surname he sits up and takes notice." Her smile was possessive, Lin thought.

If this was the relationship between husband and wife that Nicholas had been exposed to over the past years, she was hard-pressed to understand why he didn't speak more warmly of marriage.

"Do you think this boy needs to be tucked into bed?" Cleary asked his wife as Nicky toddled into his father's arms. He darted a look that seemed to hold a hidden meaning at the golden-haired woman, and Augusta smiled again.

"Whenever you say. I think Amanda was about worn out chasing him before supper. She didn't protest when you sent her about her chores a few minutes ago,'' she said to Lin.

"She needed to feed her kitten. Nicholas feels if she wants a pet, she must be responsible for its care." And then as Amanda peeped around the parlor door, Lin held out a hand in welcome. "Come in, dear. Nicky is about to be taken home and put to bed by his mama. Do you want to say good-night to him?"

Amanda nodded, her eyes lighting as the little boy half ran across the parlor carpet toward her. "I thought I'd show him my kitty, but I didn't want him to get scratched up. Maybe I should wait till Blackie learns how to pull in his claws." She looked up at Augusta solemnly. "Katie says that kitties have to learn that, and that I must be careful in the meantime not to get scratched up like Uncle Nicholas did."

"Uncle Nicholas?" Cleary said, grinning at the man in question. "Now that has a ring to it. We'll have to teach Nicky those words."

"His vocabulary is quite limited at this point, Nicholas," Augusta said. "Don't hold your breath waiting for him to spit out all those syllables any time soon."

"I won't mind," her host told her simply, rising from the floor to sit on the sofa. "I've learned in the past days to appreciate the title." He held out a hand to Amanda and she skipped to his side, glowing as his arm circled her waist.

"You begin to resemble a family man, Nick," Cleary told him beneath his breath, the sound barely reaching Lin's ear.

She glimpsed a look of chagrin that quickly turned into a frown as the two men rose in unison and walked across the room, Nicholas's arm sliding up to rest across Amanda's shoulders, Cleary carrying his son.

Nicholas would not appreciate the designation, she knew.

Yet Cleary was obviously given to teasing the man. Perhaps he thought to persuade Nicolas into a relationship matching his own. If so, he had a surprise coming. If she knew anything about it, marriage was far from what Nicholas had in mind for his future. Seduction was more to the point.

"Lin?" Beside her, Augusta called her, using the name she'd begun to respond to with such ease. Now she turned quickly to reply.

"I'm sorry, I was thinking. What did you say?"

"My thoughts probably were matching yours," Augusta said, glancing at the two men who had walked into the foyer. "I only wanted to know if I might call you by the name Nicholas has bestowed on you. Carlinda is a lovely name, but I noticed that even Amanda calls you Linnie."

"If you like. Amanda has always shortened it. She was about Nicky's age when she decided on my title, and it hasn't changed since."

"Are you coming along, Gussie?" Cleary called from the front door. "This boy of ours is settling down to sleep on my shoulder."

"Gussie?" Lin grinned as she repeated Cleary's word.

Augusta grimaced. "Rather undignified, I know, but he began it early on and there's no changing Cleary when he gets the bit in his teeth."

"I like it," Lin told her. "Let's agree on something. I'll be Lin and you can be Gussie and we'll be friends." *For as long as I'm here.*

Lin set that errant thought aside and a quick hug between the women cemented the notion. Lin watched as the petite woman hurried to join her husband on the threshold leading to the porch. *I probably won't be here long enough to keep a friend.* That thought was as daunting as the first, but the chance of gaining another woman's companionship tempted her beyond good sense. She lifted her hand as Gussie turned back, and their eyes met in understanding.

"You had a good time." It was not a question, but a statement of fact tossed in her direction as Nicholas brought Amanda back into the parlor.

"Yes, I did. They're lovely people, especially Gussie. And Nicky is a beautiful child. I can see that there's an appreciable difference in little boys and girls."

"Between big boys and girls, too," Nicholas said wisely, his eyes sparkling as he teased her. He looked down at Amanda, who was covering a wide yawn with her palm. "I think this little girl needs to go to bed."

"I agree," Lin said, willing to break the mood he'd set in place. "Come along, sweetie. I'll help you get undressed." Taking Amanda's hand, she led her to the door, but the child halted, digging in her heels.

"Wait. Just a minute, Linnie. I didn't tell Uncle Nicholas good-night."

He bent to her, holding out his arms, and she lifted her own to clutch at his neck, hugging tightly for just a moment. "Good night, Amanda," he said, lifting her from her feet for a moment before he lowered her to the carpet. His gaze remained on them as they crossed the floor, and then it lifted to touch Lin with its warmth as he spoke again. "Will you come back down?" he asked.

"Yes." Her nod lent substance to the word and then she turned to climb the stairs, Amanda chattering about the kitten and the plans she'd already made for its care.

Nicholas waited for her in his study, knowing she would seek him out there. A sheaf of papers needing his attention sat in the center of his blotter, but he could not concentrate on their contents, his mind on the two females upstairs. His life had changed drastically, and Cleary had caught on quickly to the difference in Nicholas's household.

He'd given his opinion in no uncertain terms before supper. *Have you thought of marriage to the girl? It would certainly simplify things.* Cleary had spoken his advice in an undertone during a time when the womenfolk were apart from them. The man could be depended on to get to the heart of any situation, Nicholas thought with a grimace.

For Cleary there would be no other solution but marriage. The lawman was of the old school, which decreed that once a woman came in sight with all the proper qualities of a wife-apparent, it would behoove a man to snatch her up and buy a wedding ring.

On the other hand, Nicholas had seen marriages that had begun with white lace and pretty words and ended up with division between husband and wife that tainted their lives evermore. Yet, having Amanda in his life might lead to an alliance now that there was a child to be considered.

"Are you certain you know what you're getting into, allowing Amanda to keep the kitten?" From the doorway, Lin's words were soft, as if she feared the little girl might be listening.

He waved her into his study. "Did you get her into bed already? I thought she'd keep you up there for an hour, making plans for her pet."

"I promised her we'd do all that in the morning, and she agreed. In fact, she chased me out so she could go to sleep more quickly and the night would go by faster."

"I never had a pet," Nicholas said bluntly. "If allowing Amanda to keep an animal will make her happy, it's the least I can do. In case you run off, it'll give her something to depend on." His words were teasing, but he stood stockstill as she seemed to search for an apt reply.

"If I run off, you'll be given notice," she told him after a moment "I'm not a coward, Nicholas."

He agreed with a nod. "Among other things, I'd say you were a brave lady. You brought a child halfway across the country, by yourself, and into an unknown situation, Lin. That wasn't done without some small amount of concern on your part."

"I wanted what was best for Amanda. Besides, I'd made a promise to her mother that no matter what happened, I'd take care of her."

"And had no idea where that vow would take you," he mused, waving to a chair. And then he settled behind his desk.

"Is this to be a formal interview?" she asked, watching him as he put the large piece of furniture between them.

"No. Far from it. I just want you to know that Cleary has it in his head that we should get married. You may be getting some encouragement along those same lines from Augusta if you see much of her."

"What do I call myself, Nicholas?" she asked. "Am I a combination nursemaid and companion here? Or a hostess for you, as I was tonight?"

"I enjoyed you sitting at the other end of my table, acting as my hostess, Lin. If you'll agree to that, we'll entertain often. I owe suppers to several folks in town." His hands formed a peak, his index fingers almost touching his mouth as he watched her, and his voice was quiet.

"Are you asking for more than that? If so, I've already made an offer." He watched closely as she considered his question, and her eyes refused to meet his as she spoke her reply.

"No. I've never asked a man for anything in my life." Her mind flashed a picture of herself as a younger woman. *Please don't touch me again.* And her stepfather had jeered, turning away until another opportunity should present itself.

Nicholas's voice was urgent as he noted her loss of color and the trembling of her hands. "Lin. What is it? I didn't mean to upset you. I promise I won't mention that occasion again."

Her gaze was dark with sadness as she looked up at him. "Nothing's wrong. And it wasn't anything you said. I just remembered something I'd thought was forever buried in my past.''

Prying was the furthest thing from his mind, but it pained him to see her look so bereft, as if her best and last friend had died. As indeed might have been the case, now that he considered it more fully. ''Will you tell me about it?'' he asked quietly. ''If it caused so much pain, perhaps I can help.''

''No, I'd rather not. I was foolish to let it bother me.'' She forced a smile. ''So far as you're concerned, I won't ask for marriage, Nicholas. And you, on the other hand, must not press me for any other sort of…an understanding.''

''There are things in my past…'' His hesitation was long, and then he began anew. ''I know you're familiar with my background to a certain extent, but you need to be aware that until I saw Cleary and his wife together, I wouldn't have given you two cents for any such an arrangement between a man and woman.'' He grinned suddenly, remembering.

''In fact, I knew them before such an idea entered Cleary's head, when Augusta first came to Collins Creek. I'll tell you about it someday. She was a real go-getter, and once Cleary took a good look, he was a goner.''

''They seem happy,'' she said, ''and heaven knows they're both head over heels with little Nicky.''

''Marriage worked for them. And I'm pleased on their behalf,'' he conceded.

''But you don't see it in your future.''

He shook his head. ''Not at the moment. If I did, I'd snap you up in a minute.''

''Well…'' she began, rising and walking to the door. ''I don't think I'm in danger of that happening tonight. I believe I'll go upstairs myself. I have some things to do before I go to bed.''

"Good night, Lin," he said, watching as she walked across the foyer to where the staircase wound its way to the second floor. "You're right, you know."

She halted in her tracks, one foot on the bottom step. "About what?" she asked, deigning to turn around and face him.

"You're not in danger tonight." He hesitated, and she moved up another step.

"But don't become complacent, my dear. Danger can come from many directions, you know."

He saw only the bottom half of her body now as she moved on. And then her feet touched the seventh step, for he'd been unconsciously counting as she climbed. She was unmoving, and he waited.

"I think the biggest danger is not from you, Nicholas, but from within *me*." One foot moved and then lowered again to settle beside the other. "I fear I'll make a fool of myself one of these days if I don't walk away from you."

"But not tonight?" He asked so quietly he wondered if she heard him.

Her feet shifted, then moved upward, her voice trailing behind her.

"No, not tonight."

Chapter Five

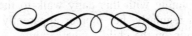

Today, as it had been for the past week, the town square was a part of Amanda's morning walk. "Linnie, let's hurry, in case Sally thinks I'm not coming." Impatience was ingrained in her character, it seemed, accompanied by an abundance of energy. It was easier, Lin decided, to include the outing in each day's plan, using it to her advantage, than to coax Amanda's cooperation with the simple lessons that had formerly been a part of every morning.

And all the time, she recognized that she was only marking time, that, as someone had once said, "The spirit is willing, but the flesh is weak." The adage, she decided, also applied to women who were in a position akin to disaster and didn't possess the strength of will to escape its entanglement.

Leaving Nicholas Garvey should be simple; just get on a train and head eastward. Surely an intelligent woman could find work somewhere between Texas and New York. Certainly she was capable of supporting herself if it came to that. She'd done it before, and could no doubt handle being on her own again.

But the reality of never seeing Nicholas again caused a pain in her breast she could hardly bear. And all this after only a couple of weeks in his presence. What would it be like should she be here for much longer, she wondered. Weeks maybe, perhaps months.

It didn't bear thinking about, for certainly her will to resist what he offered would not remain firm but eventually draw her into an illicit relationship with the man. Still she stayed, enjoying her hours with Amanda, settling into a routine, beginning with this daily walk to the park. Sally joined them regularly, her mother apparently not holding too tight a rein on the child's whereabouts.

Lin took along a book or two each day, and bargained cheerfully with Amanda as they walked the nearly half mile or so into town. "Today, we'll learn two new letters and three words," she told her, glancing upward at a sky that threatened rain before the morning touched noonday.

"I know lots of letters already," Amanda retorted, skipping ahead, uncaring of the dust she kicked up, her eagerness to play overcoming her usual decorum.

"These are new letters, sweet. There are twenty-six in all, and we've only gotten to the first dozen. You'll need to pick today's letters out from the words on the page for me. I brought two books along to use today, and one of them has a lot of pictures in it."

"I like picture books best," Amanda confided, tilting her head to the side, the better to see the cover of the book tucked beneath Lin's arm. "I know most of those letters on the front of that one already," she announced, and then, losing interest in her education, she resumed her skipping as Sally came into view.

"Sally." Her voice rang out, and the little girl she'd come to call her friend caught the ball she'd been tossing in the air and waved, running toward them. "We gotta look at books first, and then I can play," Amanda said glumly as Sally approached.

"It's gonna rain," Sally announced. "I like the books

your Linnie has, but today we need to look real quick, in case we get a gully-washer.'' She looked up at Lin and confided a small bit of knowledge. ''That's what my papa calls it when it rains extra hard. And mama said I must be home before the first drops fall,'' she announced.

With an answering smile, Lin sat on the closest bench and the little girls climbed up to sit on either side of her. The top book was opened quickly, and pictures of animals elicited an excitement that simple words on a page could not match. The girls pointed to one then another of the creatures, naming them and laughing over the elephant's trunk and the long neck of a giraffe.

Probably not the accepted way to teach, Lin thought, but more enjoyable to the student. She pointed out the letters of each animal's name, had the girls repeat them to her and then sound out the syllables. ''Effa-lint,'' Sally said studiously, and Lin held her laughter in abeyance.

''Not quite,'' she said cheerfully. ''Let's try it again.'' The time passed quickly, and in ten minutes Lin excused her pupils, closing the books and placing them beside her. She'd spend an hour this afternoon, while it rained, to review the small lessons she'd been working on for Amanda's benefit.

''Do they know how much they've learned in such a short time?'' The voice from behind her rang with a familiar note, and Lin only chuckled quietly as Nicholas rounded the bench to sit at the other end. The books lay between them and she picked them up, holding them against her breast.

''Amanda is really too young to absorb a lot at a time,'' she said. ''But she'll be reading within six months, and never even know how she got to that point.''

''You're a good teacher,'' Nicholas told her. ''You'll make a good mother one day.'' He stretched out his legs, crossing his ankles, his boot toes pointing upward. ''Why haven't you sought a husband, Lin? You're a beautiful woman. Surely there have been men who pursued you.''

"Not really," she admitted. "My stepfather was not inclined to allow me to walk out with any of the young men who showed an interest in me.''

He lifted a brow as he turned his head to her, and his words were unbelieving. "Surely your mother had something to say about that. Or did he dominate her, too?''

"He was not a kind man, unless he wanted something.''

"Something? From you?" His eyes narrowed, as if his quick mind had picked up on her unspoken meaning. He turned to her, his relaxed posture becoming more alert, his face stern as he pressed the issue. "Was he abusive to you?''

"Did he beat me?" She shook her head. "No, he left a few bruises on my arms sometimes, but he never used his fists on me.''

"Why would he do that? I doubt you were an intractable child." His hand lifted to brush a lock of hair from her cheek and she jerked from the touch, and then looked up at him quickly, an apology on her lips.

"I'm sorry. You startled me.''

"You looked frightened, Lin. And I don't believe I've given you reason to fear me, have I? Or was it that I touched you unexpectedly?''

"Perhaps." And then she shook her head. "It wasn't you." Refusing to hold his gaze, she looked toward the general store where two men sat on a bench beneath the wooden awning. "Those gentlemen are watching us," she murmured.

"Let them. I have good reason to speak with you.''

"But not to touch me.''

His hand dropped to the back of the bench. "You're right. I wouldn't do anything to damage your reputation. I want you to stay, you know that. And I want the townsfolk to respect you as Amanda's nursemaid. Most folks are aware of your position in my home."

"We haven't spoken of it as a permanent thing, Nicholas," she said. And then she looked up as a single drop of rain touched her hand. "I was afraid of this. It's going to be a downpour before we can get home. Sally says we're going to have a gully-washer." Her smile became rueful as she turned to search out her charge. "We should have stayed home, I know. I only gave in to Amanda because she loves to play here every morning, and I hated to deny her."

He rose and held out his hand. "Come on over to the bank and wait it out. There's no sense in getting soaked."

She took his extended palm and allowed his help, rising easily as he called out to his niece. "We're going to the bank to stay dry," he told the little girl, waving as Sally scampered off.

"Sally's said her mama's at the store now," Amanda announced. "She was gonna come over to talk to Linnie after she got her stuff all bought."

"Well, she'll have to do it another time," Nicholas said. "We're going to make a run for it." He snatched Amanda from her feet and lifted her, holding her with one arm as he clutched Lin's elbow with his other hand. They hastened across the park, beneath the trees, where the sudden wind blew the fresh, spring-green leaves into a frenzy. Scuffling through the rain-spattered dust beneath their feet, they crossed the street to where the double doors of the bank stood open.

Giant-size raindrops decorated their clothing as they stood inside the sheltered entrance, and Amanda laughed as Nicholas lowered her to the floor. His hat was off in an instant, and he threaded his fingers through the wayward dark strands of hair he'd ruffled, brushing them into place.

Then, with a gesture of welcome, he ushered them to his office.

"Do we have any hot water, Thomas?" he asked his clerk. "Miss Donnelly and her charge might enjoy a cup of tea."

Lin smiled at the young man, who shot her an admiring glance. "That would be wonderful," she said. "I don't know that I've ever heard of a bank that served tea to its customers."

"We don't, normally," Nicholas told her. "But I like to have it available on occasion. Thomas tends to all sorts of such things for me."

"You have a kitchen in the back room?" she asked.

He grinned at her, offering a chair and taking the precious books from her hands, handing them to Amanda. "Not a whole kitchen, but a small stove and a cupboard with odds and ends to provide me with a light meal if I decide not to go home for dinner."

Lin watched as Amanda sat on the carpet near the windows, and then she turned her attention back to Nicholas. "I've not known you to miss one of Katie's meals since we've been here."

"I've been a regular at the dinner table, haven't I? Perhaps it's the company I find there." His glance was admiring as he sat down behind his desk and leaned back in his chair. "Katie has made note of it. I don't know why I allow her to tease me so. I think she hasn't figured out yet that I'm the employer, and, as such, should be treated with great dignity."

"I think she's got you all figured out, Mr. Garvey," Lin said quietly, allowing her gaze to touch his dark hair, where his fingers had left their mark. His eyes, their brilliance masked by lowered lids, searched her own, and his smile disappeared as if a magic touch had erased it from his lips.

"And you, Lin. Have you figured me out yet?" He

leaned back, his hands lightly clasped over his vest. "I certainly haven't had much success in sorting through your thoughts and feelings. I've attempted to search out the woman beneath your cool demeanor, and until this morning, had little success."

"This morning?" Her mind sought out the few moments of conversation they'd shared in the park. "How so?"

"I think your stepfather had a lot to do with the position in which you've found yourself. Am I right?" His lips thinned, as though he contemplated the man in question and found him to be brutish and not worthy of his relationship to the woman before him.

"You wouldn't like him," she admitted.

"I don't like cruelty in any form," he said quietly. "Especially as it is directed at children or women. I think you've been the victim of a man whose actions have made you fearful of men in general." He paused, then plunged ahead, giving only a passing glance toward Amanda, who was settled on the floor with the two books open before her.

"Did he misuse you?" he asked quietly, his voice barely carrying to where she sat.

She felt a painful blush rise to cover her cheeks. With a slow movement, she shook her head. "Not really. I kept as far from him as I could. His hands were like a vulture's claws, always ready to take hold, and I had bruises to show for it."

"He would have before long, though," he said with certainty, almost as if he'd been there during those dark days. "If you hadn't left home when you did…" His words trailed off as though his thoughts were too dark to utter aloud.

She could only nod her agreement, unwilling to meet his eyes now, closing her own, embarrassed by what she'd revealed to this man. He was almost a stranger, even though they'd shared private moments. Moments she'd do well to put behind her, she thought. First and foremost, he was her employer; and she'd allowed him to poke and prod out of her the secret she'd carried for more than six years.

His voice was dark, his question barely a murmur. "You didn't tell your mother?"

"Yes, and she said I had a vivid imagination to think that a dignified man would be interested in a child." She looked up then and found he'd risen and walked to where she sat. "I wasn't a child, Nicholas. I was a woman, almost full-grown, and if I hadn't left, he'd have invaded my bed." She'd never been so outspoken in her life, even Irene had known only the very scant details of her struggle.

"But he didn't," Nicholas said softly. "And for that I'm grateful."

"Why?" She met his gaze fully, watching as he crouched before her and took her hands in his. "I'd think you'd rather have an experienced woman available for what you have in mind for me, Nicholas, rather than an old maid with no knowledge of what you propose." Her words sounded harsh in her own ears, and she bit at her lip, wishing she might take them back, unspoken.

"I'm surprised you were able to respond to me in any way the other night, Lin. But, know this. I'd never force myself on you or any woman," he told her, glancing to where Amanda sat, oblivious to their conversation. And then he looked up, a smile forming on his lips as the door opened and Thomas entered, a small tray in one hand.

"Here's our tea," Nicholas said, "and just in time.

"Miss Donnelly was feeling chilled by the rain," he told his clerk, taking the tray and placing it on his desk.

"There was no milk, sir," Thomas told him. "But I found sugar."

"I don't use milk," Lin said quickly. "This will be fine."

Thomas left, pulling the door closed behind himself, and Nicholas poured from the flowered pot. "This is from home," he said. "Katie thought I needed tea brewed in a pot as opposed to a few leaves in the bottom of a cup." He offered it to his guest and Lin took the cup carefully, lest she spill its contents. "Would you like sugar?" he asked, lifting the lid from a dainty matching container.

"No, thank you." She sipped at the brew, relishing the flavor, then felt a pang of guilt as she considered her charge. "Amanda, would you like some tea?" she asked, raising her voice to attract the child's attention.

"No, ma'am," Amanda answered, apparently unwilling to be drawn from the book before her.

"There's water if she'd like a drink," Nicholas offered. "Otherwise, I'm afraid my refreshments are in short supply."

"She's happy as she is, I think," Lin said. "And we must be getting home. I believe the rain has let up." She looked around the office. "Do you have an umbrella we could use?"

Nicholas nodded, and then, as if he'd had a sudden thought, went to the door, opening it and calling for Thomas. "Use my umbrella and run down to the livery stable and get my rig, will you?" A murmur from Thomas appeared to please him and he closed the door, his back against it as he smiled at Amanda, whose head had lifted from her book. "Would you like a ride in my buggy?" he asked.

"Oh, yes," she stated firmly. "I could even help you hold the reins. I'm very good at that. My papa used to say—" Her voice halted, and a pained expression painted her features. As if she'd unlocked a door in her mind and found sorrow behind the portal, she turned to Lin and rushed into waiting arms.

"That's all right, sweet. You can talk about your papa if you like."

"I don't want to," Amanda said stubbornly. "It makes me hurt when I remember things. And sometimes I miss my mama awful bad."

Lin lifted her to her lap. Her arms encircled the little girl, and she searched in her pocket for a clean hankie. "It's all right to cry, Amanda. We all have things in our past that make us sad sometimes."

"Do you, too?" the child asked, looking up with a teary gaze. "Do you cry sometimes, Linnie?" She allowed her eyes to be wiped and her nose blown. And then looked up into Lin's eyes, her mouth forming a soft pout. "I've never seen you cry," she announced. "I don't think ladies do that."

"I try not to." *And don't always succeed.*

"Let's wait out in the lobby," Nicholas said, apparently willing to stir Amanda from her gloomy thoughts. And, it seemed, the suggestion of a ride was just the ticket. He held the door open and they filed out, a most domestic trio, Lin thought, her lips curving in a smile as she glanced up at Nicholas.

"What's so funny?" he asked, bending to catch her reply. And then as if he read her thoughts, he grinned before she could voice them aloud. "You're thinking I look the very image of a family man, aren't you?"

"Don't let the word get around," she warned. "This town will have you at the altar before you know it."

"The day I marry, it will be because of my own choice, sweet. Not at the mercy of a bunch of gossiping women."

He took her arm and looked down to find Amanda clutching at his free hand. How he'd managed to present this picture to the townsfolk in the lobby of his bank was a mystery. Yet, he could not find it in his heart to protest. Lin had not asked for his attention; and though Amanda had almost demanded it, he knew the child had a right to expect him to cater to her a bit.

Leaving his business early was not a common thing for him, but for some reason he hadn't the heart to send these two on their way, while he sat at his desk and counted the minutes until it should be time to go home for the noon meal.

Giving of himself was becoming easier with each passing day, he realized, waiting just inside the double doors as the rain turned to a scattered sprinkling of drops. As they watched, his buggy neared the bank, Thomas dealing nicely with the reins, the mare prancing between the traces. The buggy pulled up with a flourish, and Nicholas escorted his two females to stand beside it.

With a quick movement, he lifted Amanda and settled her on the seat, then turned to Lin. "Let me help you," he said, not giving her the choice of accepting or denying his offer. He enclosed her waist with his hands, long fingers encircling the narrow span. She was neither heavy nor light, he decided, only soft and warm to his touch, and he rued the impulse that seemed to govern his actions where she was concerned.

She sat stiffly at the edge of the seat, looking down at him with eyes that glistened. A touch of anger perhaps, at his impulsive handling of her. Embarrassment perhaps, that those out and about should be privy to his casual demeanor in not allowing her to ascend the buggy in a ladylike manner. Ah, well, he thought dryly, a mark against him. And he'd done so well today.

"All set?" he asked, ignoring her rigid posture as he strode around the front of the mare to where Thomas waited, reins in hand. "Thank you, Thomas," he said nicely. "I'll be at home if you need me. It's almost time for dinner, so I'll not return until about one."

"Yes, sir, Mr. Garvey. I'll take care of things," Thomas

said, nodding at Lin and grinning widely at Amanda. "Have a nice dinner."

He glanced at Lin. "Are you comfortable? If I took you off guard, I apologize. I simply wanted you out of the drizzle as quickly as possible."

"I'm fine," she said shortly, with a quick look at Amanda. Then, perhaps ruing her aggravation, she looked back at Thomas as he stood watching them drive off. "What does he do, exactly?" she asked as Nicholas snapped the reins over the mare's back. "You said he's your clerk. What does that mean?"

"Paperwork," Nicholas said gloomily. "I hate the stuff, and he's very good at it. For such a youngster, he's come a long way. It goes against the grain with the older men in my employ for him to be in charge, but they seem to have gotten used to the idea."

"A youngster? How old is he?" she asked.

"Twenty-five, I think. Maybe twenty-six."

"I'm twenty-four," she said with a half smile. "Does that make me a youngster, too?"

"Women are different than men," he told her, his jaw clenching as he uttered the pronouncement.

"Yes, we agreed on that already." She was silent a moment. The mare had slowed her pace, and they were approaching the house. "Is he married?"

Nicholas glared outright. "Don't be making eyes at Thomas. He's too young for you to be considering."

She shot him a glare that only served to anger him further. "You're being rude, Mr. Garvey. And insulting, to boot. I only asked a question. I'm not out beating the bushes for the attentions of a man. And Thomas *is* older than I."

"We've already agreed on that," he said, wishing he'd never allowed this exchange to begin. She was madder than a wet hen, and he wasn't even sure what had gotten her in an uproar. He jumped from the rig and tied it to a tree branch, then reached for Lin as she perched on the narrow, iron step. "Let me help you," he said, aware that his voice was grumpy and his face probably matched.

Amanda jumped lithely to the wet ground and slid on the muddy approach to the sidewalk. "Be careful," Lin told her. "You'll fall and muddy your dress." Even as she spoke, her foot slipped and, in a reflex action, Nicholas grasped her, his arms around her middle as he clutched her to himself, her back sliding against his chest.

She inhaled sharply and her breasts pressed deliciously against his forearms, causing another reaction he fought against. She stiffened and attempted to straighten her posture. He only tightened his hold and muttered dark imprecations against her ear, then spoke aloud a threat that halted her movement. "Hold still, for heaven's sake, woman. You'll have us both in the mud if you don't stop wiggling."

"I'm all right, now. Let me go," she said, breathless as his grip tightened.

Ahead of them Amanda gained the porch, and after a quick swipe of her feet against the rug before the door, marched inside, alerting Katie that they were at home.

"Come on. In the house with you, Lin," Nicholas told her, shifting her to his side, his arm firmly settling around her waist. Together they plunged ahead, scraping their feet on the porch steps, lest they track mud into the house.

On the porch, they looked at each other, and he was hard-pressed not to laugh aloud. Her bonnet was askew, her hair curling in corkscrews across her forehead, and two hairpins dangled from one long lock that had come apart from the chignon she'd arranged at her nape. "I've never known a woman so unruly," he said finally, pressing his lips together to foil the amusement that begged release.

"Unruly?" Her eyes opened wide and an expression of

sheer dismay pleated her forehead and pinched her mouth. "How can you say such a thing? I'm a lady, Mr. Garvey."

"And I'm Nicholas, sweet." He caught at the pins that were headed for the ground and held them between thumb and forefinger. "We have to get you put together or Katie will think I've been misbehaving."

"Katie already does," his housekeeper's stern voice announced from the other side of the entryway. "Get on in here, the pair of you. Miss Lin, your dress is all wet."

"I'll change before dinner," Lin said quickly, looking down to where damp spots dotted the green dress she'd chosen this morning. "I won't be a minute."

"Here are your hairpins," Nicholas said gravely, holding out his hand where the two errant pins lay in the center of his palm. "You may need them." His gaze traveled up her body, past the curves of waist and breast to settle with impish delight on the unruly curls that defied the assortment of pins she used daily to subdue them into place.

She snatched the pins from his hand with a barely audible thanks and sailed up the stairs, her skirts held high so that she would not trip on them.

"You manage to get under her skin on a regular basis, don't you?" Katie asked, cocking an eyebrow at him. "You're either besotted by the lady or trying to get rid of her. Haven't figured out which it is yet."

"Neither," Nicholas answered. "She's Amanda's nursemaid and my guest. I'm in no hurry to have her leave."

"It's about as I figured then," Katie said, turning to hasten back toward the kitchen.

"And what's that supposed to mean?" Nicholas asked beneath his breath. Removing his suit coat, he hung it on the coat tree and headed for the kitchen, rolling up his sleeves to wash his hands. It would irritate Katie to have him invade her territory, and right now he couldn't think of anything he'd rather do.

New York City

"He's in Collins Creek, Texas, wherever that is. And the child is living in his house." Vincent Preston spat out the words as if they soured the very tissues of his mouth. His mood was far from serene, a fact duly noted by the men before him. "Can I count on perfection in this little task?" he asked, his dark eyes piercing, his words harsh.

"We guarantee success, or you don't pay a penny, Mr. Preston." The largest of the pair was nicely dressed, but his eyes were cold, his face devoid of expression. His partner, a slender, dapper fellow, looked to be more of a gentleman, yet guile lit his eyes as he listened to the proceedings.

"I want the child, unharmed, or it's no go. I don't care what you have to do to get her to me."

"What sort of a fella is this Garvey person?" the larger man asked.

"He's a banker. Doesn't sound like much opposition to me. But be aware that her nursemaid is in constant attendance. You may have to bring the woman along. It might be easier to handle the child if she has her nurse." He leaned back in his chair and waved a hand dismissively. "The rest is up to you. I don't want to know the details. I just want results."

"You'll have them, Mr. Preston." With a quick look at his partner, Hal Simpson left the office, Dennis Blevins at his heels.

"This is a cinch," Hal said in an undertone. "He's pretty much given us a free hand."

"We can always take the woman, too, and then if she gives us trouble, drop her off along the way." Dennis offered it casually, but Hal's eyes flashed with anger.

"I remember the last time we did a snatch and you ended up using a knife on the woman, and I had to dig the grave. You won't be pulling that stunt on me again."

"All right. All right," Dennis said, placating his partner with a shrug. "We'll settle for the child. For what he's paying us, I'll turn cartwheels in the town square while you snatch up the girl."

Hal turned the full force of his dark, soulless gaze on the shorter man and his words were a threat. "For what he's paying us, you'll mind your p's and q's and do as you're told."

"Where the hell is Collins Creek?" Dennis grumbled as they walked out of the spacious lobby into the pedestrian traffic of Wall Street.

"You ever hear about maps?" Hal asked, sarcasm oozing from his words. "My guess would be we buy tickets at the railroad station, and then, when they call out the towns along the line in Texas, we listen hard for the place we're heading."

"And then what? Act like a couple of dandies in the middle of cow country? I think we need to change our clothes before we get off a train in some dusty little burg at the end of the line."

Hal tossed him a look that resembled approval. "I knew you'd have a halfway intelligent thought in your head if I kept you around long enough. Just don't ask me to ride a horse, you hear?" What might have passed as a laugh in another man came out sounding more like a sneer as he punched his partner in the shoulder. "We'll make a stop once we get to Texas and buy some clothes that won't give us away."

"I used to ride horses back when I was a kid," Dennis said. "It's not hard to learn, once you put your mind to it, Hal. Besides, we might need to haul the kiddie off someway other than on a train."

"We'll hire a wagon," Hal said. "I'd rather sit on a wagon seat than the back of a horse any day of the week."

"Does this bird put his money on the line?" Dennis

asked. "I worked for one fella who tried to gyp me when I brought him the goods he asked for."

"He's paying up front for our expenses," Hal told him. "And Vincent Preston has too much to hide to pull any shenanigans with his *employees*." His sneer emphasized the final word he spoke as the two men crossed the busy thoroughfare.

Chapter Six

"Do you think I'll ever have a new mama?" Amanda asked. Her head was bent, as if she were intent on the ball she bounced, while one hand poised over the scattered metal jacks on the porch. And then she looked up, her gaze rising to meet Lin's, and the ball fell from her fingers, scattering the playing pieces. "I'd like it if you could be my mama," she whispered.

"I don't think that's going to happen," Lin said quietly. Her fingers pressed together and then entwined in her lap. "You may have to settle for having an uncle, Amanda. Even if he should ever get married, you won't truly have a mother."

"If he married you, I would," the child said staunchly, looking up with cunning alive on her expressive features. "You're already almost like a mama. And he could be a papa if he tried. I know he could. I think he likes me, anyway."

"You're a very likeable little girl," Lin said quickly. "I don't know why anyone wouldn't like you. And Nicholas is your uncle, so he surely thinks you're a very special person."

"I think he likes you, too, Linnie." Amanda made a

production of gathering the jacks into a pile. "I think I'll practice haystacks for a while. That's a lot easier than when they're scattered all over the place." She smiled brightly. "Maybe you and my uncle Nicholas could get married."

"I don't think your uncle is planning on marriage," Lin told her quietly. "And at any rate, it isn't something you need to worry about. He's given you a lovely home, and he's planning on taking care of you."

"Well, *I* think it'd be a good idea," the little girl said stubbornly, a determined look drawing her brows down. "Maybe I'll ask him."

"You will *not.*" There was no room for doubt as Lin spoke the words. "Children have no business interfering in adult matters, Amanda. And your uncle's plans for his future are not your concern."

Amanda shrugged, bouncing the ball again as she attempted to gather up the pile of jacks into her right hand. And then a grin lit her features as she caught the ball with her left hand. "See. I can do it if I use both hands, Linnie."

Lin laughed, as if she were unable to resist the child's shenanigans. "I think we'd better switch to jumping rope," she said. "I'm afraid you'll beat me at this game."

"If I'm very good, will you think about being my mama? I really need one," Amanda whispered mournfully.

Behind them, Nicholas watched from the doorway, half-hidden in the shadows of the foyer. Amanda's eyes held a vulnerability he ached for, and he inhaled sharply as he sensed the sadness that prompted the plea. "I *really* need a mama," Amanda said softly, repeating the cry of her heart.

His hands clenched at the child's words and he thrust them into his pockets. She hadn't asked for a new papa, he noted wryly. But that was to be expected. A little girl's mainstay in life was her mother. And that was as it should be. Amanda's plea spoke well for Irene Carmichael.

At least one of us made a success of parenthood. The thought echoed in his mind, even as he wondered about his sister. He'd lost her before he'd even known of her existence, and the only tie he would ever have to the woman was the child before him. If there had been other siblings in the unusual family they'd been a part of, Irene might have made other arrangements for her child. But Nicholas was her only choice.

At least Irene had had the opportunity to have a family of her own, he thought, his eyes intent on the two females gracing the wide boards of his front porch. And now he had the privilege—although *responsibility* might be the better word—of raising Amanda. It would take a woman living under his roof to provide the nurturing the girl needed. And for now, that area was covered by Lin's presence.

A mother for Amanda might be another thing altogether.

He'd thought not to marry, until Patience came along, and he'd been mostly tempted by the idea of having her as his hostess, gracing his table. By virtue of her position as his wife, he'd expected to extend her presence to his bedroom. He grinned knowingly as he considered those circumstances. She'd probably have a fit if her hair were mussed or her clothing wrinkled by his hand. Not to mention the perfection of the makeup that enhanced her face.

No, making love to Patience would require a deft hand. He'd never acquired the talent of smoothing feathers, and he feared Patience would require more pacifying than he was capable of giving.

On the other hand, Lin had the rare knack of making him comfortable in her presence. And she seemed not to place more emphasis than was required at her daily toilet. More often than not, he found her repairing damage to her person, smoothing her wrinkled clothing or recapturing flyaway curls in an effort to tame her luxurious, independent tresses.

Even now, as she sat on the porch beside Amanda, her

dress was wrinkled from sitting in the swing and rumpled from playing on the grass. Her hair curled against her nape, tendrils escaping from the loose knot she'd pinned high on her crown. He felt a smile curve his lips as he watched her, her head bent as long, elegant fingers scooped the jacks into her palm. The ball bounced high and she snatched it midair as Amanda chuckled in glee, then propped her chin in one hand.

"I don't know how you do that so good, Linnie," Amanda cried, her mouth forming a small pout. "I can't make my hand big enough to pick up more than three at a time, 'cause if I do, then the ball won't stay put."

"It's easier to play when your hands are as large as mine," Lin said soothingly. "And you have to bounce the ball high enough to give you time to pick up the jacks, sweetie." She bent to Amanda and dropped a quick kiss against the child's cheek. "Here," she said, handing off the ball, "try it again."

Nicholas moved, shifting his position, the better to see, and the slight sound of his boot against the floor caught Lin's attention. She glanced up, then back over her shoulder. "Did you want to play, too?" she asked, shooting him a questioning look. "I didn't know you were there."

"No, I think my talent lies in watching. Amanda thinks her fingers are too small, and I know mine are too big." He pushed the screen door open and stepped onto the porch. "Yours, on the other hand, seem to be just right."

He walked past them to where the swing hung and settled himself on the seat. Lin looked up and he caught a wary light in the depths of soft brown eyes. She allowed her gaze to linger a bit on his face, perhaps his mouth, he thought. And then it slid with approval to touch his arms, where his rolled-up shirtsleeves exposed tanned skin to her view. Even as he watched, her eyelids drooped a bit, and her tongue touched her upper lip in a hesitant movement.

"Your hands are just fine," she said quietly. "I'm sure they'd handle—" Her words broke off as if she had only just become aware of them being spoken aloud, and her eyes opened fully, then blinked as she inhaled sharply.

She rose, an awkward movement, smoothing her skirts, and he grinned, aware of what her next movement would be, even before her hands rose to tuck wayward wisps of hair into place with a set of combs on either side of her head. So well he'd come to know her in such a short time. Suddenly, the day seemed brighter, the sunshine warmer, the birdsong from his yard more sweet, and he was struck by a sense of belonging he'd never known in his life.

"Come sit with me, Lin." It was less than an order, more than a request, and she glanced at him, her hands twitching at her waistline as she tugged her bodice into place. The action accented the firm, lush lines of her bosom, and it was there his gaze became firmly fixed. She was as feminine as any creature he'd ever laid eyes on. And more appealing than any other he'd taken note of.

She stepped to the swing and turned, settling gracefully beside him. Her feet barely touched the porch, and beside him, she seemed a delicate woman, yet at the same time, totally, profusely strong—an independent creature. A paradox, indeed.

"Did you want to talk to me?" Her eyes still on Amanda, she spoke the query politely, her hands clasped loosely in her lap, and had he not known her better, he might have thought her relaxed and unaware of his proximity.

Fortunately, he knew her better, recognized the quick intake of breath that produced a flutter at her throat, noted the flush she could not control that painted her cheeks and throat with a bloom not unlike a ripe, blushing peach. Her coloring was creamy, her hair a vibrant auburn, and he wondered how he could not have noticed her rare beauty at first glance. That day in his office, when she'd appeared at his door and he'd refused her the courtesy of taking her outstretched hand.

"I've never fully apologized for my rudeness the day we met," he said, speaking aloud his thoughts.

She blinked and looked up at him in surprise. "You were rude?" And then her teeth touched one side of her bottom lip as if she recalled the event. "Yes, you were." She nodded. "I shocked you, showing up that way, and you were taken aback. I doubt you'd have been discourteous had you been better prepared for our appearance."

"Do you always make excuses for others, Lin? Or just me?"

Her smile widened as she turned the full force of dark eyes in his direction. "I try to be fair, Nicholas. You didn't purposely set out to be…unkind. And you recovered nicely, as I recall."

"Thank you," he answered, his voice solemn, feeling that she had somehow pronounced him a gentleman, even as she recognized his faults. "I hope you've been comfortable here."

She lifted a brow and he recognized the gesture, knew a retort would be heading in his direction momentarily. "Most of the time," she allowed. "My bedroom is cozy, my bed comfortable, the accommodations spacious."

"And the company you keep?"

"Usually gracious. On occasion…somewhat demanding."

"More than you feel comfortable with?" The softly uttered exchange caught Amanda's attention and she looked up at them, a question alive in her innocent gaze.

Lin smiled at her reassuringly as she offered Nicholas a subtle warning. "If I find it too difficult to cope with, I'm sure I can locate the front door.

"I wouldn't like that, Lin," he said, an unspoken threat holding her immobile.

And yet, as she turned her head to meet his gaze head-on, he noted a determination on her face that did not surprise him. "You don't frighten me," she whispered.

"I never intended to."

"What, then?"

"Linnie?" Amanda rose from the porch and extended her hand. "I don't like it when you say things I can't figure out." Her small face was troubled, and Nicholas felt a pang of regret that he'd caused the child distress.

"Linnie is only scolding me a bit," he whispered, leaning close to gather Amanda in his arms. Lifting her to settle on his lap, he set the swing into motion, his hands holding her waist as her feet rested on the wooden seat beside him.

"Did you do something bad?" she asked earnestly, peering up into his face.

"I didn't think so, but sometimes ladies and gentlemen don't agree on such things."

"I remember when my mama and papa had a fuss one day, and then my papa just picked my mama right up in the air and she hollered at him to put her down...." Her voice trailed off as she glanced up at Lin. "My papa kissed mama and she hugged him real tight." Her eyes took on a considering look.

"Would that work with you and my uncle Nicholas, Linnie?"

"Do you think I should kiss her?" Nicholas asked, barely able to conceal the smile that tugged at his lips. He furrowed his brow for Amanda's benefit, as if he considered the suggestion for a moment.

"It might work." Her words were hopeful and Amanda leaned toward Lin. "Would you stop scolding him if he kissed you?"

"I've already stopped," she blurted out, rising quickly.

"I wasn't angry with your uncle, sweetie. We were really just talking."

Amanda pursed her lips, forming a petite rosebud. And then she whispered aloud, a wistful entreaty that Nicholas could not resist. "I'd know you weren't fussing if my uncle kissed you, Linnie. Then I'd know you weren't really mad with him."

Without hesitation, Nicholas rose, Amanda in his arms. He shifted her weight to his left arm and she clung to his neck. "Let's step inside, ladies," he said, anticipation alive in each word. "I don't think we want any onlookers to be aware of this little ceremony, do we?"

He held the screen door open and Lin stepped inside the foyer ahead of him. As she would have moved away, he reached for her, his right hand firm against her waist, his arm turning her to face him.

"This could be the perfect way to solve the problem," he murmured, drawing her lithe, slender form closer.

"I wasn't aware we had a problem," she said, protesting his action quietly, as if needing to be careful not to give Amanda cause for alarm.

"Amanda," he said, allowing his voice to take on a firm edge. "I want you to kiss Lin's cheek, and then mine. Can you do that?"

She laughed aloud. "Course I can. I kiss Linnie all the time, and I'd like to kiss you, too. You smell good today."

"Does he?" Lin asked, catching on to the game, leaning closer to sniff elegantly at his cheek. She shrugged. "Not bad, I suppose."

"Well, I like the way he smells," Amanda said staunchly, and then pressed her soft lips against his cheek. A wave of pure, unadulterated affection swamped him as the child leaned back to view his response to her gesture. "Did I do that right?" she asked.

"Perfect," he announced. "Now kiss your Linnie."

Amanda obeyed, eager to perform the ritual. "Now Linnie has to do it," she crowed, her eyes glowing with anticipation.

Lin acceded to Amanda's demand, touching her lips gently against Nicholas's cheek, then turning to the child. Her touch was lingering as she blessed the soft, smooth skin with a short series of kisses, causing Amanda to giggle joyously.

"All right. Now you, Uncle Nicholas," she cried, drawing out the game to its end.

Nicholas obliged, his mouth warm against the child's face, and then he lowered her to the floor and she looked up at him, disappointment alive on her elfin features.

"I need both hands for this," he explained, winking at her, making her a part of his plan. She giggled again, her fingers rising to cover her mouth as he gathered Lin into his embrace. His mouth found hers, exploring the soft flesh gently. For only a moment he held her close, until he felt the warmth of sweet breath touch his lips, and knew she'd surrendered, for just that split second of time, to his will.

He released her, felt her tremble beneath his hands, and slid his arm around her waist to hold her firmly against himself. "How was that?" he asked Amanda, smiling for her benefit, grinning widely as she nodded her approval.

His next urge was to carry the woman up the stairs and into his bedroom. Damn the consequences, he thought impatiently. If it were not for the presence of Amanda, he'd have Lin on his bed in less than a minute.

With a simple brush of lips, a wispy gasp of honeyed breath, she had him at the end of his tether. What could she do with an encouraging gesture, a touch of slender hands against his person?

What had begun as a game to satisfy the whim of a child, had become a temptation he could barely resist. Next on the agenda would be a seduction of innocence, and that would never do. He'd made a promise. He'd told her she was safe with him, or at least implied it. Now her eyes were on him, wide and uncertain, and he could only smile, offering silent assurance.

He'd made a promise. One he'd like to banish to the four winds.

The two men elicited some raised eyebrows as they checked into the hotel. Brand-spanking-new clothing set them apart. Denim pants that had never known the dust of a corral met gleaming leather boots, not a scuff mark visible on their surfaces. Hats that needed the loving touch of a man's hands, forming the brim and creasing the crown, sat atop their heads, and long dusters hung to their knees.

They asked for rooms and were given two at the back of the hotel, in accordance with the request for cheap accommodations. Then they went into the hotel dining room to eat. The waitress answered their pointed questions, leaning over the table to point out the general store and the bank beside it across the street. And then frowned when they asked if Nicholas Garvey still ran the place.

"He owns the bank," she said sharply, darting a look of aversion to the tallest of the men. "What will you have to eat, gentlemen?"

Later, sauntering up and down the sidewalk, they came to the attention of store owners and the usual assortment of old men who staked a claim on benches in front of the establishments along the walkway.

"Everybody's smiling at us," Dennis announced in an undertone. "I think we're fitting in pretty well, don't you?"

Hal cast him a disparaging look. "Don't be a fool. They're probably thinking we're too clean to be cowhands."

"Maybe they'll take us for rich ranchers." And with those words, he preened a bit. "Or even gunfighters," he suggested, almost as an afterthought. His stride turned cocky as he glanced about beneath the brim of his hat.

"You're not carrying a gun," Hal reminded him bluntly. "At least not one that shows."

"I can get to it in a hurry if I need to," Dennis told him harshly.

"Sit down," Hal ordered beneath his breath as an empty bench before the general store lured them closer. "We'll keep an eye on the bank and watch for the Garvey fella."

"And then what?" Dennis asked, taking his seat, lifting a booted foot to the other knee in a practiced gesture.

"Find out where he lives."

"You see those two dudes out front?" Thomas asked as Nicholas rose from his desk.

Nicholas lifted his suit coat from the back of his leather chair and donned it, straightening his tie with one hand while he snatched up his hat from the rack on the wall.

"Haven't paid any attention to anything but the work in front of me for the past hour or so," he said. "Are they new in town?"

"I'd say so. Looks like they've come from the big city and are trying to fit in here. Not making a go of it, from what I can see."

"Maybe they're looking to buy land," Nicholas surmised. "If they've got money, we'll be glad to mind it for them while they look around." He grinned at Thomas. The last few days had put him in a better mood, and Thomas had shared the wealth of his good nature.

"Just seems strange to me. Couple of folks have mentioned them today. They're just lollygaggin' around town, looking things over."

"We can always use new blood," Nicholas told him, sauntering from his office. "I don't see any more customers, Thomas. Why don't you lock up and go home? That's where I'm heading right now.''

"I heard you didn't show up at the Millers' big party a couple of weeks ago, last Saturday," Thomas said with a grin. "Miss Patience went all by herself, and then to the church social, too."

Nicholas aimed a level glare at the young man. "The field's open there, son. Why don't you try your hand with the lady? Tomorrow's another Saturday. Maybe she'd like to go for a ride. You can use my buggy if you like."

"You don't mean it," Thomas said, stopping in the center of the lobby, an expectant grin lighting his face.

"Sure I do," Nicholas assured him, tilting his hat a bit as he turned toward the wide double doors. "Lock up behind me," he ordered. Then turned back. "Tell Sam Ferguson I said it was all right to take the buggy for the day if you like."

And wouldn't Miss Patience Filmore like that? Although Thomas would be an easy mark for the lady, Nicholas doubted the woman would relish being carted about in a borrowed rig. As for himself, he had two days ahead in which to draw Lin into his web.

He exited the building, looking neither right nor left, turning toward home with a lift in his step that had been more prominent of late. The day was too ripe with summer to use the buggy, the walk too short to need conveyance, at any rate. He could use the exercise, and perhaps might even suggest a walk after supper. Amanda would jump at the chance, and Lin would accede to the child's wishes.

He thought of a jaunt through the area just north of town, where wildflowers bloomed in meadows, and open spaces were surrounded by trees. Small creatures romped in the evening, even deer coming from the shelter of the forest to drink from the stream that flowed there. Collins Creek, it was called, meandering through forest and shaded glades, giving the town its name.

Rabbits were abundant, and a variety of birds had claimed the tall trees. Building nests and raising their young among the topmost branches, some of them sang at twilight, melodies that touched his soul with the beauty of nature on his occasional walks through their territory.

His stride grew longer as he anticipated the jaunt, then eyed the sun as it lay well above the horizon. There would be time before dark, should Katie have supper ready when he arrived home.

A feeling like the bite of a sharp blade touched his back, bringing him instantly alert as he turned the corner to walk toward his home. He slowed his step, aware of a presence behind him, and turned in a casual gesture to glance back toward town.

Houses on either side of the road basked in the late-afternoon sunshine and children played alongside the road, tossing a ball back and forth. One lad, astride a bicycle, was pedaling steadily as he cautiously made his way past, the front wheel wobbling as he steered it along.

And behind him were two men, pausing as if they discussed the house before them, their eyes careful not to look in his direction. Probably a hundred yards distant, they were nevertheless on his trail, he'd warrant, and he slowed his pace as he continued on. His own home was just ahead, and he hoped against hope that Amanda was not in the yard or on the porch waiting for him to appear. He'd walk on, see if they continued to follow him.

It was too much to ask for, he thought, as Amanda flew down the sidewalk to the gate, her smile wide as he opened the latch, then reached to lift her in his arms. Her hug was tight, her greeting enthusiastic, and he forgot for an instant the men he'd caught a glimpse of. With Amanda in his arms, he'd found he tended to forget most everything. The

work he'd left behind, the hour or so of paperwork in his
study, and the worries inherent in the owning of a bank
disappeared once he was in the child's presence.

Now he turned his head in a casual gesture, looking back
toward town, and found the sidewalk empty, the road bar-
ren of watchful strangers, only a handful of children playing in the dusty thoroughfare.

Probably a coincidence, he decided, and yet…there had
been that moment of danger recognized, that intense heat
of an inherently evil presence somewhere behind him. And
he marked it to be considered later, when his arms were
not filled with Amanda and his thoughts were not focused
on finding Lin waiting for him in the foyer.

They walked after supper, Amanda urging Lin's compliance as the woman would have hesitated at venturing
afield at twilight.

"It's not dark yet, Lin," Nicholas said, urging her acquiescence to the scheme.

"It will be before we return," she argued, her mouth set
stubbornly. "I'm used to being in the city, I suppose, where
wandering around after dark was not always wise."

"Well, this is the country, and we'll be very safe," he
assured her. He hesitated a moment, and then leaned closer
so that Amanda could not hear his words. "I always carry
a weapon when I leave home, Lin. Unless I'm in town or
at the house, I find it wise to be armed." His smile was
grim. "Perhaps it's from living in New York City, as you
have. Maybe I'm not the trusting soul I should be, here in
a small town. I just know I feel more secure with protection
on my person."

"All right," she said finally, watching as Amanda
danced impatiently on the sidewalk below the porch. "For
a while. But when the sun goes down, we'll return home."

Home. The word held an appeal he could not describe,
spoke by her soft, feminine voice. She considered it her

home. And so it was. For the foreseeable future at any rate. And that thought was a comfort tonight, he decided.

They made their way down the road, their pace leisurely, Lin holding a shawl in one hand, and he took it from her. ''I'll carry that for you,'' he said, waiting for her look of acquiescence as she surrendered it to his care. In the sunlight, her hair was struck by shimmering flickers of fire around her face and his fingers touched the brim of her straw bonnet.

''Take it off, please. I'd like to see your hair. It's too lovely to cover.''

''We're out in public,'' she said, glancing around.

''There's no one in sight but the three of us.'' His fingers were deft, removing the bonnet, and he watched as she automatically reached to tend the wayward tendrils that touched her face. ''Leave it be,'' he told her. ''I'd be happier if you let it down your back, to tell the truth.''

Her eyes widened and her mouth formed a round O of surprise. ''I couldn't do that, Nicholas. You know better.''

''One day I'll see it that way, Lin,'' he said quietly, offering his free arm for her touch. She placed her hand there, just inside the bend of his elbow, and they paced sedately behind Amanda, who had chosen to run ahead, then turn to skip back to them.

Ahead, the road narrowed, and off to the north a meadow stretched toward the forest. Scattered trees along its edges provided shelter, and at the furthest reach of the meadow, a doe stepped from the heavily wooded area to hesitate, nose in the air as she tested the wind. Beside her, still in the shadows, a smaller deer stood like a statue, and Nicholas heard Lin's breath catch in a sound of wonder.

''Don't move,'' he told her, reaching a hand to Amanda's shoulder as she stood before them. ''Look, Amanda,'' he instructed, pointing with a slow movement of his arm to the creatures who'd ventured forth from safety to the open meadow.

"Is that a deer?" the child asked, awe in her voice. "And a baby, too?" He felt her shiver beneath his touch and, for a moment, shared her amazement at the sight of the forest creatures.

"It's a doe," he said quietly. "That's what we call a mother deer. The small one is her fawn."

"Does it have a papa, too?" she asked innocently, ever aware of the family unit she yearned for.

"He's called a buck," Nicholas said. "And sometimes in the wild, the papa doesn't stick around much. The mama does most of the taking care of her young."

"I'll bet that baby wishes he had his papa around." Amanda's small voice was hopeful as she uttered her opinion, and Nicholas winced.

"Didn't we just go through this a while ago?" he asked Lin in an undertone.

"Oh, don't stop her now," Lin answered. "You're being drafted for the job." Her smile was warm and coaxing, and he felt his heart turn over inside his chest. The thought of such a thing happening, of his heart really performing such an impossible deed, gave him pause. And then he looked down into the dark eyes that saw beneath his jaded, pedestrian mind-set, into the depths of the man who could not resist the woman before him.

Who *must* resist, or change his whole way of life.

If barriers were ever to be constructed around his emotions, it must be now, he decided. For she had gained entry to a part of him he'd guarded well for twenty years. It could not be. He would not love the woman. He might desire her…

Might?

He *did* desire her. Might, or maybe, did not enter into it. She was in his thoughts, day and night, a constant intrusion to the work he did, to the sleep he sought. It would not do. When the time came that he chose to wed, it would be to a woman who could fit into his life without causing undue pressure on him.

The tension in the air between him and this incautious female was so thick it could be felt, so ever present he was at its mercy. Nicholas Garvey would not be possessed in this way by a woman—no matter how winsome her smiles, how enticing her windswept curls or her length of shapely legs. Nor of the whole of the lavishly endowed body in between.

"You'll understand one day, Amanda," he said, his voice ragged as he spoke the curt reproof to his niece. "Fathers cannot be wished into existence. Neither can mothers. And you're a very fortunate little girl to have an uncle who cares about you and a nurse who looks after you so well."

Amanda's face fell, her lower lip quivered and her eyes filled with tears. Without a word, Lin turned from him and swept Amanda into her arms, then turned to walk away.

"Wait," Nicholas said harshly. "I'll carry her if needs be. She's too heavy for you, Lin."

"I've carried her for years," Lin said, the sound reaching him clearly, as the sun slid to the horizon and the shadows lengthened beneath the trees by the road.

He hastened after them and took Amanda from Lin's arms after a short hesitation on her part, handing her the bonnet and shawl he still held. And then she shrugged, as if it mattered little, and followed a step behind him as they walked back to the house, Amanda stifling her sobs against his shoulder.

His heart beat with a heavy thudding pace within his chest wall, and then, as they approached the front walk and Lin reached to open the gate, it resumed its normal beat. He'd have to let the doctor in town take a look one day, he decided. For certainly, the churning in his chest was an omen of sorts, the misbehavior of that most vital organ a sign that he should return to his normal way of life.

Having these two women in his life had upset his routine, caused him to think all sorts of foolishness. And all for naught.

Yet, as he lowered Amanda to the walk before the porch steps and heard her murmur a low thanks in his ear, he felt a pang of yearning so deep it unsettled him.

Beside him, Lin looked up searchingly into his face, biting at her lip as if she would withhold the words that begged to be poured into his hearing. The soft, brown eyes were dim, the animation in her face gone as if it had never been. And her shoulders slumped in a silent admission of defeat.

She walked up the steps, across the porch and into the front door, Amanda at her side. It would not do. He must explain, let her know his reasons for backing away from the warmth she offered. But, if he did, she would think...

"Lin?" She hesitated, then bent to whisper into Amanda's ear, and the girl went on ahead, climbing the stairs to the second floor with languid movements.

"Yes?" As though her throat was clogged by tears, Lin awaited his response, offering her back, her head held high.

"My offer still stands." Cruelly, he drove home his cold, aloof attitude in those simple words. And silently, she listened to the blatantly offensive proposal. With a barely perceptible shudder, she drew herself together and walked away, her feet silent as she climbed in Amanda's wake.

He would never have her now. The knowledge burned in his mind, flashed through his body with a lurching sense of loss, and settled deep in his soul. That dark, jaded part of him that he kept tucked away, unwilling to peer too deeply into its depths, lest he find himself to still be that boy of twenty years past. That youth who had scrounged and fought for his existence in the alleys of New York City.

His soul. He smiled bitterly, hating himself in this moment, knowing that the mythical portion of himself was now even heavier, with the additional burden of this bit of cruelty on his part to weigh it down.

Chapter Seven

He'd changed. In an instant of time, he'd become a different man, his eyes turning cold, his mouth drawn into a harsh, narrowed line. Even the bones beneath his cheeks seemed to form new, stark furrows in their depths as he spoke. Harsh, hurting words that brought tears to Amanda's eyes, disappointment to her eager, loving spirit.

And a deep, fathomless sense of loss to her own aching heart, Lin thought, pressing her hand against her chest. It was still beating, the rhythm the same, slow and steady. But the pain was sharp and grievous, there beneath her breast, and she shivered at the loss he'd inflicted.

My offer still stands. He'd said the words so casually, tossing them at her as he might cast a bone to a hungry dog. *My offer still stands.* He might as well have said the words aloud that had no doubt prompted that remark. *I'll make you my mistress. You'll lack for nothing.* Nothing but self-respect.

His first offer had been couched in affectionate language. Now he made it sound like a business proposition, with him doing the buying, her the selling. Of herself, her pride and her soul.

None of which he was worthy of receiving.

She'd thought of him as a kind man, a gentleman. He was neither of those. And yet, the memories flooded her mind as she sat on the edge of the bed. His gentle ways, his smiles and patience with Amanda. The touch of his mouth as he—

She would not think about it, she decided, rocking back and forth, her arms wrapped tightly around her body. Packing her clothes was the thing to do. Leaving Amanda behind was the hardest choice she'd ever made, but it couldn't be helped. She'd known from the beginning that this day would come. No matter the dreams she'd dreamed lying here in this bed, she'd known one day down the road her final moments in this house would be spent in sorrow.

And it seemed that this was to be that day.

Outside her bedroom window, the stars glittered across the sky and the moon shone down with a radiance that brought a silver cast to the earth below. Leaves on the trees blew in a gentle dance in response to the wind, and somewhere an owl called, the sound as lonely and forlorn as the cry of Lin's heart.

The house was silent, Amanda sleeping after a session of tears, Nicholas probably still in his study, where he'd retreated behind a closed door. And she was alone.

Still, the puzzle twisted and turned in her mind. What had brought about the change? What had she done to cause his abrupt transformation from doting uncle and indulgent host to a man possessed by cold, bitter anger? For only anger could have brought forth the words he'd spoken.

The only solution was to leave, to let Nicholas fend for himself with Amanda. The child loved him. The hour was too late to awaken her now. Telling her bad news and then expecting her to go back to sleep was foolishness. It couldn't be helped. A note addressed to Amanda would have to suffice.

Lin's fingers gripped the pen as she chose her words

carefully, and tears flowed as she composed the simple note. Sealing it, she left it on her bed, consoling herself with the knowledge that the child loved Nicholas. She would forgive his lapse, and Katie would be here to comfort her. For Carlinda Donnelly there would be no comfort.

With a sigh, she rose and hauled her valise from the wardrobe, opening it on the bed. A candle waited on the table and she lit it, aware that the light would shine from beneath her bedroom door, yet caring little if he saw it and knew she was still awake. Her clothing was readily folded and packed. Her trunk holding the bulk of her belongings would have to be shipped later. Surely he would tend to that for her. Right now she only needed a few things, just enough to travel with.

The night air was chilly, but her shawl was woolen and warm. In ten minutes, she was ready, and with a last look around the room she picked up her valise, closing the door behind her as she stepped into the hallway. The tapestry bag was heavy, but she was strong, barely noticing the way it strained the muscles in her right arm.

Midway down the stairs, a sound from below alerted her to his presence and she saw him, standing in the open doorway of the study, his white shirt a blur before her tear-filled eyes. He stepped forward, meeting her at the foot of the staircase.

The sound of his voice was gruff in her ears. "Where are you going?"

Her laugh was short and unbelieving. "Does it matter?"

"Yes, it matters. I won't allow you to leave here in the middle of the night. You haven't anyplace to go."

"Sitting on a bench in the park is preferable to sleeping under your roof, Mr. Garvey." It seemed she should be better able to see him, but for some reason her eyes would not focus, and he'd become only a formidable presence, blocking her way to the front door.

"You can't leave, Lin. I won't let you go." His hand reached to relieve her of the weight of her valise and she jerked away, unwilling to give up her possessions into his keeping. "That's too heavy for you to carry," he said quietly.

The aroma of whiskey filled her nostrils, and she was suddenly aware that he'd been indulging himself, emptying a bottle of the stuff while he sat in his study. He wasn't drunk. Nicholas Garvey wouldn't permit himself the luxury of total oblivion. Being in control was too much a part of him. Yet, he was probably as close to that condition as he'd ever been.

He would not control her any longer, she decided, holding tightly to the handle of her bag. "Move out of my way," she said, proud of the firm tone she managed.

He shrugged, and his smile was apologetic. "Sorry, sweet. I can't do that."

"I'm leaving, whether you like it or not. I won't allow you to treat me like a whore, Nicholas Garvey."

His head tilted to one side as if he considered that idea. And then he nodded, a careful gesture. "I can see that you might have taken my *offer* that way. It wasn't intended as such, though. You're a beautiful woman, Lin. I want you in my bed." He shook his head again. "I've already told you all this, haven't I?" A deep sigh escaped his lips. "Maybe I need to convince you."

Off balance, she moved back, her leg ramming against the riser. With a thump, her bottom met the third step, and her valise fell from her fingers to the floor below.

"Don't touch me," she whispered as he bent over to peer intently into her face, his smile lopsided, his hair rumpled. She saw him more clearly now, and the awareness of his condition hit her broadside.

"You're drunk," she said bitterly. "You smell like a brewery, and you can't even stand up straight."

He lifted a brow, carefully, as if it required much effort. "Oh, but I can, sweet. I can stand up and I can lift you in my arms...."

His actions matched the words he spoke and she was caught up against his chest, as if her weight were nothing to the muscular strength he exhibited. With a muffled curse, using language she'd never allowed to pass her lips, she struggled with him, aware that he carried her across the threshold into his study and then leaned back against the door. The latch caught, the sound loud in the stillness.

His breathing was harsh, his arms holding her captive, and when he placed her on the sofa his heavy body pinned her against the brocade fabric.

She'd underestimated him, had unknowingly tossed a challenge in his face, and now he appeared bent on forcing her to his will. Screaming would waken Katie, frighten Amanda and bring disgrace on the man himself. If he were the subject of gossip, it would not matter, but harming Amanda was not to be countenanced.

"All your promises meant nothing, did they?" she asked, aware that her words were breathless, and bore a tinge of sorrow. He was heavy, crushing her breasts, his lips open, pressing hot, damp kisses against her throat.

"Am I hurting you?" he asked, the words slurring as he murmured them against her flesh. As if it mattered, he lifted his head, examining her face and throat as if to seek out bruises. "I only want to prove to you that we could have a wonderful time together, Lin." His eyes glittered in the pale glow of moonlight from the windows and the single candle on his desk.

"I know you like my kisses, and I can make certain you enjoy the rest of it. I promise." His mouth was damp, his breath warm as he mumbled the final words against her cheek, and then repeated them in a whisper.

"I promise."

She trembled as his lips touched the vulnerable place below her ear. She ached for what had been, and what might have been, and then hardened her heart against his coaxing. "You can force me to your will, Mr. Garvey, but you can't make me like it."

He was like a statue over her, heavy and solid, and suddenly still. "I dare say I won't have to force you," he murmured, the words a vow, delivered with a smile that tilted his mouth at one corner. His voice softened, coaxed her in an intimate whisper. "I want you to like me, sweetheart."

Her heart ached and tears flooded her eyes. "I did like you," she whispered. "Too much, perhaps." Her hands lifted, her palms finding purchase against his shoulders and pressing for her release. "Let me go, please, before you do something you'll be sorry for. You're going to hate yourself in the morning, Nicholas."

"Perhaps I will. Maybe I do already." His hold on her relaxed and he rolled from her to the floor, where he lay on his back, one knee bent, one hand behind his head as if he had chosen to take his night's rest there, beside the sofa.

Lin sat up, looking down at him, her heart aching for the loss of respect he'd garnered in this confrontation. For whatever reason, the man had become someone she didn't recognize. And yet there was about him the boyish, youthful look that had drawn her in the beginning.

His eyes appeared to be closed and she shifted on the sofa, readying herself for leaving him where he lay. "Don't go, Lin," he said, his voice low and controlled. "I'll take you to the station in the morning. Stay here for tonight."

Dark eyes glittered from beneath his heavy lids. "I won't touch you again. I won't offer an apology. I don't have adequate words. But I won't touch you."

As if a magic wand had been waved over him, he was sober. Rumpled and redolent of the whiskey he'd indulged in, he was nonetheless in control now, and she recognized the man who observed her from his spot on the floor. It didn't even make him look foolish, she thought, to lie there while she peered down at him.

Nicholas had fallen from grace, but had done it with panache. There seemed for a moment no connection between this toppled image and the man she had known.

He closed his eyes, his forearm sliding to cover them, and she curled on her side, her face at the edge of the cushion, watching him. "Don't leave," he said quietly. "Stay where you are, please."

She shivered at the sound, but she would do as he asked, and stay where she was, until sunrise, anyway. Until Katie arose and began breakfast preparations in the kitchen. By that time Nicholas would have risen from the floor and disappeared into his room. She was certain of that, positive that he would not want to be found where he lay. His pride would not allow it.

She closed her eyes, courting sleep, aware that the coming day would require much of her. Yet her body could find no rest, and by sunrise, she'd resigned herself to her sleepless state.

When Nicholas stirred, groaned and muttered darkly, then turned to his side, she held her breath. Beneath lowered lids, she watched him, noting the sudden stillness as he awoke, and recognized his circumstances.

"Damn." The single word was harsh, muttered beneath his breath, and she shut her eyes, lest he be aware that she watched his humiliation. As disappointed as she was in his behavior, she could not deliberately add to his distress now.

His clothing rustled as he rose to his feet, and she felt his gaze touch her. Then he moved away, opening and closing the study door with a stealth that told her he thought she still slept. She heard his footsteps in the foyer, then on the stairs. For several minutes she lay quiet, feigning sleep, until Katie's voice from the kitchen made her aware that Nicholas had returned from his room and gone to the back of the house.

With stealthy movements, she rose and left the study, taking care to climb silently to the second floor. Amanda's door was ajar and the child knelt before her window, turning as if she sensed Lin watching her from the doorway.

"I'm looking at the birds," she announced in a whisper. "They're right here in the tree." She pointed to where a nest of sparrows was filled with several young. "Their mama keeps bringing them worms to eat for their breakfast."

"I think Katie has *your* breakfast almost ready," Lin said. "Why don't you get dressed and go downstairs?"

"Will you help me?" Amanda smiled nicely, and Lin could not resist this last chance to hold her, these final moments in which to leave the child with words of love and affection.

"Why don't we find your clothes together?" she asked, crossing to the bureau where she'd stored Amanda's clothing. Their heads together, they chose the things she would wear, and sitting on the edge of the bed, Lin helped her into the assortment of undergarments and then a dress from the wardrobe.

She held Amanda on her lap finally, buttoning her shoes with the hook, then smoothing down the golden locks of hair into a semblance of order. A brush was brought into play, and in moments the child was ready to face the day. "Are you coming down with me?" she asked. Her eyes were troubled. "Is my uncle Nicholas still grumpy this morning?"

"No, he's fine," Lin assured her. "You go on ahead." She kept an eye on her as Amanda scampered down the staircase, leaning over the railing to watch as small hands pushed open the kitchen door belowstairs. And then she went to her room, where water from the evening before was still waiting in her pitcher on the dressing table. She washed her face, worked at her hair hurriedly, keeping watch over her shoulder lest Nicholas should return from belowstairs and come past the door. It was past time to leave. She'd dallied long enough.

"Come in and eat," Katie said from the kitchen door, her brow furrowed with worry lines. "Mr. Nicholas didn't want anything this morning. He changed his shirt in the wash room where I hung the ironing late yesterday, and he's gone already."

That solved one problem, Lin thought. She'd not have to avoid him. The way was clear. "I'll just have a bite," she told Katie, entering the kitchen where Amanda was tucked up to the table, a dish towel around her neck, the better to keep her dress clean.

"Just toast, please," Lin said, doing her best to sound calm, even as her heart raced within her. She watched as Amanda ate, and then called her to her side. "I have to leave, sweetheart," she said quietly.

Amanda tilted her head and frowned. "Can't I go along?"

"No." Lin bit her lip, searching for the right words and phrases. "I won't be living here anymore. I'm going back to New York. Your uncle will always be here to take care of you, and so will Katie," she said, swallowing against the lump in her throat.

Amanda was stricken, her eyes wide, her mouth trembling. And then she ran from the kitchen, out the back door.

"I'm leaving, Katie," Lin said quietly as the housekeeper faced her with anger alive on her expressive face. Lin lifted an appealing hand, fighting tears as she tried to explain to the woman. "I told Nicholas last night I'd be going and he persuaded me to stay until morning. I know

Amanda doesn't understand, but I've left a note on my bed for her. Perhaps it will help explain things a little better.''

''I don't know how you can just up and leave the child,'' Katie said harshly. ''You're gonna break her heart, ma'am.''

''I have to leave, Katie. I can't stay any longer, no matter how I feel about Amanda. And she'll have Nicholas,'' Lin said.

''None of that means spit when you compare it to losing the person who's been taking care of her right along.'' Katie's mouth formed a determined line as she stated her case. ''Mr. Nicholas is a fine man, that's for certain. Still, between you and me and the fencepost, he can be a bit hard to live with once in a while. I'm sure I don't know what he's done to scare you off, but whatever it is, you need to get past it for the wee one's sake.''

Her toast finished, Lin drained the coffee cup Katie had placed by her plate and then approached the housekeeper. ''Please wish me well. I hadn't planned to do it this way, but I must.''

Katie's arms were warm around Lin's shoulders and her voice trembled as she murmured a farewell. The valise still stood next to the stairs, and Lin lifted it, walking to the big entry door. From the front of the house, she could make out shoppers on the sidewalk in the center of town, two dogs running down the road, a young boy in pursuit, and a wagon at the side of the road, just beyond the front line of Nicholas's property.

She glanced over her shoulder to where Amanda stood dejectedly at the side of the house. Small fists rubbed against her eyes as the child watched Lin, and almost, she changed her mind. No, it could not be. Not even for Amanda could she compromise her beliefs, and should she stay, Nicholas would win.

The gate opened beneath her hand and she headed toward town, approaching the wagon that blocked her path beside the road. Two men stood by near the vehicle, looking down at a wheel, and she set off, walking at a fast pace in order to pass them by. With her gaze lowered, she saw only denim trousers and boots, and she quickened her step, unwilling to display an interest in their business.

"Ma'am?" The shorter of the two approached her and doffed his hat. "Ma'am? Do you know where we can find a fella to help with fixing our wagon?"

She looked up and shook her head. "Maybe the blacksmith in town. He's past the train station and around the bend," she said, pointing to the far side of Collins Creek.

"Thank you," the stranger said, eyeing her in a manner that brought her to attention. "Say," he said suddenly, as if he'd just made a discovery, "aren't you the lady that takes care of the little girl?"

"Pardon me," Lin told him, brushing past him, anxious to make her way to the station before the morning train headed into town from the east.

"Amanda. Isn't that her name?" the fellow asked, lifting his hand to stay her progress, placing it on the handle of her valise.

Lin turned to look fully at him, aware that his interest in Amanda was beyond a casual query.

"What do you want?" she asked sharply.

"Call the little girl over here," the man said, releasing his hold on her valise and grasping Lin's elbow. He turned her roughly until she faced Nicholas's house. "She's right there by the big tree, watching us. Give her a holler."

"No." Whatever the game, Lin was not willing to play it, and she balked as he drew her closer to his side.

His companion left the wagon and strolled closer. "Doesn't the lady want to cooperate?" he asked, drawling the words in a semblance of cordiality that did not impress her. "Call the girl," he muttered, capturing Lin's other arm in a painful grasp. He drew it behind her and then shifted his position until he was at her back, and her wrist was held uncomfortably high above her waist.

"You're hurting me," she gasped, fright washing over her as she recognized the danger of her position. "Who are you?"

"Hey, girlie," the larger man called out, barely raising his voice. It was enough for Amanda to hear, though, as she watched them silently, already obviously aware that something was not aright. "Come on over here to see your nursie."

"Linnie?" Amanda's voice was high, its tone uneasy as she stepped slowly across the grass toward the fence that fronted Nicholas's property. "What's happening, Linnie?"

"Go in the house, Amanda," Lin shouted, and then felt the man's hand roughly snatch at her face, covering her mouth and pressing her head back against his chest. Her teeth were driven into her lips and she tasted blood.

"Come on, little girl," he coaxed. "You don't want your nursie to get hurt, now, do you?"

"You leave my Linnie alone," Amanda cried out, hurling across the grassy expanse to the corner of the yard. There, she climbed with agile movements over the fence that enclosed Nicholas's property. Leaping from the top, she fell to the ground, a cry of pain causing Lin to jerk against the hands holding her captive.

Then, limping and crying, rubbing her eyes with grubby hands, Amanda ran toward her nursemaid, shrieking her name loudly. Within moments her face was buried in Lin's skirts, howling her anger aloud, clinging with desperate strength.

"Shut her up," the taller of the ruffians said. The other man grabbed Amanda around her waist, and the child was silent, struggling to catch her breath, kicking and squirming with an agility that made it difficult to hold her immobile.

"You shut up or I'll hurt your nursie," the big man said roughly, twisting Lin's arm to a higher position.

She groaned, closing her eyes against the pain, aware that tears streaked her cheeks. Whether seeing her Linnie in distress, or because she was too frightened to fight any longer, Amanda closed her mouth, but continued to sob beneath her breath. The two were lifted and deposited without ceremony in the back of the wagon, the large man climbing in behind them.

"Get this rig moving," he said harshly, waving a hand to order his henchman into the driver's seat. In less than a minute, the wagon was turned in the opposite direction, heading out of town, and Lin found herself on her stomach, held in place by a man who outweighed her by at least a hundred pounds. She gasped for breath, almost unconscious from the shock of being dumped into the rough, wooden wagon bed.

Beside her, Amanda whimpered, requiring no force to keep her in place, her hand patting Lin's face in an attempt at comfort. "Don't cry, my Linnie," she whispered, bending to touch her lips against Lin's almost unhearing ear. "I won't let him hurt you any more."

"Shut up, kid." Cruelty marked the words, and Lin shrank from his hard, savage touch against her tender flesh. He'd gripped her wrists so tightly her hands were numb. Her shoulders hurt from the force of his brutality, and only by making herself inhale as deeply as possible was she able to fill her lungs with enough air to keep herself conscious.

"You stay right where you are," her captor said, removing his grip on her wrist. It fell to her side and she cried out.

"I can't even move it," she said, moaning the words aloud. "You've cut off all feeling in my hand and arm."

"Good," he grunted. "That'll keep you from causin' more trouble than you already have."

"I haven't done anything." Her whisper was defiant, and he retaliated by digging his knuckles into her back. She bit back a cry, aware that Amanda would only be more upset should the bully hurt her further. "Don't hurt the child," she said, her voice quavering as she uttered the plea.

"We won't, so long as you behave yourself." His movements were efficient as he tied her hand and foot, leaving her to lie on her side in the wooden box. "Now, you stay right here beside her, little girl, you hear me?" He climbed over the seat back and situated himself next to his partner, barely sparing a second look at the two he'd left behind.

Amanda whimpered, curling closer to Lin, then lifted her arms to encircle her nursemaid's neck. "I'll take care of you, my Linnie," she whispered. "And Uncle Nicholas will come and find us," she murmured, her tone defiant. "I just know he will."

"Katie!" Nicholas burst through the hallway and into the kitchen, Lin's valise clutched in his hand. "Where the hell did they go?" He tossed the bag on the floor beside him and glared with futile anger at his housekeeper, tearing his hat from his head.

"I found Lin's bag by the neighbor's fence, and Amanda's gone, too."

Katie's eyes were reddened with tears. "I don't know, sir. I truly don't. I just went out into the yard to get the wee one." She burst into tears again, dragging a large, white handkerchief from her apron pocket.

"It's a damn good thing I turned around and came back home," he told her. "I've got to make things right with Lin. I owe her an apology." One hand ran through his hair. Although, even as he spoke, he knew it would take more than an apology or admission of guilt to mend the gulf he'd managed to place between the two of them.

"I found Lin's bag first, and one of Amanda's shoes

beside it, down the road.'' He paused for breath, his lungs pumping harshly, his mind attempting to race ahead. ''Did she say where they were going?''

''She was leaving, but she didn't take Amanda with her. I know that for a fact, because she asked me to look out for her.'' She howled in despair and lifted her apron to cover her face.

''That won't help,'' Nicholas told her harshly. ''I'm going to town to get my horse and find the sheriff.''

He turned, slamming the door against the wall as he retraced his steps to the front of the house. Shoving his hat back on his head, he crossed the porch, then cut a diagonal path through the yard. He leaped the fence, and ran full tilt toward the buildings at the edge of town.

The door of Cleary's office was ajar and Nicholas shoved it open, pausing in the doorway to lean forward and grip his thighs, gasping for breath. Cleary rose quickly, rounding his desk to stand beside his friend.

''Tell me,'' he said, his sharp eyes taking inventory as Nicholas stood erect and jabbed his index finger in the direction of a holster hanging from a hook on the wall.

''Give me that,'' he muttered, the words separated by gasping breaths.

''Damn it, Nick. Tell me what's wrong.'' It was to his credit that he lifted the holster and offered it without waiting for a reply. ''Here's the gun that goes with it,'' he said, reaching in his desk drawer and locating the revolver he kept handy for just such an occasion. His own weapon was slung over the back of his chair, and while Nicholas slid his borrowed revolver into its holster, Cleary buckled the leather belt he seldom wore around his hips.

''It looks like someone snatched up Lin and Amanda. They disappeared without a trace. Must have just happened. Not more than ten minutes or so, I'd guess.''

''Let's go,'' Cleary said without hesitation, leading the

way from his office and down the street toward the livery stable. At Sam's appearance, Cleary spoke but a single word. "Horses." And without hesitation, the tall, husky man hustled into the depths of his barn and led two horses from their stalls.

"Hold these, Cleary. I'll get your tack," Sam Ferguson said.

"I'll give you a hand," Nicholas told him, following him into the shadows of the tack room where saddles sat up-ended in a row and harness and ropes were arranged on the wall. Lugging a saddle in each hand, Sam strode past him and settled his load in the dust out front, then went back for saddle blankets.

"I've got the reins," Nicholas said, already working to insert the bit into his gelding's mouth. He slid the halter off over the horse's head, straightened the bridle and turned to Cleary's mount. The tall stallion shivered as a stranger's hands touched him, but Cleary spoke softly and the horse allowed Nicholas to have his way.

Saddle blankets were shaken and placed atop their backs, then the saddles were settled and the cinch straps tightened. The men worked feverishly, and in moments the task was complete. "Someone may have taken Nicholas's niece and her nursemaid," Cleary said briefly to Sam. "Round up half a dozen men and send them out after us." His jaw set as he stepped into the stirrup and slung his other leg over the saddle, shifting his body into it with an easy motion.

"We're heading back to Nicholas's house, and from there we'll follow whatever tracks we find," he told the livery stable owner. "Don't waste any time."

Nicholas spoke firmly as their horses set off. "They had to go the other direction, out past my place, Cleary. I'd just left home and gone to the bank, when I changed my mind and started back. If they'd come through town, I'd have seen them."

"You don't even know who you'd have been looking for," Cleary scoffed. "You develop second sight overnight?"

"I'm willing to lay money it was those two dandies who showed up in the town with their spankin' new boots all polished and their pants creased like a pair of hoodlums looking for an easy mark."

And he'd let them slip through his fingers, he thought with another surge of anger coming to the forefront. They'd been following him, and he'd been in such a damn hurry to get home, he'd ignored all the signs of trouble.

Now Lin and Amanda were paying the price for his stupidity.

Chapter Eight

"Was there a wagon pulled over here when you walked past?" Cleary asked Nicholas. Both men squatted beside the road, where wheels had dug deeply into the soft dirt beside the harder surface of the thoroughfare. As though the wagon had been turned sharply, the ruts had scuffed up the earth, and then faint impressions showed the about-face it had taken. The imprints of two horses' hooves gave evidence of a hurried departure.

"No, I'd have seen it, that's certain," Nicholas answered. "They must have waited until I left for the bank before they drove up." Heavy boot prints mixed with the daintier marks of a woman's shoe. A smaller print, probably Amanda's, Nicholas thought, marked where she'd joined the fray. His index finger touched the depression and he looked up to face Cleary head-on.

"Amanda." With that single word, he felt a surge of anger so great it impelled him to his feet. He glanced around, then pointed to a spot beside the road. "Look there," he told Cleary. "That's where Lin's bag was tossed, and where Amanda's shoe was. It must have come off when they snatched her up."

"I'm thinking maybe Amanda was the one they wanted

in the first place, and they got her by using Lin as bait,"
Cleary told him. "The question is, who'd want the child?"

"Lin told me of a man in New York who fought for
Amanda's custody. The girl's worth a fortune, Cleary. If
he has Amanda, he could very well get his hands on her
money. He was trying for custody before."

"Well, my guess is they'll figure her nursemaid is dis-
posable before long. I'd be willing to bet that Lin gave
them a run for their money."

Nicholas thought of the strength in those feminine muscles, the determination in her brown eyes, and nodded his
head in agreement. "She'd die to protect Amanda."

"With any luck, we'll catch up to them within thirty
minutes," Cleary said. "Just keep an eye on the tracks."

"Back there is where we saw the mama deer and her
baby," Amanda whispered, lifting her head to peer in the
wake of the wagon. "I think the big man is gonna make
the wagon go faster now. He's hollering at the horses, and
they're not behaving very good."

"Fold my shawl and put it under my head," Lin whispered, her skull throbbing from the constant battering it was
taking against the wagon floor as the vehicle slewed and
skidded in a sudden movement.

"All right." Amanda did as she was bid, her small hands
awkward as she slid the crumpled, woolen mass under
Lin's cheek.

Though the shawl protected her head from being bumped
against the bottom of the wagon, Lin was dizzy from the
fray and fearful of what the immediate future would hold.
Surely the kidnappers would not harm Amanda. There
would be no reason to inflict pain on her. Though if he
thought it would be to his benefit, she could imagine Vincent Preston ordering her death. Surely it was Vincent who
had brought this about.

Lin closed her eyes, recalling the day in court when the man's malevolent look had foretold today's happenings. He'd determined to get his hands on Amanda, and even knowing he was the little girl's blood kin, Lin doubted he'd spare much pity for the child's safety. Irene had marked him well, calling him evil incarnate, and Lin shuddered to think of his power, how far-reaching its extent.

Amanda was so certain that Nicholas would come. Her own thoughts ran in a different vein. The man had gone to the bank, and unless someone had seen the actual kidnapping, there would be no way for him to realize their disappearance. Not until it was too late to find them.

Katie. Perhaps Katie had gone looking for Amanda right away, and discovered she was missing. That hope lit a corner of her mind, and she opened her eyes a bit to see Amanda peering closely at her face.

"Are you awake, Linnie?" Worry lined the small forehead and tears hovered on her lower lashes as Amanda bent to brush her mouth against Lin's cheek. "I'm takin' care of you," she promised, one hand patting anxiously on Lin's shoulder.

"I'm awake," Lin said quietly. "Just be very still, Amanda. Sit close to me." She whispered softly, lest she be heard. "Take off your other shoe and let it drop over the side of the wagon," she said. "Don't ask questions. Just do as I say. Nicholas will be coming. He'll see your shoe."

Amanda nodded wisely, working at the buttons with tiny, agile fingers. "They're kinda big, Linnie," she murmured softly. "That's why the other one came off back there." With a tug, she eased the shoe from her foot and lifted it over the low side of the wagon, dropping it into the road.

Lin breathed deeply. It was the only thing she could think of to mark their trail, and surely Nicholas would spot it readily. Maybe her own handkerchief could be tossed

over the side next. She'd wait a while. Beneath her bound
arms the wagon bounced across ruts in the road, and Lin
thought of the bruises she would have, the ache in her arms
all but bringing her own tears to the surface.

Nicholas. Please find us, Nicholas. The words vibrated
in her head and became a prayer. *Send him after us. Keep
him safe.* If there was a trail to follow, Nicholas would
show up. He'd leave no stone unturned to find Amanda.

"Those birds don't know how to drive a wagon," Cleary
muttered, bending from his saddle to scan the ground.
"Look here, where they let the horses almost pull them off
the road."

"Maybe something distracted them," Nicholas said, following the curving wheel tracks where the wagon had
veered, then straightened. He could only hope and pray that
Lin had not fought them at this point, that they hadn't…
His teeth gritted at the thought of her delicate skin being
marred by hurtful hands, ire rising within him at the idea
of her flesh being bruised by harsh handling. And worse
yet, her body being violated by the men who'd taken her.

Surely not in front of Amanda. Certainly they wouldn't
do physical damage to a woman—and yet, he thought bitterly, they would if it served their purpose. Though the
roughnecks might be clumsy here, where they were out of
their element, they'd no doubt have brought with them all
the harshness of crime in the city. He should have recognized the type at first glance, and would have, had he not
been thinking of Lin.

"I don't see anything ahead," Cleary said abruptly. "We
need to split up. This road curves around a bit, and if one
of us goes cross-country we can catch up."

"Why not both of us?"

"In case they pull off the road, we'll have lost them
between here and up ahead," Cleary said. "This way, we

stand a better of chance of finding them. If one of us comes on them, we'll have to follow along and keep out of sight.

"On the other hand," he said quietly, "if the opportunity comes to step in, don't be afraid to shoot first. They won't hesitate to draw guns on us."

"Or use Amanda and Lin as shields," Nicholas surmised. "I'll go on ahead, and you cut through the woods. You know the country better than I do."

They separated, and Cleary disappeared through the trees. The tracks were straighter now, running down the middle of the rutted road, and Nicholas kept his horse to one side, the better to distinguish the freshest wagon wheel impressions from the dusty cover left by the wind that blew during the night. His gaze swept the narrow road, halted, and went on, and then his breath caught as he spied the small shoe, clearly marking the trail he followed.

"Amanda," he whispered, halting his horse to pick up the bit of leather footwear. He could buy her a hundred pair to replace it, but for some reason, he was compelled to lift the shoe with one hand, brushing the dust from the upper and wedging it beneath the heavy leather belt that circled his hips. Foolishness, he supposed, but the sight of it warmed him. She was alive, and without a doubt, Lin had told her to leave the shoe for him to find.

That was another thing to encourage his aching heart—knowing Lin trusted him to follow. No matter how bruised and battered her image of him must be this morning, she had faith in him. He hugged that bit of knowledge to himself. If she believed in him in this one small thing, he could build on it, work to redeem himself in her sight.

In a matter of four or five miles, he began slowing his pace. If the men traveled at top speed, they would still only be making half the progress he was on horseback, and if Cleary had managed to thread his way through the forest in a straight line, he would certainly be showing up before very long. Unless the wagon had a greater head start than he'd assumed, he needed to keep a sharp eye out.

He rounded a bend, trees blocking his view of the road ahead, and pulled up short. Not more than fifty yards ahead a wagon sat immobile, the horses' heads down as if they'd been pushed hard over the past hour. Unused to long hauls, the livery stable horses were hacks at best, and being driven at top speed would wear them down rapidly.

A tree lay in the road before them, blocking their path, and two men struggled to move it to one side, their curses reaching him. Nicholas narrowed his eyes, scanning the side of the road, seeking a bit of movement, certain suddenly that Cleary had something to do with the obstacle the kidnappers had encountered.

There. To his right, just inside the tree line. A flash of color caught his eye and he focused intently on the spot. Another movement alerted him, and he caught a glimpse of Cleary's hand holding a gun. No doubt fearful of shooting at the wrong angle, where a bullet might penetrate the wagon bed, the sheriff waved his revolver in a subtle motion, silently urging Nicholas forward.

He turned the horse to one side, then rode a dozen feet into the trees, sliding from the saddle as he dropped the reins. The animal obligingly lowered his head to the grass beneath his feet, and Nicholas melted into the brush, making his way toward the wagon in silence, gun in hand.

A small head peeped up over the wooden slat, and a small hand covered Amanda's mouth. With a childish gesture that made his heart ache, she lifted her other hand to wave in a furtive manner at him, and he motioned quickly for her to get back. She nodded and obeyed, probably making her way to Lin to let her know he was there—if Lin was awake and aware of what was going on.

At that thought, he deliberately put her from his mind, aware that the woman and child were between himself and his target. From the shelter of trees ahead, he watched as Cleary stepped into the open, shouting at the men, both of them lifting their heads from the tree they were dragging aside. Cleary's gun was visible, but was obviously not enough of a deterrent to the ruffians.

"There's only one of him and two of us," the larger one shouted. "Shoot him, Dennis." The other man obligingly sought his gun out, groping in the band of his trousers.

Cleary nailed him, the bullet hitting his arm, drawing a howl of pain from the kidnapper. He fell to the ground, clutching his hand and arm to his chest.

The other man, obviously the leader of the pair, drew his pistol readily and shot wildly at Cleary, stepping to one side of the road, the better to hit his target. It was all Nicholas needed, giving him a clear shot. The bullet tore through the man's right shoulder, spinning him like a top, his gun flying in the air, the expended bullet streaking upward.

"Don't move, either one of you," Cleary shouted. But Nicholas barely heard the sharp order the lawman gave, so intent was he on reaching the wagon.

He leaned over the side, his gaze meeting brown eyes that closed even as he watched. "Lin!" He called her name, but there was no response from that quarter, only a small body that hurtled over the low side of the wagon, into his arms. He gripped Amanda tightly, leaning back to look into her eager face.

"Are you all right?" he asked harshly, assured by her nodding head. And then she began to cry, as if the events were too much for her to take in.

"Uncle Nicholas, I was so scared, but Linnie said you'd come after us."

"Did she?" His heart warmed at her words.

"And I told her I knew you wouldn't let anything happen to us." Tears streaked her cheeks as she sobbed anew.

"I'm going to put you down," he said, lowering her to the road. "I need to see to Lin, now."

"I think she went to sleep," Amanda said in a whisper, peering up at him, then clambering up into the wagon bed.

Fainted is more like it. Glancing for a moment at Cleary, he received a nod of encouragement, then climbed into the wagon bed. His fingers worked quickly, untying the rope that bound her, but Lin lay like a stone, limp and unresponsive. His fingers trembling, he slid his hand to her throat to feel her pulse. It was erratic, but strong, and he lifted her carefully from the rough wooden floor into his lap.

"Lin." He spoke her name quietly, unwilling to startle her awake, and bent his head to press his lips against her forehead. "Lin, open your eyes," he said, his voice sharper, as if sheer volume would rouse her.

"Draw your gun and hold it on these fellas," Cleary said from beside the wagon. "I'm going to tie them up and I want that barrel aimed at a vital part of the big man while I'm getting my rope from my saddle."

"I can do that," Nicholas told him. Shifting Lin to his left arm, he drew his gun. "You know, mister," he said, speaking to the nearest thug. "I'd really like a chance to shoot you in your tracks. Maybe you could move just a little and give me a good excuse."

"Not me, mister. I'm not budgin' from this spot," the cowed gunman said. "It's against the law to shoot an unarmed man, anyway."

"And is it against the law to kidnap a woman and child and abuse them?"

"We didn't hurt them none, neither one of 'em." He nudged his partner with the toe of his boot. "Tell him, Dennis. Tell him we didn't touch that woman."

"I'll bet you left bruises on her," Dennis grumbled.

"This whole thing was all your doing, Hal. Don't try to make me the fall guy here."

"Who hired you?" Nicholas asked, drawing back the hammer on his revolver, the sound a threat in itself.

"Some big shot in New York," Dennis blurted. "He hired Hal and I was talked into coming along."

"What was his name?" And even as he asked he spoke the syllables in his mind. *Vincent Preston.* He'd bet every cent he owned on it.

But the stubborn look passing between the two men on the ground told Nicholas that his question would go unanswered for now. No doubt they feared their employer as much as they did the cocked gun he held on them.

Beyond them, Cleary stood with the rope in his hand, a grin saluting Nicholas's shenanigans. "You gents ready to be trussed up for jail?" he asked cheerfully. He looked up at Nicholas again. "Has your lady managed to sit up and take notice yet?"

"I'm all right." From his left arm, where he'd cradled her head, Lin spoke quietly but firmly in answer to Cleary's words. She stirred a bit, as if gauging the hurt she'd suffered, and winced as her body shifted against the wagon bed. "I'll probably be black and blue from bouncing around in here," she said, closing her eyes against the sunlight.

Her voice softened and he bent closer to hear the words she spoke. "I knew you'd come for us, Nicholas. I prayed."

"You're not leaving me," he said firmly, watching as her eyelids unfurled and her brown eyes examined him dubiously. "I mean it, Lin. I won't let you go."

She shook her head. "I can't do what you want. That hasn't changed."

"Hush," he admonished her gently. "I know that. But what I *want* has changed." He kissed her gently, holding her with tenderness, fearful of what might lie beneath her clothing, what harm she'd been dealt.

"You won't…" She halted, unable or unwilling to remind him of the night before when he'd handled her roughly, when he'd come close to forcing the issue. She couldn't bear it should he not desire her, not need her in his life. But the circumstances must be different.

As though he understood her dilemma, he smiled. "I want you to marry me, Lin. We're going to make a life together."

"Can we go home now?" Amanda's plaintive cry brought Lin to attention, and she struggled to sit upright. Another sound caught her ear, and she turned to see five riders heading in their direction.

"Where were you when I needed you?" Cleary called out. He grinned as the men slid to the ground, almost as one, then surrounded the downed kidnappers.

"These fellas ready for the hangin' tree?" Sam Ferguson asked, his burly form resembling that of a man set on revenge.

"I see Cleary's got the rope handy," another man said, his thumbs wedged in his pockets.

The two men, well terrified by this time, uttered cries of disbelief as the posse circled them. Lin could not work up a moment's sympathy for the pair of them, even as she recognized the tomfoolery being bandied about. The men might hang for their crimes, but not today. Not while Cleary was sheriff.

"Well, I don't know," the lawman said laconically. "Maybe it would save having the judge make a trip here from Dallas if we just went ahead and took care of things ourselves." His expression was stern, but the look he darted in her direction let her in on the plot and she settled back to enjoy the shenanigans of the men.

Now that the whole thing was wrapped up, tension eased,

even Nicholas relaxing beside her. Until she moved without thinking and uttered a stifled groan. He looked down at her and his features grew stern and angry.

"You are hurt, aren't you?" he asked. He looked up at their audience. "One of you help me get her on my horse. I'm taking her home. When you get back to town, somebody stop by and send the doctor over to my place. I want him to take a look at her."

Against her protests, he signaled Sam Ferguson, and the burly giant lifted her tenderly from the wagon bed into muscled arms that surrounded her carefully. Nicholas mounted his gelding, then held out his arms, and Sam deposited her in his embrace.

"Cleary, bring Amanda along," Nicholas said.

"Do I get to really ride on top of a horse?" Amanda asked, smiling at the sheriff as lifted her out of the wagon and settled her in front of him on his saddle.

"You bet," he replied. Then he turned to the men. "Just don't forget to load this pair of vermin into the wagon before y'all leave me here."

With hands that lacked tenderness and attitudes sorely wanting in respect, the men tossed the bound prisoners into the wagon bed and one climbed onto the seat, turning the wagon in a half circle in an empty area off to one side, before he headed back to town.

Lin rested her head on Nicholas's chest, content to be quiet as he traveled at a sedate pace. The wagon and all the horsemen, including Cleary, soon passed them by, Amanda waving a farewell over Cleary's shoulder.

"Thank you, Nicholas," Lin said quietly. "I knew you'd come after Amanda. There was never a doubt. If I'd been more aware of my surroundings, I might have noticed the men waiting for me. I fear this is all my fault."

"I won't deny that Amanda was a big concern," he said

after a moment. "But you have to know that I feel more guilt about this whole thing than you could ever scrape up."

"You?" She lifted her head, the better to see his face.

"I'm the one who chased you out of the house, Lin. Might as well have just turned you out in the middle of the night as to treat you the way I did. I'll warrant you bear bruises from my hands, alongside those you gathered up today."

"How long will you be paying penance for last night?" This was getting interesting, she decided. Nicholas on his knees was something she'd never thought to see, even if the position was not literal. Although she had a notion it could come to that.

His jaw set stubbornly. "For as long as it takes."

"You said that once before," she reminded him.

"So I did," he answered. "I believe we were referring to Amanda's future that day. And I think her future is settled now. Am I right?"

"You'll be keeping her, I assume." Her heart was beating heavily, and she wondered that he could not feel the vibration, his arm surrounding her, his chest firm beneath her weight.

"You know I will." He was silent, only the song of birds filling the stillness as they rode through shade and sun, the road twisting and turning beneath trees, then back into the blinding light of day.

"How long will you make me wait until you forgive me, Lin?" He looked down, and his eyes were haunted. "I know I hurt you badly. I told you last night there were no words to offer as an excuse or apology. I drank half a bottle of whiskey and still couldn't put you out of my mind. All I could think of was that I'd been harsh and crude and you'd be leaving me.

"I've never treated another woman that way," he confessed.

She focused on his profile, looking upward from where he cradled her in his arm. "Do you love me?" The words were hard to come by, and she spoke them slowly, dreading it should he totally deny the emotion.

His mouth tightened and he looked down as if he searched for an answer in her eyes. "I don't know," he said finally.

Well, that wasn't as bad as a negative answer. He hadn't said an outright no.

"Do you love Amanda?" she asked.

"She makes me feel protective and I enjoy her company," he began, then hesitated. "Damn, I don't know what it's supposed to be like, this loving another person. I've never been sure what the word means, Lin. I care about people, like Cleary and Augusta and little Nicky. I care more than that for Amanda, and I feel differently about you than any other human being I've known. But whether or not the feeling is what you're calling *love* is a question I can't answer."

"I've made you uncomfortable," she said. "I'm sorry."

"No." The single word was harsh, sudden and emphatic. "You never have to apologize to me for anything, sweet. You can say or do whatever you please around me."

"You're giving me a blank page to write on," she said smugly, shifting as sore muscles clenched in protest to her unnatural posture.

"I'll give you anything you want," he vowed. "Just ask away."

"Don't make me see the doctor, please," she whispered politely.

"Anything but that," he amended. "I want to be certain you're all right."

"I am, I promise you. I'll even let you look at my arms and legs and see for yourself."

He leaned back and looked down his nose at her, his expression dubious. "You'll expose your skin to me?"

"Within reason," she said, tempering the offer.

"All right, we'll forget the doctor visit. Just don't plan on reneging when the time comes for my inspection."

"Well…" Her hesitation was long, and then she smiled. "If we're going to be married, I suppose you'll see most of me anyway, won't you?"

"*Most* of you?" His eyes lit with a fire that threatened to melt her where she lay. She was vulnerable, stretched across his lap, leaning against his left arm, and his gaze did a slow survey of her, the clothing she wore not seeming to hamper his ability to see beneath the surface of cotton and lace.

"You can count on that being *all* of you, ma'am." He drew back on the reins, and his horse responded readily, coming to a halt by the side of the road.

She felt a slow flush rise from her breasts to her throat, and then heat washed over her cheeks as he lowered his head. With a groan, he took her mouth, parting her lips and invading the dark warmth within, teeth and tongue joining the foray as he took possession of that almost virgin place.

She'd never been kissed so thoroughly. Indeed, she'd only been the recipient of small pecks on the cheek or lips by two young men who had managed to brave her father's anger long enough to snatch a forbidden kiss. Nicholas had the dubious privilege of being the only man to ever truly give her the caress of a man, full grown.

His touch was addictive, she'd found, and her mouth opened to his coaxing without hesitation. He groaned and moved, his hand busy beneath her shoulder, looping the reins over the saddle horn, if she was any judge. And then those long, gentle fingers returned to her, sliding beneath the buttons of her dress, releasing them from the bound buttonholes and spreading the opening wide to reveal the fine batiste of her vest.

"I don't think you're supposed to look until after we get married," she said, her voice catching as his hand released the dainty buttons remaining. His index finger touched her skin and she tilted her head down to watch its progress. "Nicholas?"

"Did either of those men touch you?" he asked gruffly.

She looked up into eyes that were dark with pain, as if that thought alone was enough to cause him despair. "No. Not that way."

"Thank God," he whispered. "I couldn't have stood it, for you to be stained by their filth."

"Would you have not wanted me, if that had happened?" And before he spoke, she knew the answer he would give.

"I'll always want you. I'd just have been sorry for whatever damage they caused. And then I'd have killed them both."

She believed him, knew that his sense of justice would not have been satisfied by mere courtroom tactics. Nicholas was a man of honor. He would die to uphold hers, or to keep harm from his own.

His hand stilled, warm against the skin between her breasts. "I only want to kiss you here," he said, tacitly asking her consent.

"Yes." She breathed the word, heard the faint hissing as she drew it out, then tilted her head back, welcoming the caress of his mouth as he lifted her higher in his arms, his head bending to accomplish his aim.

His lips were warm as he nuzzled against the soft fullness of her breasts, kissing and suckling the flesh into his mouth, careful not to expose her fully. "I think I'd better stop," he murmured, looking down at his handiwork.

"Help me button you together," he said roughly.

"I don't want Katie to see you all undone. She'll have my scalp if she thinks I've taken advantage of you." He nudged the horse into an easy gait as she glared up at him again.

"And haven't you?" she murmured, sounding a bit grumpy to his ears. Embarrassed, most likely, he decided. And he would not have it.

"Don't you believe it, love. Now, if you were my mistress, I'd tote you right upstairs when we reach the house, and take you to my bed and then I'd—" He grunted in response to her elbow in his midriff, then laughed aloud. They rode past the edge of town and Nicholas sobered as he thought of his last glimpse of this piece of roadway. They'd been most fortunate, he decided, and he was thankful.

The gate was before them and he lifted her to the ground. "Stand still," he ordered, then joined her, clasping her waist in one long arm as he tied his gelding to the gatepost. He lifted her, swinging her up in his arms and carrying her to the porch, up the steps and to the front door.

"Land sakes," Katie said, red-faced and puffing as she opened wide the portal. "There was a whole flock of riders went past pretty near fifteen minutes ago, hauling a wagon with a couple of bully-looking fellas in the bed. Was they the ones that took you, Miss? The sheriff dropped Amanda off out in front and I've got her in a tub of warm water in the kitchen, scrubbing all the dirt away."

"We're going upstairs," Nicholas said briskly. "When the doctor comes by, tell him we won't be needing him. Lin's going to be fine. She just needs to rest for a while. If you'd like to bring up a pitcher of warm water, that would help, Katie."

"But who's going to tend her?" the housekeeper said, eyes widening as she watched her employer carry his burden up the flight of stairs.

"I will," Nicholas answered. "Just leave the water outside the door."

"I'm not your mistress, Nicholas," Lin reminded him. "You'll leave me at the door of my room."

"Ah, that's where you're wrong, my dear. You'll be spending the rest of your life in my bed. You'd might as well begin now."

Chapter Nine

Lin was beyond protesting. It seemed she'd managed to set loose a tiger. By now, after the time she'd spent with him here, the knowledge should have been clear in her mind that he was not what he appeared to be. Nicholas's suave, gentlemanly appearance was but a facade. Beneath it lay the heart of a man determined on success, no matter what endeavor he set out upon.

He'd decided to claim her, and there would be no stopping him. Being deposited upon his bed was only the beginning. Nicholas had the bit between his teeth, and if the hard, determined jut of his jaw was anything to go by, she'd might as well hang on for the ride. His touch, though, was tender, his hands careful with her as he placed her upright on the quilted coverlet, settling her against the pillows.

"Loosen your sleeves," he said, gruffness tingeing his words, and she looked up quickly into eyes that burned with an intensity she'd found there only last night. They had glittered in the moonlight as he hovered over her on his sofa, halting her protests with the force of his unyielding will. Yet now, his fingers were gentle as he rolled up the full sleeves of her dress, his gaze absorbed as he inspected each inch of exposed skin, from the palms of her hands almost to her shoulders.

She was silent, eyes half-closed as she watched his movements, aware he sought only to ensure her comfort, that his touch was not that of a man beset by passion. Not for now, at any rate. His nod seemed satisfied as he moved to the foot of the bed, then leaned over to remove her shoes and lift her skirt to her knees. Lacy garters held her stockings, peeking beneath the ruffle of her drawers.

"Don't curl your toes," he said, amusement alive in the look he bent toward her. "I'm only going to take your stockings off, sweet. I've already seen the backs of these," he said, touching the spot just below her left knee.

"Somehow, that doesn't make me feel any better," she murmured, her throat tight with anticipation.

Her stockings were fine black cotton, and his fingers were nimble, pulling both stockings and garters down the length of her legs, then her feet. "You've got a few bruises, Lin, but the skin's not broken," he said, lifting one foot to his lap as he settled on the edge of the mattress. The exposure of her undergarments was embarrassment enough without him touching her bare foot, she decided, and she jerked it from his hand.

"I'm fine, Nicholas." Her voice wasn't quite as firm as she'd hoped, but the man was beyond belief. "If you'll please bring me my dressing gown, I'll take off these dusty clothes. Your quilt is going to be filthy."

He glanced down at the bed and shrugged, dismissing her argument. "I'll get your dressing gown, if you'll promise to stay right where you are until I get back."

"Yes, all right." She was impatient with his shenanigans now, knowing he both teased and taunted with the power he held over her. Yet, it was pleasant to be so coddled and tended. She'd had little experience with being waited on during her life, and if Nicholas was intent on pampering her, she'd allow him his way. At least for a while.

He was gone but a moment, returning with her dressing gown and a fresh nightgown from her drawer. "Put these on," he said, "then I'll take a look."

"You already have," she stated firmly, and was granted a look of supreme patience from brilliant blue eyes that promised no quarter.

"You have three minutes to change into the nightgown," he told her. He held it aloft, frowning as he inspected the full sleeves and high neckline. Embroidery trimmed the front, and buttons reached almost to the waist. "I don't like it," he said. "You deserve something softer and finer."

"It cost me eighty-five cents from the Sears and Roebuck catalog," she told him. "There are almost seven yards of good, sturdy cotton in that gown. It'll last for years."

"Don't count on it," he said, handing it to her. "I'll be finding something else for you to wear, if I have to send to New York City for it."

The door closed behind him and she rose from the bed. When Nicholas said three minutes, she had a notion he'd be timing her to the second. She could envision him glaring down at the watch he wore daily. Made of gold, it was attached to a heavy chain that stretched across his vest, beneath his suit coat when he went to the bank every morning. And unless she missed her guess, that suit would never be the same again, even with Katie's diligent care.

Her clothing fell to the floor in a circle around her and she slid into the nightgown, feeling muscles she hadn't known existed before now. Several tears in the skirt and sleeves of her dress warned her of what she would find, and she moved in front of the mirror, leaving her nightgown unbuttoned as she lowered one sleeve and looked over her shoulder. The gouge was shallow and dried blood edged it.

Bruising surrounded it, a deep maroon in color, and she suspected it would be black and blue by evening.

"Don't move." Nicholas voice gave her little warning as he strode through the doorway and she turned, tugging the sleeve back up, wincing as the fabric snagged on the crusted blood.

"Damn it, Lin, stand still," he said, his voice a low growl, his hands reaching for her. With a gentleness she wouldn't have believed he possessed, he moved the cotton fabric from the abrasion and bent to look closer.

"Now this time, I want you to listen to me," he told her. If she had not been looking up at him, she'd have thought him angry with her, his words harsh, his jaw firm. But the pain he felt on her behalf was clear in the gaze he shed on her damaged skin.

"Where else?" he asked roughly, moving her other sleeve down the slope of her shoulder and seeking a closer look.

"Please, Nicholas. This isn't…it isn't proper for you to see me this way." She bent her head, averting her face from his, wishing she'd had the forethought to ask Katie for her help. Though whether or not Nicholas would have given in to that notion was doubtful.

"Proper be damned, Lin. You're hurt, and I'm not going to let anyone else take care of you." He led her to a comfortable chair near the bed. "Just sit there a minute while I get some salve. I'll wash that first and then see about a bandage."

She sat down, shivering a bit. Whether the chill she felt was from the strain she'd undergone or the fact that Nicholas was bent on stripping her naked, she didn't know. Both theories held equal merit, she decided. Suddenly too weary to make a fuss, she sank limply against the soft cushion, lowering her forehead to rest against one hand.

He was gone from the room, and she heard his voice

calling to Katie from the top of the staircase. Aching in every conceivable spot, she felt tears rising to the surface, and she fought against the need to lean on Nicholas's chest and allow them to flow.

"Why not let me take care of Lin, Mr. Nicholas," Katie insisted. "She'll do better with another woman tending her."

"I have another task for you, Katie," Nicholas said tersely. "I'd like you to get Amanda dressed and then take a walk to the parsonage and bring the minister back here. Keep a close eye out, will you? I don't think there's any danger to Amanda right now, but I'm not taking any more chances. I want them both watched over closely until this thing is straightened out. With you on hand Amanda's care doesn't pose a problem, but the only way to keep Lin close is for me to marry her, here and now."

"And then what?" Katie asked smartly. "You don't get married just to keep a woman safe, sir. There has to be more involved than that, if you don't mind my saying so."

"Trust me," Nicholas told her bluntly. "There's much more than that involved. I'm not going to embarrass you by listing my reasons, but if you insist I'll begin with the most important one."

"I don't think that'll be necessary," Katie said hastily. "I knew there was something stirrin' between the two of you from the very beginning. I'm just glad you saw the light, sir. I hated to think she would be leavin' us."

"If she goes anywhere, it'll be with me beside her."

And wasn't that just dandy? Lin rubbed her forehead, aware of a persistent headache that had only worsened over the past minutes. The man was determined to put a ring on her finger whether she liked the idea or not. Although finding a ring in the middle of a weekday morning in Collins Creek might put a crimp in his plans.

She shook her head, wincing as the movement produced

fresh pain, its site just above her left ear. With her index finger, she explored the area. A lump about the size of a pullet egg met her inquiring touch. She closed her eyes, recalling the initial thump when she'd been tossed over the side of the wagon, unable to protect her head.

Nicholas moved silently from the doorway, bandages and a metal tin of salve in his hand. A clean cloth and matching towel were slung over his shoulder, and he carried a water pitcher, with steam rising from the top. His movements sure and certain, he rinsed out the basin and poured a measure of warm water into it. And then he stood over her.

"I want you to drop your gown to your waist, Lin."

She looked up quickly, and winced again, aware of the pain behind her eyes in even greater measure. "I want Katie," she said stubbornly.

"She's tending to Amanda, and then they're going to get the minister from town."

"I heard," she said, her lips pressing firmly together as she defied him. "I can do this myself if you'll just give me the chance."

"Lin." He sighed, then squatted in front of her, taking her hands in his and kissing the backs in a gesture that spoke of his affection and concern. As if he'd made up his mind and there would be no turning back, he held them immobile in one broad palm, then lifted his other hand, touching her chin with a brush of his knuckles.

"That man is going to be here before you know it, and I'd like to have you sufficiently covered before he arrives. Please don't cause a fuss, sweetheart."

"Wait, let me get you the quilt," he said, rising and snatching up the covering. He handed it to her and turned his back. "Now. Slip your gown down and hold the quilt in front of you. I promise not to look. I only want to wash your bruises and put salve on them. Please."

She lowered the gown to her waist and covered herself

with the quilt, holding it against her breasts with both hands.

As if he sensed her cooperation, he turned, casting a quick glance, then faced her fully, satisfaction clear as he nodded his head. "I'm going to wash your back. You've got several places where it looks like you scraped across the wood and they need to be cleaned."

She closed her eyes and endured. There was little pain, for his hands were skilled and the measured touch of his fingers as they smoothed the pungent salve over four different places above her waist, and then applied soft cloth with plaster holding it in place, told her he was competent at the task. It was the knowledge that Nicholas was looking at her body, that his hands were tracing the line of her spine and smoothing her skin beneath his fingertips that set her stomach churning.

"I'm going to pull your gown back up," he said after several long minutes had passed. "I want you to look at your legs above your knees, Lin. If you've got this sort of damage there, I want you to wash the skin well and apply the salve. You can tend to the front, and if necessary, I'll do the back. All right?"

"Yes, fine," she whispered, thankful for the fullness of her gown as she buttoned the placket. He held her dressing gown open and she slid her arms into the sleeves, then wrapped it around her waist and tied it.

"I'll change the water and you can wash your face with a clean cloth." He turned his back again and rinsed out the cloth for her, then busied himself while she stroked the warm, damp fabric over her face and neck. Carrying the basin to her, he placed it on her lap and watched as she washed her hands thoroughly.

"We'll leave you in your dressing gown," he decided. "For right now, I want you beneath a quilt until you stop shivering." He leaned to look directly into her eyes, and his hand tilted her chin as he inspected them. "Is your vision blurry?"

"No, but I have a headache. There's a lump above my left ear," she told him. "My head hit the wagon bed when they dumped me in." She watched his mouth tighten as she spoke and he held her head, tilting it a bit, cupping it within one hand while he examined the sore spot. She felt his fingers parting the strands of hair that covered the bump, and heard the muttered expletive he uttered beneath his breath.

"All the more reason to stay in bed for the rest of the day," he told her, releasing her from his hands. She felt, for a moment, bereft by the absence of his touch, aware that she craved the warmth of his hands and mouth and the solid feel of his body. As if he were a bulwark behind which she could rest, unafraid, she yearned to be held once more in his embrace. Instead, she cleared her throat and asked the most mundane of queries.

"Don't you have to go to the bank?"

"I don't have to do anything but take care of you and Amanda," he said firmly. "And at this moment, you're the one needing me. Katie is looking after Amanda, and half the folks in town will be making a fuss over her. She's safe for now."

"All right." She blinked and focused on him. He was changed, she decided. No longer the man she'd met on the day of her arrival here, Nicholas had undergone a transformation. From a man who found it simple to be cynical, who was unwilling to allow his emotions to blossom into anything resembling love, he'd managed to assume the responsibility for herself and the child he'd been presented with.

Gone forever, it seemed, was the distance he had imposed between himself and the niece he'd accepted. With no reservations he was prepared to do whatever it took to

accomplish their safety. And because of that, it was easier
to give in to his maneuvering, she decided, than it was to
argue, and by far the more enjoyable option. "I think I
need to lie down," she said, her mind weary from the
thoughts that had circled and finally settled to rest, allowing
her peace.

"I agree." Lifting her from the chair, he made short
work of placing her between the sheets, then pulled the
quilt high on her chest, tucking her arms beneath the covering. "You're going to be married from this very spot,"
he whispered, sitting beside her, one hand on her forehead
as he leaned close. He turned her head with a gentle movement and eased her hairpins from the bun at the nape of
her neck.

"Is that better?" His fingers massaged the muscles there,
then threaded through the tangled curls.

"Um…yes." It was an effort to speak, and she wondered
whether she'd be awake to greet the clergyman when he
arrived, so great was the lethargy that swooped down upon
her.

The sound of voices roused her, and her eyes opened to
see a kindly face above her. "I understand you've been
having quite a day." The minister's words were soft, his
expression sympathetic. "I brought my wife along to be a
witness, if you don't mind," he said to Nicholas, who nodded his agreement. "I think we'll skip the odds and ends
and get right to the important parts," the gentleman said.
"I don't think this young lady is up to a long ceremony."

Lin repeated a few choice phrases, obeying the instructions given, and then felt Nicholas take her hand and slide
a cool, metal circle on her finger. He bent to press his lips
against her forehead and placed her hand beneath the quilt
once more.

"Was that my wedding kiss?" Her tongue seemed thick,

her voice too soft to be heard, but Nicholas's response let her know he'd deciphered the words.

"Would you like me to try again?"

"Please." His lips touched hers, a soft, undemanding caress that elicited a murmur of pleasure.

"I'll do better later on, sweet," he promised, whispering the words in her ear. And then he was gone, the voices moving beyond the room and down the stairs. She lifted her hand from beneath the covers and touched her lips with one finger, there, where so recently his own had lingered.

"I'm married." The words were barely audible, and she wondered for a moment if perhaps she'd dreamed the whole thing. Her eyelids lifted just far enough for her to peer at the ring finger of her left hand, and she caught her breath in wonder.

Somewhere, Nicholas had found a wide gold band, a wedding ring.

She slept, awakening once to feel his hands touching her, lifting her head above the pillow, coaxing her with a spoon of liquid. *Water.* She relished the cool taste and murmured beneath her breath.

"More?" he asked, offering the spoon again. "Your mouth looks sore. Can you drink from a glass?"

"Um…" The sound was faint, but he apparently heard, for in seconds he was holding a water glass to her lips. They were indeed sore, she found, and then recalled the hand that had closed against her mouth with rough pressure, lest she cry out and attract attention. The thug had apparently bruised the soft tissue inside her lips. Her body felt battered from head to toe, and she groaned as she shifted in the bed.

"The doctor left a sedative for you, to help with the pain, but Katie said you'd do as well with a tea she knows of. Would you try a little?"

She nodded, more awake and aware of her surroundings. The windows reflected back the interior of the room. "It's dark out," she whispered, careful not to move her lips as she spoke. Looking up at him, she attempted a smile and failed miserably. It hurt too much.

"Tea, please," she said, trusting that Katie would know just the thing to give her.

"She's making it now," he said, easing his arm from beneath her neck, making her comfortable against the pillows. Beside the bed was an easy chair, one he'd apparently carried from another room. He settled back in it now, peaking his fingers and watching her closely, as if she might explode should he take his eyes from her.

"I've been worried," he said quietly. "You slept a long time. The doctor dropped by and poked his head in the door. He told me you'd no doubt sleep the day away, but I kept wanting you to wake, so I could be sure you were all right."

"I'm fine," she said, and indeed, she discovered that she could move a bit without groaning. By tomorrow she'd be fit as a fiddle, perhaps.

An awareness of pain in her back caught her attention, burning like the very dickens where bandages covered the sore spots. Her arm ached, too, as if she'd been slammed against a wall. Or a wagon bed. And at that remembrance, she shuddered.

But she was alive, and Nicholas was here beside her and he'd married her. Unless that, too, was a dream. One to match the others that had marched through her head during the hours when sleep had overtaken her so completely. She lifted her left hand and blinked, concentrating on the shiny circle on her ring finger.

"Where'd you get the ring?"

"I bought it several years ago."

"Who for?" She felt a stirring in her chest that might

be jealousy, she decided. If she was wearing a ring intended for another woman, he could just take it back. She'd go without before she stooped to being second choice.

As if he sensed her agitation, he shifted from the easy chair to settle on the side of the bed, reaching to hold the hand wearing his token. "I bought it in the city, before I ever came to Texas. It was a foolish thing, a spur-of-the-moment idea. I thought if I ever found a woman I wanted to marry, I'd be ready."

He grinned and she thought, for the first time, that he possessed the soul of a dreamer. Why else would he buy a wedding ring for a woman who might never materialize?

"It fits," she murmured, turning her hand, watching as the lamp light reflected from the shiny surface. "You got the right size."

He smiled, the expression softening the lines of his face, thawing the stern look of worried eyes. "Maybe it was meant to be, you and me coming together the way we did. I just guessed at the size. The jeweler thought I was out of my mind as it was, buying a wedding ring for a woman I'd yet to choose as my bride."

"Hmm." Her hand felt heavy, her arm weary and she allowed it to drop to her side. "I didn't look to marry you, Nicholas."

He bent and kissed her forehead. "You weren't exactly what I had in mind, Lin. I have to admit I'd considered the idea of a wife I could tuck away and show off on occasion, sort of a trophy I might win if I succeeded in life." He lifted a length of curls from her pillow. "And then you walked into my office at the bank, and everything I'd planned went out the door like Katie's wash water."

He looked up as a movement at the door caught his eye. "And here she is now," he said, rising to take the tray from Katie's hands. "Is Amanda in bed?"

"No. She won't hear of it until she sees for herself that

Linnie is safe and sound. She's poked her head in the door half a dozen times today, miss, and you've slept away the whole of the afternoon, right into evening. Do you feel like waving to her?''

"Send her in," Lin said, looking toward the door with anticipation. "Is she all right? She wasn't hurt?"

"No. She took a nap and got up full of vinegar, just like always," Katie said. "I've heard nothing all day but how brave you were, miss, and how those bad men mistreated you. The little one is about worried to death."

Lin watched as Amanda slipped through the doorway and approached, eyes wary, as if she were not accustomed to seeing her stalwart nanny lying abed.

"Are you bleeding?" she asked. "There was blood on your dress before, Linnie. Katie said my uncle Nicholas fixed you up just fine, but I don't like it when you get hurt." She edged closer and bent toward Lin. "Katie said you got married to—" her index finger pointed toward Nicholas, settled once more in the chair "—to him. Did you really?"

"She really did, Amanda," Nicholas said, his eyes dancing as if he withheld laughter. "Come and sit on my lap for a moment and we'll tell you about it. Or at least I will. I think your Linnie is about worn out."

Amanda went to him, relief alive on her vibrant features. "I'm so glad. Does that mean that we'll all live together from now on?"

"Yes, that's exactly right," Nicholas told her. "In a few days, Lin will be feeling right as rain and we'll have a party to celebrate. Would you like that?"

The child clapped her hands with enthusiasm. "Oh, yes. And I'll help Katie make stuff to eat."

Lin closed her eyes, weary from the commotion, fearful of tears flowing from beneath her lashes, lest she frighten Amanda, yet unable to work up much excitement for the events of the day. Nicholas whispered words she didn't even attempt to understand, and in moments the door closed, almost silently, as though someone had very carefully turned the handle to suppress the sound.

The bed moved as he joined her again. "Drink the tea, love," he said quietly, and she roused herself to obey. It had cooled and she drank it quickly.

"Are you hungry?" he asked and she shook her head, aware of the pain the movement caused. "All right, then. I'll settle the house for the night and be right back."

He left and Lin closed her eyes. He'd no doubt sit in the chair all night, and she felt a pang of guilt for his discomfort. She should tell him to use her room, since he'd given over his own for her comfort.

A movement of the mattress beneath her roused her again, and in the dark she heard his whisper. "Shh, it's only me, love. I'm shifting you over a bit to make room."

"For what?" she asked, floundering as his arms lifted her and placed her on a cool spot on the sheet. "What—"

"I'm sorry," Nicholas said. "I tried not to wake you. I just needed more room than you left for me."

Even now, he was beside her, covering them both with the sheet, arranging it to his satisfaction as he bent over her prone form. "I won't bother you," he told her. "I just need to be here where I can watch over you."

"What's wrong with the chair?" she muttered, aghast at the thought of sleeping in the same bed with a man.

"It's my bed," he reminded her.

"I'll sit in the chair, then," she said, struggling to sit up. It was no use. Between his strong arm across her middle and the pain that surged through her head, she was no match for his determination. Head back on the pillow, she looked away from him, feeling the tears begin again.

"Are you crying?" he asked softly, lifting on one elbow to peer down at her. "Damn it all, Lin. We're married. I don't have to apologize for sleeping in the same bed with you. Especially since it's my bed, and not six hours ago you promised to love, honor and obey me.''

''I was leaving this morning,'' she whispered, the events of the day flooding her mind with a kaleidoscope of color and sound that seemed almost intimidating, given her state of body and mind.

''You wouldn't have gotten far. I was on my way home to change your mind when all this happened. I'd have hunted you down, no matter where you went,'' he told her. And then his strong arms enfolded her, one sliding beneath her neck to provide support to her aching head, the other turning her to face him, careful not to handle the bruised and battered parts of her body.

He was cross as an old bear, she thought, and yet he was gentle, as caring of her as if she were a child and he the father who doted on her. The thought gave her comfort.

''This isn't the way I'd planned on spending my wedding night,'' he whispered in her ear. ''I'm having a hard time being patient, Lin, but in a day or two, when you've recovered enough, I'll make up for it.''

Her eyes opened wide, and she looked up, barely able to see any details in the light from the window. His mouth touched hers, a soft, gentle caress that soothed her sore lips, passion set aside for tonight.

Then one large, wide palm settled at her throat and he undid the buttons of her gown. Long fingers slid through the opening he'd created and in an instant, his hand cupped her breast. Carefully, tenderly, as if he cherished the firm, full weight.

''Nicholas?'' She whispered his name, and he shushed her with a soft murmur. How she would ever sleep with his masculine body beside her was a problem, she decided. How she could think of anything but the warmth of his palm, the pressure of fingers clasping that feminine part of her, was another puzzle. And yet, her eyes closed and she was aware only of his breathing, his scent, the length of his leg beside hers, and the feeling of safety and security his presence offered.

New York City

"The fools are in jail." Vincent Preston slapped the single sheet of paper against the surface of his desk and spoke vile utterances that obviously offended the man before him. "I sent two of them to handle one child and a puny woman and they ended up in the jailhouse of a speck on the map in Texas."

"You were dealing with a former U.S. marshal, sir," the gentleman said harshly. "I think you underestimated your quarry."

"The uncle was a lawman? I thought he owned a bank."

"Not the uncle, but the sheriff in the town. A good friend of the banker, I understand. And the woman and child were under their joint protection. Those two hooligans didn't stand a chance."

"And can you do better?" Vincent's eyes shot fury across the room to where his visitor lounged in a chair, obviously not impressed by his temper.

"For a price." His mouth settled into a smug smile, and the well-clad businessman rose. "It's up to you to pay the price, Mr. Preston. Then I'll begin the negotiations."

"Are you sure you have the judge in your pocket?"

"Try me." Spoken with confidence, the words were a challenge, one Vincent could not ignore.

"I expect to see the child in my parlor within two weeks' time. With or without the nursemaid."

"Witnesses are not a good idea, sir," his visitor said bluntly. "The lady will be left behind, and it will be to her advantage if she sees nothing of the transaction when the child comes into our possession.''

''Get a court date, then, and locate the child.''

With a nod of agreement, the visitor left. Vincent stood, stalking to the window, where he gazed out upon the street below. Irene had thought to leave him empty-handed, but he'd have the child and money both before he was done. And sole ownership of his business. The woman had lied and connived and cheated him. Revenge would be sweet, he decided.

He hoped the girl resembled her mother.

Chapter Ten

"Something went on at the jail last night." Cleary stood in Nicholas's office, his face set in lines that measured his concern. "I found horse tracks around the back and footprints leading right up to the window."

"Were the bars intact?" Nicholas asked. The two men waiting in that cell had been much on his mind this morning, and the thought that they might find a way of escape made it imperative that they be dealt with rapidly. Though Cleary excelled at his position in Collins Creek, there were ways of challenging the system here, where so little crime existed and the facilities were less than foolproof.

"Yeah, I checked that out." Cleary frowned. "I sure as hell hate the thought of parking my backside in my office every night till we hear from a judge as to what those two will be finally be charged with. I figure I'll have to ship them off to Dallas for trial, but in the meantime Gussie isn't going to like it one little bit when I tell her I'll be standing guard instead of coming home."

The thought of the petite, golden-haired woman giving Cleary a hard time made Nicholas come near to smiling, and then he subsided, registering the lawman's grim features. Considering the night to come, Cleary might be in need of a backup. "Are they sending a marshal? Will he arrive today, maybe?"

Cleary shrugged. "Who knows when the red tape will be cut and they'll get a man out here? But it should be any time now. Kidnapping is a serious offense. I'd think there'll be a couple of men here shortly. They won't send just one for this job."

Nicholas leaned back in his chair, the primitive sense of justice he favored in this case almost overwhelming his better instincts. "I'm all for a hanging," he said shortly. "I'll even spring for a couple of new ropes."

"Don't let that news get out and around," Cleary warned him. "You'll shoot your classy image all to hell and back, Nick." His mouth twisted in a grin of recognition as he surveyed his friend. "That's the alley rat in you comin' out, you know."

"I can see I never should have confided my beginnings to you, Sheriff." Good humor overcame his quick temper for a moment as Nicholas eyed the lawman. "These folks think I'm a gentleman. I'd hate to let them in on the facts of the matter. They'd never trust me with their money."

"Well, you've got my share in that safe in the back room." Cleary moved from the doorway and settled into a chair. "Not that there's much to brag about. But Gussie trusts you, and we both know she's got a dandy nest egg. I won't let the cat out of the bag, Nick. Your secret's safe with me."

"Why don't you get yourself a deputy?" Nicholas asked, reverting to the sober frown he'd been wearing during the past two days. "I'd come down tonight and take turns patrolling the place, but I need to stay with Amanda and Lin. I'm afraid to let them out of my sight. I almost stayed home again today, but Lin was beginning to suspect my motives, and I don't want her worrying."

"I think we need to talk about this," Cleary said, stretching his long legs before him and crossing his ankles. His slouch suggested relaxation, but the sharp look he sent Nicholas's way denied that theory. "It's not safe here for your womenfolk, Nick."

"You've got a better idea?"

Cleary nodded. "I know of a place about forty or fifty miles north from here. There's a ranch house and outbuildings, sittin' a ways off the road, on about a thousand acres, give or take a few. Lots of meadow and pastureland, and not far out of town. The folks who own it moved on and the place is empty."

"I'd lay odds you own it," Nicholas said without hesitation. "You planning on moving?" he asked, recognizing Cleary's line of thought.

"No, not for some time probably, but I'd like to see you and your family put down some temporary roots there. Just for a few weeks, maybe, till this thing is cleared up."

Nicholas grinned, leaning back in his chair. "You want me to turn into a rancher? I'll lose my big-city image, Cleary. And I'm not sure Lin could cope with roughing it in a ranch house kitchen."

"It sure beats having her roughed up again by New York City hoodlums." Cleary's eyes darkened as he spoke the words, his voice soft, even as his jaw was taut with anger. "I don't want to think what could happen to her if the gentleman sends more of his troops here, Nick."

"If we were found there, I'd be on my own," Nicholas said bluntly.

"No one but me knows of the place. With the right moves, you can be in residence and a part of the community without making a stir. I'll have the local lawman keep an eye on things for me." His slouched position underwent a swift movement as he stood and faced his friend.

"I don't want to bury your bride. And neither do you. This fella is playing for keeps. He made a mistake with his first move, but I think he's sharp and I've got a feeling he's ready to send in another crew."

"Can we do anything legally?"

"If the birds we've got in jail now decide to sing out, we'd have all we need to send him away for a good long stretch."

"I know his name," Nicholas said bluntly. "Lin told me she's certain it's the other half of Joseph Carmichael's firm."

"Yeah, Vincent Preston." Cleary said, with a trace of disgust. "I've heard that name before, just this morning, in fact. On paper, he's clean cut, and we don't have any proof otherwise."

Nicholas stood and crossed the room. "I'll tell you what, Cleary," he said smoothly. "Give me ten minutes alone with those two, and I'll give you chapter and verse. We're talking about my family here, and I won't draw any lines when it comes to looking out for them."

"You know, Gussie told me once she thought you had the look of a man with secrets. I'll bet you could kill a man a dozen different ways, Nick."

"Let's just say my education came from the streets," Nicholas told him. "I got my book learning in the university, but I was well versed in survival before I was sixteen years old."

Cleary stood to face his friend. "Trust me on this one, will you? I want Lin and Amanda out of town, and I can still smooth your tracks behind you if you'll leave today."

"Today?" Nicholas's mind raced as he considered the thought. Loading up their basic necessities wouldn't take long, and Katie could stay with friends if she didn't want to be alone in the big house. The bottom line was safety, and if Cleary was certain of his plan, Nicholas might do well to follow along.

"Today." Cleary emphasized the word. "Someone in

town carried a message to the station and a wire was sent off to New York yesterday. Our prisoners whistled down a boy and paid him to deliver a note to Henry. He was bright enough to bring it to me. You're probably going to think I'm foolhardy, but I let him dispatch it.''

Nicholas felt the stirring of anger. If Cleary had jeopardized… ''What did it say?'' he asked harshly.

Cleary grinned suddenly. '''Caged birds learn to sing.' I'd never have given them credit for enough intelligence to put their threat quite that way, but I figured it's going to bring results from New York, one way or another.''

''You think—''

''I think it'll take Vincent Preston less than two days to set things in motion, and this time it won't be a couple of amateur thugs. I plan to be ready for them.''

''All right. Write out directions to the place and I'll get things rolling at home.'' Nicholas frowned, his mind moving rapidly. ''I'll need more than my revolver. Get me a repeating rifle and plenty of rounds. Bring it to the house.'' He opened the door of his office, waiting as Cleary walked out ahead of him.

They crossed the lobby together, Nicholas slowing his stride as he caught sight of his clerk. ''Thomas, take over here until further notice.''

To the man's credit, he neither frowned nor flinched, just nodded and turned to watch his employer pass through the double doors, onto the sidewalk.

''Tell Sam Ferguson to send a heavy wagon to the house. I want his two best horses, and my gelding tied on behind. I'll need my tack for the gelding and enough oats for a week for all three animals.''

His words were spoken in an undertone, and the men parted company abruptly as Cleary veered off toward the livery stable. Nicholas moved with a single-mindedness that was a basic part of his character, one he'd not been forced to employ for the past months, and his mind moved rapidly along with his long strides as he headed for his home.

His wedding night might be on the back burner for a few days, he decided wryly. His prime concern now was convincing Lin that they must flee the town and settle for a more primitive lifestyle until Cleary had a chance to set things in order.

He opened the front door and entered his wide foyer, glancing into the parlor and then the dining room in search of his family. Katie came from the kitchen, wiping her hands on her apron.

"You're home early for dinner, Mr. Nicholas. Miss Carlinda is out back with Amanda. They're playing under the tree with the kitten."

"I need to talk to you, Katie," he said quietly.

"Uncle Nicholas is home." Amanda looked up with a joyous light in her eyes, and Lin's gaze followed her direction. Nicholas stood on the back stoop, watching them. She felt a chill of foreboding as he stepped to the ground and headed in their direction. His eyes were intent on her, his jaw set in a determined fashion, and she rose from the ground to meet him, her movements a bit awkward due to her bruises.

"What's wrong?" Her heart fluttered in her chest as she met his gaze. It wasn't anger alone that gleamed from those blue eyes, but a measure of concern that frightened her.

"Nicholas? Has something happened?"

He nodded, reaching for her, drawing her against himself. She leaned readily against his strength, aware of the solid, measured beat of his heart as he held her close. "We need to leave town," he said, his words barely audible as he bent his head to murmur them for her alone. "Cleary is sending a wagon for us. Can you be ready in an hour?"

"Where are we going?" she asked.

"North of here. An empty ranch house. Cleary says it's safe, and I'd trust him with my life."

She nodded in silent agreement. "How much shall I pack?"

He leaned back from her and tilted her head upward, cupping her chin. "Just like that, Lin? No questions?" His eyes warmed as he gazed into hers, and she felt a jolt of heat travel from the spot where his hand touched her back. "You trust me?"

"At least as much as you trust Cleary," she told him. "I'll do whatever you say, Nicholas."

"That's my girl," he whispered. His attention was diverted as Amanda rose, the kitten in her arms, her eyes wary as she faced the two adults.

"What's wrong?" she asked.

"We're going on an adventure," Nicholas told her, releasing Lin to crouch before his niece. His smile was quick as he gathered the child into his arms, then stood with her clinging to his neck. The kitten mewed, and Amanda laughed.

"You scared her, Uncle Nicholas. Are you going to carry us both?"

He nodded, and indicated the back door with a nod. Lin stepped quickly to the stoop and opened the door, waiting as Nicholas passed her, his nose nuzzling Amanda's cheek, his words soft as he spoke reassuringly to the child.

"I want you to mind Lin now, sweetie. She'll help you get your things together for a long ride. Run along upstairs, and I'll be there in a moment." He touched Lin's shoulder, catching her attention. "Don't lift anything. I'll do the toting down the stairs."

"Can I take my kitty along?" Her priorities obvious, Amanda stood hesitantly before them, and Nicholas did not quibble.

"Of course you can. I'll have Katie find a box for her."

Lin hastened up the stairs, hearing Nicholas issuing orders in the kitchen behind her. Whatever he had in mind, she was certain of his motives. Keeping Amanda safe and secure was uppermost in his mind, and she could only second the decisions he made.

The wagon was large and sturdy, loaded with essentials that would keep them from hunger and harm. The sight of three guns being placed beneath the seat was enough to unhinge Lin, but Nicholas shot her a reassuring glance as she contemplated the armory he planned to travel with. "We need to be ready for anything," he said soberly.

"Katie has about loaded up the whole pantry, and that crate—" she motioned toward a large container "—has enough linens and pillows to fill a closet." Her own belongings were packed, not neatly perhaps, but with a degree of haste that had not allowed for her usual methodical style of doing things. Amanda's clothing and books filled a trunk, and Cleary had muttered dark words as he lifted it to his shoulder and carried it from the back door.

The wagon had been pulled up at the rear of the house, and between the two men, they had filled it in less than a half hour with what Katie deemed necessary for their survival.

"I want you to go roundabout," Cleary said, his long fingers unfolding a map for Nicholas's perusal. Hastily drawn, it nevertheless was in detail, and Nicholas nodded as Cleary explained the route he would have them take. "I'll know where you are, and I'll come as soon as things settle down here. Once we get the marshal in on this, I'll feel better. In the meantime, I'll have three less to worry about."

A road led northwest from town, little-traveled but easy enough to follow, and it was there that Nicholas directed the team of horses an hour later. "We haven't come this way before, have we?" Lin asked.

Behind them, Amanda was perched comfortably on a feather tick, nestled in the pillowy bed that provided a nest in one corner for her and her kitten. Her head drooped and a yawn escaped her lips, even as Lin watched. She turned back to Nicholas as he spoke.

"It's a roundabout way to travel, but Cleary wants us to leave with the least number of folks aware of what's going on. If we're very lucky, Sam will do as he's told and no one will find out we've gone until it's too late to track us."

"Is it so dangerous for us here?" she asked.

"Yeah, I'd say so," Nicholas answered. "Cleary doesn't scare easy. And today, he's convinced that we need to be in a safe place. I trust his judgment, Lin."

"And I trust you," she said quietly, snaking her hand beneath his elbow to clutch at his forearm. He squeezed it against his side and she was reassured by the gesture.

Nicholas loved Amanda. She was certain of that. And his affections spilled over onto her. If not to the depth of the devotion he gave his niece, at least he cared enough to give her his name and his promise of safekeeping.

Perhaps someday…sometime soon, she hoped, he would return the love she'd come to acknowledge over the past days. Her gaze touched his dark hair and sought the strength of purpose in the depths of his blue eyes. Resting her fingers against his arm, she recognized the tensing of muscles beneath her touch and was swept with helpless admiration for the varied roles he was capable of playing in the game of life.

More than a cultured man of the world, he was also a man who moved with assurance in the place he had chosen. Yet, he was an enigma. Dressed as a professional man of business, he offered a facade of gentility to the public eye, even as he owned a primitive measure of strength that promised protection for those who sheltered in his care.

He belongs to me. The words vibrated in her mind, and she rejoiced in the truth of them.

Her thigh pressed with blatant familiarity against his, and heat rushed to her face as she thought of the past two nights when he'd been beside her in his bed. She'd almost wished last night that his gentlemanly instincts would vanish and his arms would have drawn her beneath him in a consummation of their wedding vows. But it seemed that Nicholas would not so readily claim his bride.

His murmurs in her ear had given her another night to recover from the injuries she'd suffered, and even as she drifted off to sleep in his arms, she sensed the tension of masculine desire surrounding her. His body was firm, his male parts making themselves known against her soft flesh, and yet he did not press her to accept him.

In many ways, Nicholas was a gentle man, she decided. More than aware of the bruises she wore, he'd been satisfied to wait. Yet, his eyes were ever on her, his face set in stern lines of constraint, and she felt most pampered and cosseted by his patience.

Now he was faced by another obstacle, and he'd been able to turn in another direction without hesitation. The man held hidden depths she'd only begun to explore. The next days would perhaps allow her access to the total persona of Nicholas Garvey, and she felt anticipation soar within her as she contemplated the venture ahead.

"How long will it take us?" she asked quietly, and met Nicholas's gaze as he glanced at her momentarily. His hat was pulled low over his forehead and his eyes were in shadow, narrowing as he searched the horizon quickly before returning his attention to her. A new image of the man filled her mind, a hard-edged version of the Nicholas she'd come to recognize, a glimpse into the mystery she intended to unwrap.

Gone was the banker, the elegantly dressed gentleman who left the house each morning to go to his place of business. In his place was a man who might be taken for a gunfighter at first glance. His leather coat hung open, allowing quick access to the holster he wore. Denim trousers fit long, muscular thighs and calves with precision, and worn boots she had not seen before today covered his feet, rising halfway to his knees.

"We'll travel through the night," he said quietly. "I don't think we'll be followed, but I'm not taking any chances with making camp. You and Amanda can stretch out in the back and sleep."

"Amanda can. I'll be here, beside you," she said, her words soft, but determined.

He looked down at her quickly. "Stubborn little cuss, aren't you?" A grin touched his stern mouth and vanished in an instant, but the momentary warming of his features lifted her spirits.

"I never said I'd be easy to get along with, Nicholas," she said lightly.

"So long as you do what I tell you, we'll be fine." Beneath the quiet words lurked a warning, and she knew, without a doubt, that he was capable of enforcing his ultimatum, should the need arise.

She nodded in agreement, leaning her head to rest against his shoulder, a sigh escaping her lips.

"Are you tired?" he asked, switching the reins to his left hand and shifting in the seat, his right arm moving to circle her waist. "I don't want you to overdo, sweet. There'll be a lot for you to cope with once we arrive."

"I just want to be close to you," she said, speaking the words that were the cry of her heart. "I need you, Nicholas." Those words of confession hung between them for a moment, and then she continued, as she revealed the thoughts she'd been harboring.

"I've never known what it was to feel this way." It was perhaps not the right time for the admission, she supposed. But he deserved to know her thoughts and feelings.

He tightened his grip and she felt his warmth radiate from his body to hers, knew the pleasure of long fingers that spread against her side, sinking into the flesh of her hip and nestling her closer. He dipped his head and his kiss touched her temple, the brush of lips a tender caress.

"I fear our marriage isn't getting off to a good start," he murmured. "You deserve a soft bed and the luxury of a comfortable home, Lin. Instead, I'm about to present you with a deserted ranch and a house that probably hasn't been lived in for some time. I hope you'll find it in your heart to understand the need for all this."

"If this is what it takes to keep Amanda safe, then I'm in it for the long haul," she told him firmly. "I can cope with most anything, Nicholas. You forget, I'm not from the upper crust. I'm just a very ordinary woman, and I can make do nicely."

He laughed, a throaty chuckle that sent shards of excitement down the length of her spine. "You're far from ordinary, sweetheart. You outshine any other woman I've ever known. You have the nicest little bottom on you, and the softest curves I've ever—"

Halting his words abruptly, he sighed. "I need to change this conversation, I think. Or you'll find yourself in a compromising position." At her quick glance into the back of the wagon, he laughed softly. "Amanda's sound asleep, all tucked into her nest."

"I'm not certain you can compromise me, Nicholas," she said, her heartbeat increasing with the movement of his hand as he slid it upward to cup the underside of her breast.

"That word doesn't apply any longer. I'm your wife, remember?"

"Not yet, you're not," he reminded her with a heated glance. "But you will be. And soon." His head dipped quickly and his mouth was hot and open against hers. It was a quick kiss, hard and filled with promise, and she inhaled the scent of male desire as he shifted in the seat beside her.

It was not an unknown aroma, for he'd come to her the past two nights with a complete lack of covering. Obviously, the man slept without benefit of nightshirt or drawers and she'd been exposed to knowledge of his male parts, aware of the musky scent of him as he responded to her presence beside him. The sensual thrust of masculine desire against her body had told her of the restraint he held over himself.

He was her husband, yet he waited for the claiming of her body, and she knew a moment of pure love for the man who would not give her pain, but be satisfied to await the time when she could respond to him.

"I love you, Nicholas." She spoke the words softly, quietly and without prompting, knowing she must tell him of the emotion that filled her to overflowing. "I never knew I had the ability to feel so much for a man."

His body was taut, his arm like a steel trap around her, and he growled an inaudible reply. "You needn't feel obliged to answer," she said quickly. "I know you care about me, and you love Amanda, and that's all that matters right now. I just wanted…"

He glanced down again and she saw desire in his eyes, saw the brilliant blue turn dark with a glittering, midnight flare of passion leashed, held on a short rein. His lids almost closed, and she sensed she would be consumed in the flame of his desire should he but halt the team and turn to her. If Amanda were not asleep just feet away, she would no doubt find herself tossed into the back of the wagon, Nicholas beside her.

As it was, he set her apart from himself and shot a warning glare in her direction. "You're messing with a man who's about as randy as—" He halted and his eyes sought her mouth and then swept to where her breasts filled the bodice of her dress.

"Don't touch me, Lin. I'm about that close—" He held up two fingers with barely space between.

"All right," she said, smothering the satisfaction that would have brought a smile to her lips. Recognition of her power over him filled her with a new, gratifying pleasure. She'd never before known the sensation of being the focus of a man's desire, and though it carried with it the natural fear of virginity about to be breached by a man's most potent need, she held the sensation close. Even the nagging notion of pain Irene had once warned her of could not subdue her anticipation of the moment when Nicholas would truly make her his bride.

"Can I just lean on you?" she asked, the query spoken meekly.

He cast her a look of suspicion. "You're enjoying this, aren't you?" At her quick glance, taking in the sparkle she could not hide in the depths of brown eyes, he frowned.

"Do you know what you're doing, sweet?" he asked. He'd already decided the woman was a temptress.

He could bide his time. Patience was a virtue he'd learned years ago. Especially when the prize was as warm and welcoming as Lin's arms promised to be. The anticipation would only grow, and though his desire provided him with a degree of discomfort, he set it aside, turning his mind to the job at hand.

He could wait. Tomorrow evening would find them safe and secure, behind locked and barred doors if he knew anything about Cleary's foresight. The sheriff had assured him of a safe house, and Cleary was a man to be trusted.

There would be time spent testing the security of their haven, gauging the strength of doors and shutters, and carrying in their provisions. Certainly there would be enough to do to keep them all busy for hours. Lin surely knew the basics of settling in, of lighting a cooking fire and preparing food. They'd be ready for bed before nightfall, in case there was a dearth of lanterns.

He smiled in satisfaction. Lanterns be hanged. There would be no need of staying up late. Amanda would be tired and Lin ready for a good night's sleep. But first...

His heart sped up, the cadence rapid as he anticipated the moment when he would seek out his bride and make her his wife.

She'd worn herself to a frazzle, what with learning how to build a fire in the black monster Nicholas called a cookstove, then sweeping with the poor excuse for a broom she'd found in the cobweb-laden pantry. Katie had sent soap and a bucket of rags, deeming them worthy of a space on the wagon, and Lin was fervently grateful at the sight of the equipment she would require to turn the kitchen into a place fit for the cooking and eating of food.

Her knees ached from crawling over the wide boards of the floor, scrub rag in one hand, brush in the other, tackling the accumulation of dirt and unexplained small piles of leavings she shuddered at. Her hair was clinging to temples and neck alike, curling and damp with perspiration, and she felt in desperate need of a bath.

Smack in the middle of the room, a wooden table sat with three chairs surrounding it, a wide bench against one wall obviously meant to provide additional seating. A kitchen cabinet stood with doors askew, one leg shorter than the other three, causing it to lean precariously toward the pantry. Lin found a block of wood that brought the piece of furniture almost to a level stance. By dint of much lifting and dark muttering, she had managed to fit it into place.

She stepped back to admire the results. The dirt on the inside of the cubbyholes and shelves had given way to soap and water, and she placed her provisions neatly within, polishing the remaining glass in the doors with a clean cloth.

The filled mason jars Katie had thought to include with their provisions looked lonely on the pantry shelves, and Lin stood before her store of goods, wondering how long she could make them last. In addition to several items of cookware, an iron skillet and another saucepan from the pantry were cleaned with a ready supply of gritty sand and an overflowing horse trough. Her mother had said no soap must touch the skillets at home, lest the finish be ruined for cooking.

With a critical eye, Lin decided finally that the one she possessed today could not be further damaged no matter how much soap she used on its surface. And with a smile of remembrance, she set the utensils aside.

Nicholas carried the mattress and feather tick up the stairs to bedrooms on the second floor, then repeated the trip, delivering trunks and boxes into the rooms overhead. A series of thumps and scraping noises made her aware of his activities and she left him to his chores, satisfied that her own would keep her occupied for the rest of the day.

They'd arrived after the noonday sun was high in the sky, and Amanda had jumped from the wagon, running across the yard from house to barn, the kitten at her heels.

"Wish I could harness all that energy," Nicholas muttered, lifting his saddle from the wagon, and leading his horse to the barn. "I'll need to set that corral fence to rights before I can let the horses loose," he told Lin. "As soon as I empty the wagon I'll get to it."

Once inside the house he'd looked around and contemplated the work facing them. "I hate to see you killing yourself in this kitchen," he said finally, "but if you can get it clean enough to work in, I'll see what I can do to help set things to rights."

"I assure you I'm capable of doing it," she said stubbornly.

"Probably," he agreed, slanting her a look of appraisal. "But you're not over the beating you took the other day, being banged around on that wagon bed, and I didn't plan for you to put in a full day's work so soon."

"We don't always get what we want in life," she reminded him.

His steps were quick as he approached her, his hands firm on her waist as he pulled her off balance and into his embrace. "Well, I sure got what I wanted," he murmured against her throat, his head bent as he nuzzled the soft flesh beneath her ear.

"Or, at least, I'm *gonna* get what I want, sweetheart." He straightened and sought her gaze. "Are you too tired and sore for some snuggling tonight?"

"Snuggling?" One brow lifted as she repeated his word. "Is that what you call it?"

He grinned. "There's a whole slew of other descriptive words I could use, but that one seems best for your tender ears to handle." He watched her as a blush rose to cover her cheeks, and his smile became tender, his eyes sparkling with a degree of satisfaction she could not mistake.

"If you can figure out a way for me to have a bath, I'll agree to some *snuggling*," she told him, daring to meet his look with a vow of cooperation, should he satisfy her demand for cleanliness.

"Damn, there has to be a washtub somewhere around here," he muttered. "I'll check out the barn. Or maybe the fruit cellar under the house."

"Fruit cellar?" she asked, her ears catching the promise inherent in that phrase.

"It's probably empty," he said, as if he would warn her of another chamber filled with cobwebs and small creatures in the corners. "Let me go and take a look."

She pumped water while she waited, priming the incongruously red pump that looked to be fairly new, then using the handle with a vigorous motion. Water spewed forth and she waited until it cleared, then stuck a bucket under the flow. The stove was hot beneath two of its burners and she eased the bucket atop the likeliest spot to heat.

"You won't believe the gold mine I just discovered," Nicholas said, standing in the kitchen doorway. "There must be a hundred or more jars of canned vegetables and even what looks like beef down there. There's a barrel of apples, and I turned them out on the floor. Some of them are all withered up, but there's enough to put together a dozen pies or make a couple of kettles of applesauce if you know how to do it."

"I wonder why they left their foodstuffs behind," Lin mused.

"Cleary said they were heading back East and just wanted someone to take the place off their hands, so he bought it for a song." He smiled, his look cocky, she decided. "There's also a nice square washtub down there, complete with handles. A little session with a scrub rag should get it into shape for your bath."

"You'll have my everlasting gratitude," she said emphatically, and then she replayed his words in her mind. "This ranch belongs to Cleary?" she asked, dumbfounded by that bit of information.

"He thought of making it his home before he met Gussie. Once he settled in as sheriff, he decided to stay in Collins Creek for a while. I suspect he'll be back here one day, when he gets ready to run some cattle and horses on the high pastures north of here."

She thought for a moment that Nicholas's eyes darkened with yearning as he spoke, and her thoughts were voiced aloud before she could contain the words. "Is that what you'd like to do? Live on a ranch, and make a living with horses and cattle."

He grinned, and the moment was gone. "You're a city girl, Lin. I wouldn't ask you to take on the work of a ranch. I'll be satisfied to run a bank and raise our family in town, I think.

"Now I believe I'll drag that washtub up out of the cellar and scrub it out good for you by the horse trough. You got a rag I can use?"

She sought the pile she'd folded and placed on the pantry shelf and snatched up an old towel Katie had sent along. "This ought to do it," she said, pressing a bar of lye soap into his other hand. "At least I'll have a tub to wash our clothes in."

He left the kitchen, and she heard the sound of hinges creaking as he opened the doors to the cellar beneath the house. If it weren't for her aching muscles and the unending pile of work to be tackled over the next days, she could almost be happy here, she thought, looking through a pane of glass that begged for a vinegar-soaked rag to be applied to its surface.

No matter. Nicholas was giving up the operation of his bank to conceal her from the danger she faced. The least she could do was dispense with groaning over her sore knees and aching back and do her share.

The sound of Amanda in the yard carried into the kitchen, and Lin searched the area, catching a glimpse of blue as Amanda scampered between the trees planted in neatly designed rows off to one side of the yard. Fully leafed out, they seemed to be fruit trees of some sort, and she thought of the woman who had watched them bloom and form fruit last year.

Life went on, it seemed, no matter who the observer. Her heart lifted with joy as she considered the place Nicholas had brought her, her sore muscles seeming of little matter as she considered the days ahead.

They would begin here, working together, making a home no matter how temporary it might be. It would be a time out of their lives set apart. She might even learn how to do all the things Katie did so well in Nicholas's bright, cheery kitchen in Collins Creek. At least she would give it her best shot.

Chapter Eleven

She was asleep, her body sprawled in the middle of the mattress, her glorious mass of russet hair dark on the pale pillow slip beneath her head. Nicholas, his disappointment at war with his raging desire, stripped from the denim trousers he'd donned after his bath in the kitchen and tossed them aside. His better instincts won out and he vowed to spend yet another night holding her while she slept. Kneeling on the edge of the mattress, he lifted her, rolling her to her back, making room for himself beside her.

Despite his care, she woke, blinking up at him for a moment. And then her smile appeared, broken by a yawn that caught her unawares. "I fell asleep," she whispered, reaching to circle his neck with her forearm. Tugging him close, she nestled her face against his shoulder and opened her lips to press a damp kiss against his skin.

Not only awake, but willing.

"You smell like wildflowers," she murmured. "You must have used my soap."

"Once I got squatted down in that blasted washtub, I couldn't reach anything else," he told her. "You'll have to put up with wildflowers for tonight."

"Hmm…I don't mind." She turned her head, and the

long line of his throat was blessed by a blend of nuzzling and tasting, her lips and teeth testing his flesh. Her sigh was deep as he circled her with his arms, drawing her against the long length of his body, her nightgown riding up to free her legs from its folds.

''You don't have any clothes on,'' she whispered. ''I noticed that when you slept with me before.'' She touched his back, a restless movement of her fingers that settled into a caress as she opened her hand. ''Don't you ever sleep in nightclothes? What if Amanda comes in here, Nicholas?''

''She won't,'' he said firmly. ''There's a nice little latch on the door, and I used it. We have all the privacy you could ask for.'' His fingers tugged at the white gown, and she murmured a protest.

''Get used to it, sweetheart,'' he told her, lifting to bend over her, supported by his elbow against the mattress. ''Let's get this thing off. I want you as close to me as you can be, with nothing in the way.''

Warily, she looked up at him, and he was silent as she made up her mind. Patiently he allowed her the time she needed, hoping he hadn't pushed her beyond the limits of propriety so firmly ingrained in her behavior. Then he spoke, urging her compliance. ''You're my wife, Lin. We'll be together every night from now on, and your life is about to undergo a definite change.''

He bent to kiss her and she was unresponsive for a moment beneath him, as if he'd thrust a challenge before her that warranted consideration. His mouth lingered against hers, brushing, pressing lightly, coaxing her to return the caress, and for a long moment he rued his words. He'd pushed her too far, too fast, it seemed, not wooing her as he'd ought.

''In other words, you've been as patient as you're going

to be?'' She whispered the query against his mouth, and he nodded, one slow, measured movement of his head.

''You expect me to take off my nightgown?'' she asked as he tilted her face upward, the better to meet her gaze. In the evening sky, stars and a moon on the wane provided barely enough light to penetrate the darkness of the room, but he could not mistake the sober look she wore.

''I'd be happy to do it for you,'' he offered.

''No,'' she said quietly. ''I think I can manage.'' She sat up and he released her from his hold, watching as she unbuttoned the front of her bodice, then unloosed her arms from the long sleeves before tugging the voluminous yards of fabric over her head. She wiggled against the mattress, pulling the gown from beneath her, and he smiled at the sight, watching as she emerged finally from the hemline. Her hair was tousled, falling down her back as she brushed it from her face, and he reached to catch a handful.

''I love your curls,'' he said, casting aside the white gown.

''You wouldn't if you were the one who had to keep them in order,'' she grumbled.

''They needn't be in order tonight,'' he told her, looking up at her, her face in shadow now, her breasts limned in moonlight. He spread his hand against her waist and slid it upward, cupping his palm under the soft weight of that feminine part.

Her breath caught, and he heard a hum of pleasure radiate from her throat as he explored the tender flesh, his fingers squeezing the peak lightly, causing the dark, pebbled surface to pucker beneath his coaxing touch.

''Nicholas.'' She spoke his name in a hissing whisper, and he repeated the caress.

''Do you know how that feels?'' she asked.

''Tell me.'' His words were a dark, husky demand as he lowered her to the bed, tucking the pillow beneath her head and rising over her. His mouth found the place he'd readied for his tongue, and she lifted herself from the bed in an involuntary movement that pleased him. Holding her firmly, he let his fingers splay across her stomach, pressing against the softness.

"Tell me," he said again, breathing deliberately against the damp flesh he suckled. She responded with a shiver, her words almost inaudible.

"I've never…no one ever…."

The message implicit in her confession touched him, reducing his yearning for completion into a tenderness he was not familiar with. She was truly virgin, truly untouched, and he was struck with the need to give her pleasure with whatever degree of skill he'd learned in the past years. Control was a definite necessity, and he rued the demands of his body, aching with the dark craving for fulfillment that rode him with burning talons of desire. He counted the months of his abstinence and decreed them more than any man could be expected to endure. Yet tonight he must be patient, and that particular lack in his nature might prove to be his undoing.

He called upon that last thread of self-control, that slender rein he held on desire. She was worth the wait, worth the constraint he would impose on himself, keeping him from the quick, urgent coupling he craved. Lin deserved gentleness of touch, the tenderness of coaxing caresses. Even though it brought him to the edge of reason, he would make this time of awakening a pleasure for her…for both of them.

"Nicholas?" She turned in his arms, seeking his embrace, and he lifted his head. "I'm not afraid," she said. "You needn't be worried about my bruises any longer."

Her mouth touched his, her lips opening with the urging of his tongue, and she accepted its presence. Then in a tentative gesture she met the thrust with an answering movement, suckling his flesh, seeking the penetration he offered into the depths of her mouth. A shiver, a soft murmur and the tensing of her fingers against the back of his head sent the message he'd hoped for.

Again his hand found the rounding of her breasts, measuring the soft weight, teasing the taut nubbins that pressed against his palm, and she responded with an agile thrust of her hips. Her indrawn breath told him of new sensations, her shuddering intake of air becoming a lingering gasp of pleasure. The grasp of searching fingers left his head, traveling the width of his shoulders, then spreading wide over the muscles of his back as if she sought to satisfy the yearning for intimacy she'd only just discovered.

His thighs tense, his buttocks taut, he held his breath as she allowed her hands a greater degree of freedom, venturing toward his apex of sensation. With shuddering delight he reveled in the promise fulfilled as slender fingers touched that part of him—the throbbing length that threatened to burst from the pressure of months of celibacy.

Fingertips fluttered into the nest of curls, and he forbade himself the pleasure of thrusting into her palm, holding himself rigid as she explored the length of him, curling her fingers to encircle the pulsing ache he could barely control.

She was eager, unafraid by her own admission, and he blessed the day he'd found the good sense to urge her into the hasty marriage vows they'd spoken. And then a dubious whisper reached his ear. "I don't think this is going to fit, Nicholas," she said, and he smiled softly at her doubts.

"Oh, yes. We'll fit just fine," he told her, edging away from her gentle caress, even as his body urged him to move with longer strokes within the circling fingers. He clasped her hand, moving it to lie beside her head. "It's my turn," he decreed. "Let me touch you, Lin."

"You are," she murmured, her hand escaping his grasp to return to the exploration she'd only begun. Her move-

ments slowed upon reaching his waist, her fingers spreading
wide as she shifted to his hip, and then shaped the slope
of his flank.

It seemed she would not be halted, and he gritted his
teeth against the temptation she offered, then murmured his
intentions aloud. ''I've touched only a bit, sweetheart. But
not where I need to.''

She stilled, almost ceasing to breathe as he rolled her
fully to her back and lifted himself to rise over her. His
hands caressed her inner thighs, urging them apart, a firm
pressure she allowed. And then he knelt there between her
knees, watching her, only too aware he might have gone
beyond whatever degree of modesty she clung to. Her
hands twitched against the sheet, then rose, her fingers
moving along the muscular length of his thighs, testing the
sinews that firmed beneath their pressure.

''You're beautiful, Lin,'' he said, barely able to speak
the words, his throat almost closing as he appraised the
trusting smile she offered, noting her trembling lips. He
moved slowly, allowing his hands to trace the length of her
body, forming her breasts, measuring the slender circle of
her waist. He enclosed the fullness of her hips in his wide
palms and then brushed with tender care across the vulnerable flesh of her belly.

Long fingers threaded through the curls that guarded her
most tender parts, and he eased gently through the layers
of sensitive flesh, finding a satisfying dampness. Then he
discovered hot, wet moisture, there where he would seek
to join them for the first time. His index finger explored,
circling and entering carefully, and she lifted her hips to
allow him entry.

''I won't hurt you, sweet,'' he whispered, even as he
prayed the words would prove to be the truth. His experience had never included a virgin, but in his earlier years in
the city he'd heard tales that had chilled him—stories of

blood and screams of pain from first couplings. Perhaps most of them had been exaggerated by youthful egos in need of sustenance, but probably some of those adventures held a germ of truth. This, he determined, would not be such an ordeal, no matter how long it took to ready Lin for his taking.

Yet she seemed eager, willing to believe his promise, allowing his touch. He watched her face as he tested the depths of that narrow sheath, sensed the moment he reached the fragile veil of her maidenhood. It was but a thin membrane, yet it gave promise of a bride untouched, a woman pure and unsullied by any other hand but his own. And he rejoiced in the knowledge that she came to him a virgin, even as he acknowledged the unfairness of it all.

Women lived under restriction that had never applied to the men of the world. And having reached his mid-thirties, Nicholas was well versed in the sexual arts. Yet, in this moment, he felt almost as untried as the woman before him. This was new territory for him, a fresh beginning, and he, who had not darkened a church door in his life, sought strength from whatever gods might be listening as he prepared to take his bride.

"I love you, Nicholas," she whispered, and his heart surged in his breast at the softly spoken pledge she gave. He'd not asked for her love, only her desire and passion. Yet it seemed they came as a whole, a gift given into his care.

His fingers moved against her, teasing the sensitive places he sought out, urging her into a rhythm that would bring fulfillment. She obeyed his coaxing, and her head jerked to the side as her breath caught in a quick spasm.

"Nicholas?" It was a cry of surprise, a plea he responded to as he recognized her first taste of the dark flavor of sensual adventure. Never ceasing the movement he'd set into motion, he bent low over her, opening his mouth against her breast, suckling hard, holding the crest against the roof of his mouth and drawing it deep.

She jerked against him, her hips rising and falling in the age-old rhythm he recognized, and her hands clasped him, nails digging for purchase against his back. Again she cried out his name, a sob accompanied by the syllables, sounding them in a drawn-out bewildered wail.

"Nicholas!" It was a cry of release, a sound of pleasure sought and found, and he thrust against her, rising to join their bodies even as she lifted her hips, offering herself, joyously accepting his invasion.

The membrane gave without protest and he was deep inside, where hot, pulsing muscles tugged at him. He withdrew and she groaned, grasping his shoulders as if she would cling to each increment of flesh he denied her. "Don't leave me."

"I'm here, sweet," he assured her, his voice husky with the urgency of his need. Again he slid to the depths of the channel he'd invaded, then eased back, only to return, establishing the rhythm that would bring them to the peak of pleasure.

She shivered, trembled and held him close, her knees bent, her hips rising to meet each thrust he offered. Tight, almost unbearably tight, her muscles tensing with each stroke, she held him prisoner within her. And then he could hold back no longer, felt the hot rush of release, knew the heartrending moment of delivering his seed into the depths of her feminine heat. He was without defense, his control at an end as he emptied himself of this most intimate of gifts.

She possessed him, her arms and legs enveloping him, even as shuddering cries escaped her lips and tears slid in silver streaks across her face, visible in the moonlight as he chanced a look, fearful of finding her tears to be a sign of pain. He was heavy, pressing her into the mattress with his long, powerful frame. Yet she clung, as if she would pull him into herself, make him a part of her soft, welcoming feminine body. He tilted his head, the better to kiss the dampness from her cheek, and felt a pang of guilt for the pain he had caused.

"I'm sorry, sweet," he said. "I told you I wouldn't hurt you."

"Just a bit," she answered, her eyelids fluttering open, the dark depths mysterious in the moonlight. "I knew it would hurt some, but it was…" She hesitated as if she searched for words to describe the moment of her passage from innocence to knowledge. Her smile was quick, fleeting, but filled with satisfaction. "You're a part of me now, Nicholas. We're one flesh."

"Yeah, I guess you could say that," he agreed, his fingers tangling in the lush curls that lay close to his face. She carried the scent of her soap and another aroma he recognized as the slaking of desire, of her female essence.

She touched his cheek, drawing his attention.

"You haven't read the Bible much, I suppose. Or have you?" she asked, and he shook his head, strangely embarrassed that he must make such an admission of ignorance.

"There's a place where it speaks of a man and woman…being together, like we are. I thought the words were strange, and almost forbidden, when I was younger and read it the first time."

"In the Bible? There are words to describe making love?"

She nodded. "I think I understand now what it meant when it said they would become one flesh."

"Maybe there's more to this Bible reading than I thought," he said, amusement tingeing the words.

"Don't make fun, Nicholas."

"Oh, I'm not. I've just never been exposed to religion much in my life."

"I didn't think you were much of a churchgoer," she whispered. "But it doesn't matter. I'm sure you'll find it an interesting avenue to explore."

"You're going to make me go to church?"

She smiled again. "I won't force you to do anything you don't want. But I'd like you to give it a chance."

If she only knew the power she held in those slender hands. He shuddered to think what lengths he would go to in order to please the woman. "You have me at a disadvantage, you know," he said, lifting his weight to his forearms. "Right this minute I'd do about anything you asked of me."

Her mouth trembled a bit as if she tried to cover a smile, and then she lost the battle and a grin appeared, followed by soft laughter. "Anything, Nicholas?"

Hesitating, he quibbled a bit. "Most anything, I suspect."

"Would you kiss me?" Her arms slid around his neck and she pressed her hands against the back of his head. It was an invitation he didn't think to turn from, and his mouth took hers in a deep, intimate blending of lips and tongue. She gasped for air as he lifted his head, and her eyes were wide.

"I'm thinking the night's not over," she whispered. "I'm beginning to wonder—" Her nostrils flared as she drew another deep breath. "Are you still interested in…I mean, can you *do* that again?"

"Oh, yes. I'm still interested," he said, his lips returning to press a series of short kisses against her throat. "And yes, I can do that again. But the problem may lie with you, sweetheart. I don't want you to be hurting in the morning." He eased from her and rose from the mattress. "I'll be back," he said, sliding into his trousers and opening the door, just in time to see her snatch at the sheet.

Lin moved gingerly, stretching out one leg, then the other. She was aching with a delicious tenderness in places she'd never before thought much about. Her breasts felt swollen to the touch, and the sheet brushing against them reminded her of the sensation those female parts were capable of. She'd never before considered herself a sensual person. Even Irene's short, embarrassed monologue when she'd considered it late enough in Lin's life to be made aware of the usual events of a wedding night, had not made much of an impression.

She'd known there would be a degree of pain, known she could anticipate a certain amount of familiarity from whomever she chose to marry. But the reality had gone far beyond expectation. That Nicholas would come to her without nightclothes was not a surprise, but his swift disrobing of her had come as a shock.

Her panic had mounted to new heights when he'd knelt between her splayed thighs and taken her measure. With heated gaze and warm hands he'd inspected her from top to bottom, and then, to her surprise and pleasure, had pronounced her beautiful.

Whether she was truly as lovely as he supposed it mattered little. That he thought it was true was what counted. His close scrutiny and his murmured words of appreciation as he'd elaborated on each and every portion of her body at great length was enough to raise her spirits beyond belief.

She'd somehow managed to satisfy the man, and heaven above was well aware that her own expectations had been swallowed up in the reality of his claiming. Even now she felt tingling nerve ends vibrate as she shifted to her side, knew the aching reality of flesh newly introduced to the marriage act.

"I'm his wife," she whispered. "Mrs. Nicholas Garvey. Lin Garvey." And then she bit at her lip, recalling the

words she'd offered so willingly. Words he had not repeated, only accepted as a part of this night.

I love you, Nicholas. She could not recant, could never
regret the speaking of that vow. And if this…this shattering
expression of passion was all she ever received at his hand,
she would accept it gladly and be pleased that his desire
for her body ran strong.

"Lin?" He stood in the doorway, his body pale in the
darkness, and she whispered his name.

"Nicholas. I'm awake."

"I brought a warm cloth to wash you with," he said,
closing the door quietly behind him. He bent to her, offering the cloth. "Shall I do it?" he asked.

"No. I can." Now this, she decided, was more than she'd
bargained for. That he would come back to her, expecting
to help her bathe the tender tissues, the secret, feminine
parts of her body, was not to be considered. And yet he
banished those thoughts as he sat down beside her.

"Don't be ashamed of your body, sweet," he said quietly. "I've seen most all of it, and it's beyond perfect."

"Nothing is *beyond perfect*," she said firmly. "Me, least
of all."

"I think we're going to argue this point, here and now,"
Nicholas informed her. He took the cloth from her hand
and tugged the sheet aside, exposing her to his view once
more. With gentle touches and murmurs of praise for the
curves and hollows he touched, he washed the residue of
his passion from her, then wiped the dampness from her
skin with a clean towel.

"If we're truly one flesh, as you said, dear heart, then I
have the right to tend you and set to rights the damage I
did to you tonight."

She retrieved the sheet with haste, burrowing beneath it,
and he smiled at her action. It probably wasn't fair to expect instant intimacy from a young woman who'd never

been exposed to a sexual relationship, but all in all, Lin had managed to accept everything he'd offered her tonight. And if tucking the sheet under her arms made her feel better, he'd just have to crawl in beside her and share the covering with her.

Setting aside the cloth, he bent to kiss her again. "Just think of it as a part of our wedding night."

"Well, it's a part I hadn't planned on," she told him. "No one has ever…" She waved a hand at the damp cloth and towel he'd used.

"I'll let you wash my back the next time I get into that washtub," he offered, succeeding in prompting a smile as she chuckled at his nonsense. "But for now, let's just see if we can get a few hours' sleep. Tomorrow will be a long day."

He crossed to the other side of the mattress and stretched his long length out beside her, offering his shoulder for her use. Without hesitation she rolled toward him, snuggled against his warmth and made herself comfortable. The curves of her breasts pressed firmly against his side and she entwined her leg with his, rubbing the sole of her foot against his shinbone.

"You sure you're comfortable?" he asked, well pleased with the familiarity she assumed with his body.

"Oh, yes, I'm fine." A yawn followed her words of assurance and, with a bit of reluctance, he set aside his half-formed plans. She'd no doubt be agreeable, but it seemed only fair to allow her a few hours for her tender flesh to heal from the initiation she'd undergone tonight.

"You *sure* you're all right?" he asked softly, scooping her even closer.

Her head nodded, and a muttered reply was muffled against his chest. "Umm…" she murmured. "Fine, thank you." And then she was limp, her body twitching once as she slid with ease into a depth of slumber he envied.

His own thoughts were in too much turmoil to allow the luxury of dreamless sleep tonight. The doors and windows were secure, his gun was at hand and he'd checked the outbuildings at dusk. Cleary's methodical mind had seen to it that locks were installed, and each door was capable of withstanding a nominal amount of force. There was nothing else to be done for tonight.

Tomorrow he could set about cleaning up the barn and putting the corral fence to rights. The hay on the wagon and the oats they'd brought were sufficient for several days. Then the horses could be put to pasture, where the grass was tall and green, heavy with the lush growth of summer.

He closed his eyes, listening to the measured breathing of the woman he held. She'd told him she loved him, and he'd given her no reply. He'd admitted freely just the other day to feeling more for her than any other woman in his life, and she'd accepted that, it seemed. Beside her declaration, his own paled.

She loves me. He savored the thought, reveling in the memory of the hour just past. Lin had given herself without reservation, allowed him total freedom of her body, and he'd been able to bring her satisfaction and pleasure. His sigh was deep, and he bent to touch his lips to her forehead. She murmured, lifting her face a bit, and he obliged with a brush of his mouth against hers.

And then returned for a deeper caress. He couldn't have asked for more.

She loved him.

Chapter Twelve

Six days. They'd been here for six days already. Lin looked out the kitchen window, watching as Nicholas rode from the pasture on the far side of the corral and across the yard. He sat proudly atop the horse, straight in the saddle. And in front of him, perched high above the ground, Amanda viewed the world around her with no trace of fear or foreboding to mar her small, perfect features.

She rode with her shoulders back, and yet seemed relaxed, in a stance very much like that of her uncle, rolling with the gait of the gelding as though she were a part of the creature. Nicholas was proud of the child. His feelings gleamed from blue eyes that watched her every move, shone with each flashing smile he cast in her direction. Acceptance had come easily to him, as if Amanda gave him a living link with the sister he'd never known.

"She has my eyes," he'd said, late in the night when Lin had thought him asleep, silent beside her for so long she'd closed her eyelids, courting slumber.

"You think so?" she'd asked idly, and had not been surprised when he rolled to face her.

"Don't you?" His query held a note of doubt, and she couldn't bear to tease him further.

"Of course she resembles you," she'd whispered. "She's your blood kin, Nicholas. She wears the look of you." A look that gave him perfect male features, a face guaranteed to cause women's hearts to flutter at first sight of that handsome profile.

Lin sighed, remembering. Her hand had risen to touch his cheek, and he'd turned his mouth to press a kiss against her palm. Then had enclosed her in his embrace.

She shivered at the memory, recalling the scent of clean sheets and the aroma of desire that surrounded Nicholas when his need for her drew her into that world they'd begun to create.

Inhaling deeply, she stood in the doorway, drawing the smell of fresh air into her lungs, that same crisp and clean scent that permeated the laundry she hung to dry on the clothesline in the yard. There was a certain amount of pride to be gained by the knowledge of her own ability to wash the garments they wore, she decided, and even the struggle she undertook as she wrestled with the wind as she hung to dry the bedding they used.

The air was fresh in the mornings, the sun hot, warming her bones as she stepped through the kitchen doorway to stand on the edge of the porch. Her gaze moved to where her washing blew in the wind, and she felt the mantle of marriage fall on her shoulders as she surveyed the work of her hands.

It fit her well, she'd decided. She was more than a nanny, had more value than a young woman trained simply to teach and care for a child. Being a wife encompassed all of that and yet held promise of a satisfaction she'd only begun to appreciate.

A sense of belonging swept through her as she watched Nicholas now, recognized the pride and pleasure in his smile as he brought Amanda to the back of the house and bent to deposit her on the ground in front of the porch.

"Lin." He spoke her name, and she was aware of underlying warmth in the single syllable, as he smiled. "Amanda's had her ride, and I'm off for the back of the pasture. The fence needs bolstering." His gaze held her immobile, touching her with heated knowledge, and warmth swept through the length of her body. Then he lifted his reins and shot a look of promise over Amanda's head. "I won't be too long."

"I'm going to play with my kitten, Linnie," the child said, bending to peer beneath the porch to where her pet had claimed a dark corner as her own. A tattered piece of saddle blanket, cadged from the tack room in the barn, provided a nest, and, true to her nature, the kitten curled in the center of her bed, content to sleep away the major portion of the day. Amanda leaned in to lift the small creature and brought her to nestle against her chest. With a yawn and a curving of her back, the small, black kitty accepted the attention and curled obligingly into place.

"Don't go far from the house." Lin reluctantly turned her gaze from Nicholas to offer the soft warning. "I need to be able to see you from the kitchen."

Amanda nodded and shot her uncle's retreating back a long look of patience. "I know. Uncle Nicholas already told me the rules." Her arms held the kitten close, and she climbed the four steps, turning at the top to settle on the edge of the porch. "Can we do our lessons out here, Linnie? It's more fun than at the table."

Lin nodded agreeably. Reading could be done anywhere, and going back indoors when the alternative was sitting in the sunshine was hardly an option. "I'll get your book, as soon as I finish putting the soup to cook."

"Nicholas?" She called his name and he brought his horse to a halt, turning to look back at her. "Don't be long. We'll eat in a couple of hours. I'm making soup. I'm about ready to add the vegetables and put the kettle on the back of the stove to simmer.''

He acknowledged her message with an uplifted hand and urged his horse into a trot, disappearing behind the barn in moments.

Lin opened the door with a last look at Amanda and entered the cool haven that was her kitchen. It was strange, she thought, how carrots and potatoes took on a different aspect when you were the one washing and paring. She'd never known the attraction of putting food together before, had always watched from the sidelines as another prepared the meals in whatever place she lived.

Now, having ventured beneath the house, into that dark, musty place where some other woman had stored the harvest from her garden, she appreciated each aspect of putting together a meal, from the preparing of the food to the final serving of it.

The spiders below ground level were off-putting, and the sound of scampering mice sent a chill down her spine each time she invaded their territory, intent on searching out the withering carrots and potatoes for cooking. Yet there was that silent presence of the woman who had lived here before, who had left that part of herself behind, and Lin found herself wondering at the passage of lives through the doors of this house.

The hours and days spent in returning this house to a portion of its former beauty brought a sense of pride to Lin's soul. At the cost of blisters and aching muscles, she'd learned the price to be paid for clean floors and sparkling widows. The meals came from her hands, the comfort of clean bedding and clothing from her long hours of work.

Sad irons found in the pantry had been cleaned and set atop the cook stove to heat, in readiness for the ironing to be done. The maids in Irene's mansion had been adept at the chore, and it apparently was a skill not easily gained.

But Lin's efforts had shown improvement after the first brown, iron-shaped impression appeared on the back of Nicholas' second-best shirt. He'd worn it without a murmur, only casting her a grin as he held it up to view the scorched area.

Thankfully, the furniture took little care, there being a dearth of usable objects in the parlor. Only a sofa remained from the previous occupants, a lumpy, ancient relic of better days. But the windows were clean, the curtains free of dust, and she'd swept the faded carpet vigorously.

Lin looked around the kitchen, admiring the mason jar of wildflowers that were Amanda's contribution to the decor. As if she'd never lived in luxury, the little girl found joy in small comforts. Taking on the task of setting the table, drying silverware, what scant supply there was, and toting and carrying in Lin's wake, she'd been ever cheerful. The sun's rays brought new color to her cheeks, the fresh air and the energy dispensed by chasing her kitten and romping beneath the trees gave her sound slumber each night.

''She's fit in here as if she were born in this place,'' Lin murmured, cutting up carrots into the simmering broth. The events of their kidnaping seemed forgotten, if the little girl's frame of mind was any indication. Lin's own memory was not so easily erased. She'd woken from a sound sleep only last night to find Nicholas's hands on her, his voice soothing as he sought to pierce the nightmare she struggled to escape. His arms provided comfort and then a greater degree of pleasure as she turned to him and murmured her thanks.

Being married was the best part of this venture, she decided smugly, settling the lid of the soup kettle in place. Nicholas admired her, complimented her every accomplishment as if he knew that her background had not prepared her for this place. Offering her the scrub board on their second day, he'd grinned apologetically.

"Katie has life easier than you, I fear," he'd said. "She only has to turn a crank to do the laundry."

"I don't mind." Lin recalled her words of assurance with a wry smile. In truth, she hadn't minded, had almost enjoyed the scrubbing and wringing out, had been invigorated by the wind that attempted to snatch the sheets from her grasp and then blew them like the sails of a ship as they dried.

"Mm...smells good." Nicholas's faint praise was enough, she'd decided, remembering the fresh scent of clean air their bedding had captured. "Almost as good as you," he'd murmured, reaching for her with arms that held her close, hands that cherished her feminine flesh. His lips caressed her skin, skimmed the surface with a teasing touch she could not resist.

"I'm a brazen hussy," she whispered, recalling the newfound joy of cuddling, the sweet taste of pleasure found in another's presence. "But he doesn't seem to mind." A smile curved her lips as she sought and found Amanda's book. It slid into her pocket as she returned to the stove, her fingers holding a dish towel as she lifted the pot lid to peer into the steaming broth. Steadfastly, she put Nicholas from her mind as she returned to the child who waited on the porch.

Supper that evening was cut short by a call from the yard. Riding a plodding horse, a man made his way to the hitching rail and slid from his mount. Behind him, at the end of a rope was a brown-and-white cow, her big, mournful eyes winning Lin's heart at first sight.

"I asked the man at the general store to locate us a cow, Lin. I'd say he didn't let any grass grow under his feet. Looks like we're about to buy our milk supply." Nicholas rose from the table and stepped out onto the porch, greeting the visitor warmly.

Within minutes, he'd drawn money from his pocket and taken possession of the cow, shaking hands with the gentleman and exchanging a few pleasantries. Lin and Amanda watched from the porch for a while, then went back in the house to clear the table and put Nicholas's plate in the warming oven. It looked like he'd be busy for a while, settling their new purchase into the barn.

"She's pretty," Amanda decided. "I like cows."

"You'll need to stay back from her till we find out if she's friendly," Lin told her firmly. "I don't know much about their moods."

"Well, her eyes look real pretty," Amanda said. "I think she's nice."

Lin nodded, glancing out the window as the neighboring farmer untied his horse and settled his long frame atop the creature. "Let's go out and see what Nicholas has to say," she said, removing her apron and hanging it on a nail by the door.

They watched as their first visitor departed, his feet hanging on either side of the plow horse he rode, his hat perched squarely atop his head. The cow he'd left behind lifted her head and uttered a long, low sound that seemed to offer her former owner a sad farewell. Then, bending her head to the swatch of greenery before her, she set about the process of turning grass into milk, chewing contentedly as Nicholas strode toward her.

"Come on, Bossie," he said coaxingly. "You'll do better for now in your stall. We'll settle for hay tonight, and tomorrow you can be turned loose in the pasture."

"Bossie?" Lin repeated curiously. "What a strange name for a cow."

"What would you call her?" he asked, grasping the lead

rope the animal had come equipped with. "Something more elegant, I suppose."

"I've never named a cow," Lin admitted. "But if she's going to supply us with some of the essentials of living, we'd ought to come up with something more dignified than *Bossie,* I'd think." She tilted her head to one side. "How about Precious?"

She thought for a moment Nicholas would choke. He coughed, then grinned widely. "Maybe Belle would work," he offered. "I remember a cow with that name when I was a boy."

Lin was willing to compromise. "Belle sounds fine," she agreed. "Do you know how to milk her?"

Nicholas lifted an eyebrow. "Of course I can milk her. As I understand it, the process is quite simple. Her equipment is standard, I would think, and we have a new bucket in the pantry."

Lin shrugged. "Well, I'm glad you have that chore. I wouldn't have the first idea how to go about it." Relieved at his nonchalance, she watched as the docile cow followed her new owner into the barn.

It was almost dark when Nicholas saw fit to admit defeat, announcing he apparently lacked the basic knowledge necessary to coax the milk from the cow's udder. "It seems a simple enough process," he said, obviously embarrassed by his frustration. "Would you like to give it a shot?"

The sound of Belle's discomfort reached the porch as Lin considered the idea. "She's not happy, is she?"

Nicholas shook his head. "And she's impatient with my attempts."

"I'll try," Lin said, stepping to his side, and then looked up in surprise as the gelding in the corral issued a shrill challenge. "What's wrong?" she asked, peering past Nicholas to see the horse reaching his head over the fence.

"Company, I suspect," Nicholas answered shortly.

From the twilight beyond the barn, a pale horse approached, a woman astride his bare back, and the gelding again snorted and whinnied. The woman lifted a hand in greeting and nudged her mount into a quick canter as she rode past the corral fence and across the yard.

Nicholas relaxed visibly and stepped forward. "We weren't expecting visitors," he said. Tilting his hat back a bit, he smiled a welcome. "Are you a neighbor?"

"You could call me that," the woman answered. She was graceful, her dismount accomplished with barely a whisper of fabric as she slid to the ground and dropped her horse's reins. Fair hair shone like a halo around her head, and her skin gleamed as if lit from within in the faint light shed from the kitchen windows.

"I was riding back home from the woods north of here when I heard your cow protesting." She waved a hand vaguely in the direction of a forested area beyond the pasture as she spoke and then looked directly at Lin. "I thought she might be tangled in the fencing. Now," she said with a smile that invited a response, "from the sounds of it, I've decided she just needs to be milked."

"I fear you're right," Lin said, and then freely admitted her own inadequacy. "I haven't the faintest idea how to go about the job, and Nicholas has just admitted defeat." She tilted her head and considered the visitor. "I don't suppose…"

"You're in luck." The woman held out a hand. "I'm Faith Hudson, and I learned how to coax milk from a cow a couple of years ago."

"I could use a lesson," Lin said thankfully. She looked up at Nicholas. "You don't mind if I take over this chore, do you?"

He handed her the shiny bucket with a bow. "You have my permission, sweetheart. I'll just stand by and watch."

The next hour was a revelation to Lin. She found herself

admiring the slim creature who had come out of the twilight to their rescue. There was a sense of kindred spirits in the easy laughter they shared, as the self-effacing woman answered her questions and laughed gently at her tentative efforts to persuade the cow into releasing her burden. The pail was gradually filled past the halfway point, the milk foaming as Lin successfully gained the knack of coaxing Belle into compliance.

"Do you have a separator?" Faith asked, looking from the barn door toward the house. She searched the yard a moment, and Lin met her returning gaze with a shrug of defeat.

"I don't even know what a separator is," she admitted. "What gets separated?"

"The milk from the cream," Faith said. "But you can let it rise to the top and just ladle it off almost as easily."

"Can't we just drink it as it is?" Lin feared she sounded almost as ignorant as she felt.

"Certainly. But if you want to make butter, you'll have to use just the cream."

"Butter." She hadn't thought that far ahead. The golden round brought from Katie's kitchen was almost gone, and replacing it had not been an issue. But by tomorrow it would be.

"There's probably a churn somewhere around here," Faith said. "The folks who lived here left a lot of their belongings behind when they sold the place. I'll warrant they didn't tote their churn on board the train when they headed for the city."

"Maybe it's in the cellar," Lin suggested. "I've been down there, but I didn't notice it." Her pause was long and then she put forth a new query. "What would it look like?" That she'd never been involved with the making of butter was something she hated to admit. This stranger seemed to be well equipped to survive on a farm, and Lin was definitely a woman born and raised in town.

Faith laughed aloud and lifted the bucket of milk. "Let's take this in the house and set it aside while we search out the churn," she said cheerfully. "I hope your family has had their evening meal already. This may take a while."

"She was a lifesaver, wasn't she?" Lin stripped from her stockings and shook them out, then turned to where Nicholas waited in the bed. Invigorated by the events of the evening, she grinned widely. "I didn't know there was so much involved in keeping a house." As she spoke she picked up his soiled clothing from the chair and deposited it in the basket, then added her own.

"You've taken to it well," he conceded. "A stranger would never know how pampered you've been all your life." And then he laughed aloud as she spun and darted toward him, pouncing on him in mock anger.

"What a way to talk to the woman who's been gathering blisters all week," she said between gasps of laughter. His fingers were busy, poking and tickling as he pulled her across the mattress. Beneath her nightgown she was naked, available and tempting, he decided, and he wasn't about to lose any opportunity to touch the softness she concealed beneath yards of pale cotton fabric.

"Is this all you think about?" she asked him, peering up through waves of disheveled hair. She blew distractedly at a strand that covered her mouth and he reached to tuck it behind her ear, smoothing the dark, russet locks from her face.

"Not *all*," he said with a husky tone invading his words. "Just mostly."

"Did you ever consider that I might be tired after learning how to milk a cow and hunting through crates and stacks of leftovers for a butter churn?"

He bent to bless her mouth with a warm caress. ''Can you figure out how to use it?''

''Faith will be back in the morning to help me,'' she admitted. ''I think she was trying hard not to laugh at my questions.''

''I wonder where she lives,'' he mused, his eyes narrowing as he considered the woman who had dropped by in such a casual manner. ''I haven't seen another farmhouse down the road toward town that wasn't occupied by a family.''

Lin shrugged. ''I don't know. I'll ask her tomorrow. We're going to make butter, and she said she'd bring me some fresh vegetables from her garden. She has peas and green beans ready to eat. I won't turn them down, even if we have a good supply in glass jars in the cellar.''

It seemed they would have this conversation whether he liked it or not, Nicholas decided. ''Find out about her family,'' he told Lin. ''I'd like to know a little more about her. She seems to be genuine, but I'm afraid I'm looking for trouble in every corner.''

''I got the feeling she lives alone.'' Lin's brows pulled together as she considered the idea. ''She didn't say so in so many words, but I just have an idea she's on her own in the world.'' Her brow unfurled and she relaxed. ''I trust her, Nicholas. And I'm usually pretty good at sorting people out.''

''Her living alone is odd.'' Nicholas said. ''A beautiful woman by herself, when the men in this area are hard put to find good wives hereabouts.''

Lin's mouth twitched and her eyes lit with warning, signs he'd learned to accept as a prelude to trouble, as if she formed her words carefully for the best possible effect. ''A *beautiful* woman? You noticed that? A bridegroom for a mere two weeks and already you're casting longing looks at another woman?''

He growled, low in his throat, and his mouth descended again, this time to nuzzle against the tender skin of her throat. "The only woman who interests me is right here in this bed." Her indrawn breath was the signal he hoped for and his hand swept to enclose the soft curve of her breast. "I'd like it better if you weren't wearing this gown," he muttered darkly.

"Hmm...I'd say that's easily solved," she returned with a look he recognized. Lin had rapidly become a seductress of the very best sort, and he gloried in the joy she found beneath his touch. Now she sat upright, pushing aside his embrace as she lifted the gown over her head and dropped it to the floor. With a wisdom as old as Eve, she turned to him, offering herself.

"I love you," she whispered, and the lines of her face softened as she received his kiss and the tenderness of his embrace.

Churning butter was a revelation. The cream they poured into the upright, wooden container bore little resemblance to the double handful of butter they removed a short while later, and Lin was exultant over the transformation. Faith showed her how to press it into a wooden bowl, causing the excess moisture to gather, using the flat paddle she'd brought with her to form the pale butter into a round that resembled Katie's own finished product.

"I feel so proud of myself," Lin said gaily, holding the plate aloft as she admired her finished product.

"You should only need to do this twice a week," Faith told her. "That ought to do you for three or four days. The rest of the milk you can drink or use to cook with, but with the way that cow produces, I'm sure you'll have lots left over."

"Can you use any?" Lin asked quickly. "Or do you have a cow?"

Faith shook her head. "I'd be glad to buy some from you a couple of times a week. I used to come here to help with things," she said. "The woman who lived here was sickly for a while and I milked her cow and lent a hand. In turn, they gave me milk and kept a good eye on my comings and goings."

"Well, you won't be buying milk, or anything else from us," Lin said firmly. "You'll take what you need, and be welcome to it. I can't say how much I appreciate what you've done for me." She viewed the bread tins sitting in the warming oven. "I'll warrant that will be a whole lot better than what I baked the other day."

"You have to knead it well," Faith told her. "You've got the knack now."

"Will you stay for supper?" Lin asked. "Or would you rather get home before dark?"

Faith shrugged. "I'll stay. Riding at night is no problem. There's nothing in the woods that frightens me."

"How far away is your place?" Lin asked reluctantly, fearful of being intrusive.

"Maybe fifteen minutes from here, if I let the horse take her time." She smiled knowingly. "I suspect you'd like to know where, wouldn't you?"

"You'll think I'm being nosy." Lin felt a blush steal across her cheeks as she made the admission. "I really wondered because Nicholas mentioned it. He wanted to know if you were alone in the world. I think he's concerned about you."

"No need for that," Faith said quietly. "I'm fine on my own. I've no one here. No husband. No children. Just me and my cat and a few chickens." She opened the oven door and poked her hand inside, removing it quickly as if the heat threatened to burn her fingers. "That's hot enough for the bread now," she said.

"How can you tell?" Lin asked, reaching for the three bread tins and placing them on the oven rack carefully.

"If it feels hot enough to burn your flesh as soon as you stick your hand in, it's ready to bake." Faith shrugged. "You'll learn soon enough."

Lin washed the bread pan and dried it, then hung it on the pantry wall. "How long have you lived alone?" she asked, pausing in the doorway as Faith settled in a chair before the table.

"Nearly two years. I came from back East, found a place I could handle on my own and settled in." The coffee cup she held was lifted to her lips and she looked up at Lin as she sipped the hot brew. "I'm glad to have neighbors again. The woman who lived here before you was kind to me, and her husband didn't mind my using the empty cabin."

"I'm glad," Lin told her. "I hope we can be friends, too."

Faith grinned widely. "Aren't we already?"

"Where in the woods?" Nicholas asked as they watched their visitor ride into the night. The moon provided light while Faith crossed the pasture and meadow beyond, and then she disappeared among the trees, fading into the depths like a pale shadow atop her golden horse.

"She didn't say," Lin answered. "I'm not certain she wanted us to know."

"She's somewhat of a mystery, I'd say. I'd sure like to know where she got that mare," Nicholas said. "That color's rare, you know. I read about a herd of them owned by one of the Indian chiefs a few years back, but they're harder than hell to breed. You never know what color you'll come up with, from what I've heard. One fella said a sorrel stud works best."

"Her mare's beautiful," Lin agreed, and cast him a side-long glance. "Almost as *beautiful* as its owner."

Nicholas groaned. "I'll never hear the end of that, will I?"

Lin turned into his embrace and they laughed softly together. From the kitchen behind them Amanda called out. "Are you comin' in now? I'm ready for my story, Linnie." She appeared inside the doorway, garbed in her nightgown, book in hand. "It's dark out. Will Faith be all right all by herself?"

"She's fine," Lin assured her, backing from Nicholas and offering her hand to the child. "Let's sit at the table and read tonight. The light is better than using a candle in your bedroom." She lifted the child in her arms as she sat and held her close, opening the book to the first page.

Nicholas sat across the table, leaning back in his chair, and Lin was aware of his watchfulness and the attention he shed on both woman and child. The sense of family, of belonging together, was strong as she read from a collection of verses Amanda was familiar with. The child's whisper accompanied Lin's reading, and when the next page was turned, Lin halted her reading to look down at the small, relaxed figure in her lap.

"Why don't you read this verse?" she asked, pointing to an illustration of a child in a swing.

"I can't read what it says," Amanda said. "You know those words are too hard for me, Linnie."

"I'll bet you know them already. Why don't I put my finger on every word and you recite the poem. It's the one that begins—"

"I know! I know!" Amanda said, lifting her hand to touch Lin's lips, silencing her effectively. "It starts out, 'How would you like to go up in the air?' doesn't it?"

"See," Lin said, chuckling at the child's quick response. "I knew you could tell what the words are. Let's try it together."

"I can do it," Amanda said proudly, her index finger already pointing at the words on the page.

That she sped ahead, her finger lagging several words behind, was not important, Lin decided, even though she captured the tiny digit and helped the girl keep pace. The whole idea was to expose Amanda to the idea of sounds and words belonging together.

When bedtime had been celebrated with a song and prayers and Amanda was tucked between the covers, Nicholas led Lin from the child's bedroom and back to the kitchen. "She's either very bright or you're a good teacher," he said as Lin poured two cups of coffee.

"I'd like to think I have a knack for it," Lin said, "but I can't deny that she's advanced for a child her age." She settled across the table from him. "She's already memorized a good number of the poems in that book."

"How long have you been reading them to her?" he asked.

"Since the first day she sat on my lap." Lin smiled in memory. "I love Robert Louis Stevenson's work. He knew the mind of a child so well."

"So do you," Nicholas told her. "At least this child. You're a wonderful mother for her."

"I've wished more than once that she were my own," Lin confessed quietly. "I couldn't love her more if she'd been born from my body."

"Well, she is your own now." Nicholas picked up his cup and looked at her over the rim. "And one day, we'll give her brothers and sisters."

Lin looked up quickly. "Do you want a large family?"

"As many as we can take care of," he said firmly. "We can afford it, Lin. And I think we ought to be thinking about it while we're still young enough to raise them to adulthood and see our grandchildren born."

"I haven't looked that far ahead," she admitted, and a

smile flashed as she met his gaze. "It pleases me that you have."

"Let's go to bed," he said, tilting his cup to swallow the last drops. "We've got a full day tomorrow. Are you planning on washing clothes again? Or shall we take a ride to town in the wagon?"

"A ride to town?" she asked, excitement rising as she thought of walking through a general store, perhaps finding a piece of oilcloth for the kitchen table.

Nicholas lifted a brow as he shot her a look of surprise. "You'd think I'd just offered a trip to New York City."

"New York City doesn't interest me," she told him, watching as he lifted the globe on the lamp over the table and blew out the flame, leaving them in darkness, except for the faint gleam of starlight that shone through the windows.

"It doesn't? Well I'm glad to hear that. I don't have any immediate plans to go there myself."

Chapter Thirteen

New York City

"They've vanished. No one seems to know where they are, and I've had a search put into place everywhere within ten miles of Collins Creek."

Vincent Preston's eyes were flat, radiating cold anger in the direction of his visitor. "You told me your men were the best."

"The best available," the gentleman said agreeably. "I warned you the last time that we were dealing with men who could hold their own in any company. Sheriff Cleary is capable of running a town the size of Dallas, maybe even New York. Why the man has chosen to hide out in the two-bit village of Collins Creek is beyond me."

"Can he be bought?"

Vincent's visitor shook his head, a definite denial of the suggestion. "He's top-notch, Mr. Preston. A lawman above reproach, and there'll be no bribery taking place within the boundaries of his jurisdiction. We're going to have to look further afield for our targets."

"Do you have any more ideas to suggest?" Vincent asked, his voice impatient.

"I'm working on it. I've sent wires to several of my associates in towns within a fifty-mile radius of Nicholas Garvey's home, asking them to check into any new residents of the area. That may get some results. They've obviously gone into hiding, but I can't imagine they'd go any farther than that from the bank. Garvey's too good at what he does to leave someone else in charge for an indefinite period of time."

"How do you know that?" Vincent's interest swung in a new direction, and he leaned back in his chair. "What else about the man is common knowledge?"

"You knew he was from here in the city," the visitor said. "He's had his finger in a dozen different pies over the past years. Inherited money from his benefactor and invested it well. I have no idea why he chose to live in Collins Creek, Texas. He could be a millionaire in New York if he'd chosen to remain here."

"Dig into his background," Vincent said abruptly. "We may be facing the man in court before we're done, and I need to have all the ammunition I can find when that time comes. If there are secrets I can use, I want them ferreted out."

"I'll put someone on it right away. And in the meantime, I'll wire my associates in Texas to keep an eye out for our man."

Benning, Texas

"You're new in town, ain't ya?" The storekeeper greeted Nicholas with a friendly gesture, hand outstretched in welcome.

"Yes, we've just moved into the area. I'm Jake Henderson and this is my wife, Amelia."

Lin smiled, not at all surprised at Nicholas's ability to provide new names for them on such short notice. "I need a few things," she told the man behind the counter. "A length of oilcloth for the kitchen table and—" she consulted her list "—a slab of bacon, some flour and coffee."

"Well, you're in luck. Fella just outside of town brought in a couple slabs of bacon yesterday. We can fix you up in no time," the man said, turning to scan the shelf behind him. "Twenty-five pounds of flour enough?"

"Yes, and three pounds of coffee," Lin said. "I'll look at the oilcloth while you weigh it out for me." She strolled to a rack, where a dozen patterns of the useful fabric hung in rolls and pulled out one, then another, to examine the flowered surfaces.

"I believe I like this one," she told the man, unrolling a six-foot length and examining it.

"About two yards?" he asked, lifting it to the counter and measuring as he spoke. At her nod of agreement, he took a long-bladed pair of scissors and cut the length to measure, folded it and placed it next to the packages he'd made ready. "Will that do it?"

"Some penny candy for our daughter," Nicholas said. "An assortment. Twenty-five cents worth should do it."

"Where is she?" the storekeeper asked, looking around the large room.

"On the wagon, out front," Lin replied. She turned to Nicholas. "I'll go on out. You can bring the purchases."

"You folks must be about settled by now?" the man said casually as Lin opened the door to leave.

"Just about," she heard Nicholas say as she pulled the door shut behind herself.

She stood by the wagon, nodding at passersby and listening to Amanda's chatter with half an ear. The little girl sat on a pile of hay, holding her kitten, absorbed in the wagons and horsemen who rode by, her eyes taking in the sights as if she'd been isolated for months instead of a mere week or so.

"It's fun going to town, Linnie," she said brightly. "My kitty likes it, too."

"Just make sure you hang on tight to her," Lin warned. "I'm not about to go chasing after a kitten if she runs off. We probably should have left her at home."

"She needed to go for a ride," Amanda said. "Just like me." She glanced toward the door where Nicholas had just made his appearance, the shopkeeper behind him, bearing the side of bacon. "Do you think Uncle Nicholas got me some candy?"

"I wouldn't be surprised," Lin told her, her gaze intent on Nicholas's face.

The cloth-wrapped bacon was placed in the rear of the wagon and, with a wave and a look that took in every detail of the wagon and Nicholas's family, the storekeeper went back into the store.

"Everything all right?" Lin asked in an undertone.

Nicholas grinned, as if he had not a care in the world, but his words were cautious. "Let's get on our way. I don't feel safe here."

The wagon was untied and Lin lifted to the seat in moments. Nicholas turned it around and headed for home.

Lin felt a pang of disappointment at his words. It seemed they would be marooned for a longer time than she'd expected, and the isolation she already felt would be magnified. "Do you think—"

Nicholas shook his head in warning, glancing back at Amanda. "We'll talk about it later, sweetheart. I just don't have a good feeling about this."

Yet, the child didn't appear to share his apprehension. Her soft whispers to her kitten and the song she whispered beneath her breath gave assurance to Lin that Amanda was pleasantly occupied, no matter the fears of her uncle. Lin settled beside Nicholas, unwilling to distract from his constant surveillance of the surrounding countryside, only resting her hand against his thigh, seeking to give him assurance.

With a sigh, Amanda shifted on the wagon bed, and alerted by the rustle of her movements, Lin glanced over her shoulder to find the kitten curled up against Amanda's tummy, the child's eyes closed in slumber.

"She's asleep," Lin said, looking ahead to where the northward road could be seen off to their right. "We're almost at the place where the woods begins, aren't we?"

"Yeah," Nicholas agreed. "Just to the northeast from here is where I suspect your new friend lives."

"In the middle of the woods?"

"Cleary said there was a small clearing on the east side of his property where a fella had built a one-room place, and then moved on. It's a part of the property, but no one else ever claimed it. I'll lay odds that that's where Faith Hudson is living."

"I'm surprised Cleary didn't know about her. You'd think the last owners of his place would have told him she was there, especially if she's living on his land."

"They may have and he just didn't mention it. I doubt anyone cares if she squats in the shack or not. She's not hurting anything or taking advantage of anyone."

"Squats?" Lin raised an eyebrow at the word.

"Squatters usually take over a bit of someone else's land and establish a claim of one sort or another. It's not uncommon in the West for people who can't afford a place of their own to hunker down and make a living on someone else's land, especially if no one takes them to task for it."

"And you think that's what Faith has done?" She considered that thought. "That doesn't sound like a very honest thing to do, does it? And I'd have given her credit for being above reproach."

"She may very well be," Nicholas agreed. "Squatting on a bit of Cleary's thousand acres doesn't make her a criminal. I think she probably has a past she's not going to make public. At least, that's the impression I got. A woman like that is wasted out here, which tells me we don't know a whole lot about Faith Hudson.''

"Well, I like her," Lin told him, lifting her chin in a defensive motion.

Nicholas grinned down at her. "You make a stout defense of the lady, Lin. I'm glad you're on my side. I wouldn't want you for an enemy. I fear you'd be a savage, given good reason."

"Savage? I've never thought of myself in that way."

"Given reason, I'd say you'd defend your own tooth and nail, lady."

She nodded. "You may be right there. I defy anyone to touch Amanda. Or you, for that matter. Which reminds me. I need a lesson on shooting one of the guns you brought here."

"I agree," Nicholas said quickly. "We'll tend to that this afternoon."

The lesson went well, Nicholas setting up a target on the far side of the barn, against a straw stack, where any stray shotgun blasts would be captured by the dense mountain of dirty, yellow straw. Lin held the heavy gun to her shoulder and lined up the sights with the metal bucket and an assortment of battered tin cans Nicholas had placed atop a makeshift table. Two sawhorses with a long piece of lumber stretched out between them provided a place for the targets, and Lin stood thirty feet away, ready to fire.

The scattered shot from her first shell spun the bucket from the table, then buried themselves in the straw. The second hit a large can, blowing it into the depths of the straw stack. She looked up at Nicholas with a wide grin.

"How'm I doin', mister?" she asked, assuming a drawl that pleased him.

"Hot shot," he declared. "You don't need lessons, lady. You're a natural."

"This is easy," she said, lowering the shotgun, then rubbing her shoulder. "You didn't tell me it would punch back though."

He moved her fingers, replacing them with his wide palm. "Just part of the game, sweet. It gives me a chance to give you a nice massage later on. I'll put some liniment on that shoulder tonight." The movement of strong fingertips eased the buffeting her shoulder had taken, and Lin wiggled beneath his touch.

"That feels good," she said, leaning her head back to rest against his shoulder.

His fingers ceased their movement and he bent to kiss her temple. "Do you feel better about shooting a gun now? More secure?"

"Yes. Though I doubt I'll have reason to use it, it's a comfort to know how to load the thing and know that I can come somewhere close to my target should I find the need."

"Do you ever wonder about your father?" Nicholas was silent and Lin, for a moment, regretted her impulsive question. He'd had put his past in a box, it seemed, one she was forbidden to open. Causing a rift between them was not her intention, yet she could not help but wish for Nicholas to attain peace of mind regarding his sister and the family he'd never known.

It seemed that tonight was not to be the time for such a thing to come to pass, and she turned to her side, looking toward the open window of their bedroom. Behind her, Nicholas rose from the bed and she heard the rustle of clothing as he moved softly in the darkness.

"Have I chased you from my presence?" she asked quietly. "I'm truly sorry." Sitting up, she swung her feet from the bed and tossed back the sheet. "I'll leave you to your solitude."

Her robe lay over a nearby chair and she slid into it quickly, then turned toward the bedroom door. Nicholas stood in front of it, a worthy opponent should she attempt to make her escape past his muscular form.

"You're not going anywhere," he said, his voice rough with emotion. "I chose not to get into a fuss with you tonight. There was no need for you to get out of bed. You need your rest after working hard all day."

"And you don't?" she asked sharply. "It seems to me I saw you using a scythe to cut hay this afternoon in the hayfield. For about six hours, if I'm not mistaken. Doesn't that qualify as hard work?"

He shrugged, his shoulders pale in the faint light of stars and moon that shone through the windows. "I'm more than capable of physical labor. You're a lady, and I've expected you to do more than should be required of a woman during the past weeks."

"Not any more than Katie does back in Collins Creek," she answered. "I'm a woman, Nicholas. A lady, to my mind, is designated as someone who pours tea for the garden club and arranges flowers for her parlor. I do neither, unless you want to count the Queen Anne's lace and dandelions I stuck in a water glass yesterday."

"I'm not certain why we're arguing, Lin. This is what I was trying to avoid by retreating a moment ago."

"Then I'd suggest you get back in bed and get a good night's sleep," she retorted. "Either that, or expect some company in your night walk."

"My *night walk?*"

"The little stroll you've taken a couple of times when you thought I was asleep and you seemed to need time alone." She folded her arms around her waist, feeling chilled suddenly by the air of unpleasantness that filled the room. Somehow she'd managed to open a can of worms with her query concerning his father, and now she must deal with the results.

"I have a lot on my mind," he said stubbornly. "I find it difficult to sleep once in a while."

"And that can't ever be attributed to the fact that you've taken on the upbringing of your sister's child? Plus the care and tending of a woman you had no knowledge of before I turned up in your office? Not to mention the fact that we've brought to the light of day the reminder of a family you've spent years putting behind you.

"I'd think there was a lot in your past that needs to be brought out into the open," she said bluntly. "Then, perhaps you can find a measure of serenity that will allow you to sleep through the night. Every night."

He tilted his head a bit, as if he were taken aback by her words. "I beg your pardon if I've disturbed your sleep with my—" He halted abruptly, and then, with a measure of anger she flinched from, he spoke again, the words low, but forceful.

"I didn't balk at taking on the responsibility of raising Amanda. And I asked you, without coercion, to marry me. As to my past, you've told me everything I needed to know about Amanda's mother, I think."

"And you're not interested in knowing anything about your father?" she asked pointedly. "You don't even want to know who he was?"

His shrug was off-putting, as he'd no doubt meant it to be. "I know he was a womanizer, a man who took advantage of my mother and left her with a child she didn't want. I'm aware he never acknowledged my existence, and for all I know he's dead and buried. There's no reason to talk about him."

Lin took a different tack, her voice softening as she spoke words she knew to be the truth. "Irene would have loved you, Nicholas. She wanted so badly to own you as her brother. She admired you from afar, you know.''

''So you've said.'' His words were clipped, his manner flippant. ''I managed to live my life adequately without associating with my relatives for a number of years, Lin. I see no point in dragging all this up tonight.''

''Perhaps you're right.'' She felt the starch trickle from her spine, recognized the moment her shoulders slumped in defeat. And rued the first words she'd spoken in this verbal sparring between them.

Turning toward the window, she stepped to stand beside the open pane, drawing back the lace curtain to look out upon the orchard where fruit trees stood in neat rows.

There would be fruit borne on those trees in a few months' time, fruit she would never see. And the time they spent here would be gone, like leaves torn from a calendar, tossed aside and forgotten. A sadness, pervasive and intense, filled her heart, and she fought the tears its presence brought about. Crying would not solve the problems she and Nicholas shared.

For though they were compatible in many ways, she could never hope to know the man beneath the facade he presented, unless he chose to allow it. A gentleman with his emotions neatly in place, he'd won her heart, but refused to allow her access to his.

''Do you think you'll ever come to love me?'' she asked, and heard his indrawn breath from directly behind her back. He'd managed to approach her in silence, or she had been too intent on her train of thought to note his approach. Either way, he was a presence to be dealt with.

''Where did that come from?'' he asked quietly. ''Do you doubt my feelings for you, Lin? Haven't I made it clear that I care about you? That you and Amanda are the most important people in my life?''

"There's a wide gap between *caring* about a woman and pledging your love," she said simply. And then she relented, her sigh repentant.

"I'm sorry, Nicholas. I have no right to ask such a question." Her head bent as hot tears fell, escaping from closed eyelids to trail down her cheek and soak into the fabric of her dressing gown.

"You have the right to ask me anything you please," he said. "Just don't be angry if I can't give you the answers you'd like." It seemed his ire had vanished, replaced by a need for reconciliation.

"I wonder if I really know you," she said in a whisper, fearing to speak aloud, lest her voice quiver.

"Oh, I think you know me quite well," he said, his hands lifting to grip her shoulders, turning her to face him. "Probably better than any other person I've met up with in my life." He bent to kiss her, muttering as his mouth came in contact with her tears. "Have I made you cry?"

"No. My weakness has given me leave to shed tears," she said. "I'm not strong when it comes to you. I've managed to face the world as a woman alone. I've taken my place as hired help in a household, then traveled halfway across the country on public transport. All that in order to face up to a man who was set on turning aside a child who I felt was his responsibility.

"All of that," she said quietly and without rancor, "was a cakewalk compared to what *you* did to me."

"What I did?" he asked.

She nodded, lifting her gaze to meet his. "I was doing just fine...until you made me love you."

His voice softened as he formed a reply. "You have no idea how it makes me feel to know that you have that depth of emotion where I'm concerned. I've never been told in my entire life that another person loves me."

"Perhaps because you've never allowed anyone the opportunity. I'd say it's about time you learned how to return it, to some degree, Nicholas. Your niece absolute adores you. Katie thinks you're the best man walking, and your wife—" She broke off suddenly, unable to speak.

"My wife?" he prompted, his mouth touching hers briefly. "Don't stop now, Lin. Is my wife having second thoughts about me?"

"You know better than that," she said, her words broken. "I can't help loving you. I owe you my life, Nicholas. You've given me all a woman could ask for in a marriage."

He laughed, a dry, harsh sound that expressed no joy. "Sure, I have. We're on the run. You've been battered by criminals, bruised by my own hands, and now you're working from dawn till dark, trying to make a home in a ramshackle farmhouse, with broken-down furniture and a total lack of the necessities of life."

"I think we differ on that," she said quietly. "I have all I need."

"How about what you *want*, Lin? Needs are easily met. What you *want* is my undying expression of love, and I don't seem to be able to put my feelings into words that will please you, do I?"

"I won't ask you to speak words that aren't heartfelt."

"I'm honored to be Amanda's uncle. I delight in the child. She makes my heart swell with some emotion I can't describe when she wraps her arms around my neck and tells me she loves me. Is that *heartfelt* enough for you?"

"You truly don't recognize that as love?" Lin asked.

"I don't know. I admire Katie. She's loyal and honest and fills a need in my life that no one else ever has. She's like a favorite aunt I never had—she's my family, I suppose you could say." He paused to press his mouth against her lips again, seeking her response, a response she turned from, her head moving sharply to one side, knowing he thought to placate her with kisses.

He shook her, just hard enough to gain her attention, and his voice darkened with emotion. "You'll make me say it, won't you?"

"Not unless you feel it, and know it to be the truth." She held her breath as he looked down at her, his eyes narrowing, as if he hid from her behind the lashes.

"And then there's you, Lin. My wife. Just those two words make my chest tight with a feeling I've never known for another woman.

"Do I love you? If I knew for certain what that phrase means, I'd say it aloud. I'd shout it from the rooftop.

"If it means I'd lay down my life for you, that I want to live with you the rest of my days, then, yes...." His pause was long, but the words that left his lips sounded raw and rasping as they were spoken aloud in the silence of the dark room.

"...I love you."

She closed her eyes. "Please. Please, say it again, Nicholas. I want to hear you speak the words again."

His voice was softer now, the phrase lingering beside her ear as he spoke it with an intensity she could not miss. "I love you, Lin. So far as I know the meaning of those words, they express my feelings for you. It's not a fairy-tale thing we're talking about here. This is real life. This is a man pledging his future into your hands. I'm being as honest as I know how to be, sweetheart."

"Do you know," she asked quietly, lifting her face to his, "do you know, you've said more to me in these few minutes than you have in the past weeks?"

"It seems you've opened the floodgates, love," he said quietly. "I can't lose you, Lin. I'll do whatever it takes to keep you with me." He kissed her with a solemnity she cherished, and then his words warmed her as he broke the silence of years, requesting her knowledge of his past.

"What do you know about my father?"

"His name, his reputation, his background and a way in which he can help us."

"Tell me."

"I've sent off a wire," Nicholas said, swinging his leg over the saddle, and turning to face Lin. "It was probably the most difficult thing I've ever done."

"Asking for help?"

He shook his head. "No, not the act of being a suppliant, but by asking the one person I never thought to approach for help."

"I didn't mean for you to be embarrassed by this," Lin said quietly. "I just didn't know any other way to solve the problem. And he may be willing to acknowledge that he owes you a debt. One you've never laid claim to."

"We'll soon find out," Nicholas told her, leading his horse toward the barn. The animal followed, tossing her head, white flecks of foam flying through the air, a testament to the speed at which she'd been ridden. "My mare needs a good rubdown. And then I'll be in for dinner."

Lin watched him go, biting at her lip, her thoughts in turmoil. At her suggestion, Nicholas had done this thing, had wired to ask for his father's help. And if it came to pass that the gentleman in question did not give it, without strings attached, the fragile relationship so newly formed— her marriage, for that matter—might be damaged by her interference.

And yet, it had seemed right to her. And still did. She sighed, turning back to the house, and climbing the porch steps wearily. It had truly seemed the right thing to do. And so she must dwell on that belief.

New York City

"I'm claiming the child as my own," Vincent said gravely, facing the man who watched him intently. "She should have been mine from the beginning, but I refused to be involved in the sordid mess, once her mother walked away from me. That was my first mistake." He managed a look of regret as he continued.

"The girl was born a Carmichael, only because my business partner took pity on the mother and married her." His hands clenched into fists, hidden beneath the surface of the desk.

Dignified and obviously unimpressed by Vincent's words, his visitor shrugged. "And now you've changed your mind about the girl? Does her inheritance come into the picture?"

The judge pulled no punches, Victor thought, anger rising as he remembered his henchman's assurance.

Are you sure you have the judge in your pocket?

Try me....

The words rang in his head, and he swallowed his rage. Perhaps his feelers might yet locate Garvey and solve this problem without going to court.

"I don't care about the money." Vincent waved out the window where the city of New York lay at his feet. "I have all I need, except for someone to inherit my wealth when I'm gone."

"Why not marry?" his visitor asked mildly, steepling his fingers beneath his chin, elbows resting on the arms of the chair he occupied. "Surely there must be an eligible woman handy to provide you with a legitimate heir? A son, perhaps?"

Vincent shook his head. "I'm not interested in marriage. I like my life the way it is." That his life included a mistress who made no demands on his time was a point in her favor, he'd long since decided.

The judge sounded noncommittal, Vincent thought, listening to the query the man offered. "And you want to include a small child in your household?"

Aware that he could be charming when the need arose, Vincent smiled nicely. "It's my responsibility to give her the life she deserves. An education and a future." His hand lifted from his lap and slashed the air with a derogatory gesture.

"What can Mr. Garvey offer her? A cowboy rounded up from a ranch? Or perhaps a farmer with dirt under his fingernails and straw in his hair?" And if he had his way, Mr. Garvey might yet meet his death, and thus neatly solve the whole problem.

The judge nodded, as if deep in thought. "I'll consider your case very carefully, Mr. Preston. The hearing will be next month. It's the soonest I can put it on my docket."

Vincent stifled his impatience, nodding politely. "I understand." His eyelids flickered as he met the judge's implacable gaze. "You know I will be more than grateful if you see things in the light of—"

The judge nodded, speaking sharply. "I'll certainly do what is best in this case."

Chapter Fourteen

The sheriff rode a pure black gelding and apparently, Lin decided, thought his own getup should match the ebony of his mount. Dressed from head to toe in what surely resembled funeral garb, relieved only by the shining silver star decorating his vest, he stood before her. He peered past her through the screened door as though he sought out the presence of another.

His words verified her thoughts. "There a fella here called Jake Henderson?" he asked, his voice lending a dubious note to the name Nicholas had used in town.

"My husband," Lin answered. "He's out in the hay field, loading up the wagon."

The sheriff grinned suddenly, relieving the dour expression he'd worn. "He wouldn't by chance also be known as Nicholas Garvey, would he, ma'am?"

Lin hesitated. Cleary had said the sheriff in Benning was a friend. Yet, even a lawman could be bought, and she would put nothing past Vincent Preston.

"Ma'am?" the sheriff waited, a bit of impatience glittering from dark eyes. "I was told by Cleary that you were staying on his place. Then I got a message from the storekeeper that a stranger by the name of Henderson was in town, and I'll tell you, ma'am—''

His hesitation was prolonged as one long finger rose to nudge his hat back a bit. ''—I'm just a bit confused, here,'' he finished dryly. ''So far as I know, there ain't any other new folks to these parts.''

''You're truly a friend of Cleary's?'' Feeling as if she had stepped out onto a thin sheet of ice, Lin proposed the question, then held her breath for the reply.

''You could say that,'' the sheriff answered. ''We've worked together a time or two. My name's Brace Caulfield.''

''My husband is in the hay field, Mr. Caulfield. Right where he's been for the past two weeks,'' Lin said. ''And, yes, his name is Nicholas Garvey. He felt it a good idea not to bandy that fact around town. There are those who might come looking for us should our whereabouts be known.''

''That's why I'm here,'' the sheriff said. ''I think there's someone scouting out your location right now. Got a wire from Cleary this morning, and he said to offer my help, should you need it.''

''Cleary?'' Lin held her breath. ''Does someone know where we are? Is that what he said?''

''No, ma'am. Not exactly. But he did say that somebody out there was offering a nice reward, just waiting for the right person to come up with Nicholas Garvey.'' His grin faded. ''And that somebody doesn't care whether he's found dead or alive.''

''What can we do?'' She heard the desperate edge in her voice and rued the quick panic that washed over her.

''Just lay low, I'd think. In the meantime, I'll see what I can do to cover up your tracks.'' He tilted his hat forward a bit, and his eyes were shadowed once more. ''Right now,

I'm going to ride out and round up your husband. I think we need to talk.''

The sun was hot against his back and the shirt clung there damply as Nicholas watched the rider approach. The man rode easily in the saddle, a dark figure atop a satanic looking creature, a horse who might conceivably be named for one of the demons of the netherworld.

''Whoa, Devil,'' the visitor said, almost beneath his breath, and Nicholas could not hide the smile that curved his lips. He'd certainly pegged that right.

''You Nicholas Garvey?''

''I was the last time I looked in the mirror,'' Nicholas answered quietly, his attention drawn to the silver star. Unless he missed his guess, this was the man Cleary had said would be his ally, should the need arise. He measured the man's apparent height, gauged the width of broad shoulders, and noted the lean body that rode the black horse as if they were one and the same being.

A strong hand reached for his, and Nicholas wiped his palm against his pant leg before he offered it. ''I'm Brace Caulfield.''

Nicholas nodded shortly. ''Caulfield.'' He'd have felt better had he known more about this lawman right from the start. But his departure had been too rushed for details to be given, too hurried for information to be exchanged. He'd been working in the dark for almost a month already. And to finally see something happening, be it good or bad, was a relief, he decided. And then, knowing that this visit was not accidental, that some event had precipitated it, he spoke.

''What's happened?'' he asked, leaning on his pitchfork.

Brace Caulfield glanced over Nicholas's shoulder at the wagon, already filled with dried hay. ''I see you've been busy,'' he said. ''Cleary oughta appreciate you tending to his chores for him.''

"It's given me something to do, waiting for the hay to dry so I can put it in the barn."

"Yeah, this business of farming's a lot of hurry up and wait, I've found," the sheriff said, tugging his hat lower to shade his eyes from the sun.

Nicholas was silent now, aware that the conversation was headed in another direction, willing to wait for the sheriff to define its path. He was not long in doing so.

"Cleary says there's trouble afoot," the lawman said bluntly. "There's a price on your head, Garvey."

"That doesn't surprise me." And yet a small current of dismay troubled his mind as he considered what might take place. "There's a man in New York who wants me out of the way."

The lawman's brow rose. "New York, you say? How'd he manage to track you all the way to Texas?"

"I didn't try to hide my trail," Nicholas said simply. "I left the city some time ago. Opened a bank in Collins Creek, and I've lived there ever since. At least up until a month ago."

"What's the big-city man's problem?"

A man after his own heart, Nicholas decided. Short of words and right to the point. "I've got my niece with me. Vincent Preston wants her."

"He got any rights in the matter?"

"None. The child's mother was my half sister. She was awarded to me after the death of her parents a while back, and her nurse brought her to me."

Caulfield slid from his horse and dropped the reins. The animal's head bent to the ground, nosing at bits of hay. "Where's the nurse now?" And then his features brightened. "That woman back at the house? Your wife?"

"My wife," Nicholas said firmly. "She was Amanda's nurse, and we were married a short while ago."

"Right handy."

He might have taken offense, Nicholas thought, but the remark was cheerfully spoken, with no hint of derision attached, and so he smiled his agreement. "You might say so."

"She know how to handle a gun?"

Nicholas thought of the lesson he'd given behind the barn, recalling Lin's sassy pride in her shooting ability. "Yes," he said. "A shotgun, anyway."

"That's good enough." And then the lawman took a different tack. "You got a dog, maybe?"

Nicholas shook his head. "Didn't think I'd need one. I don't know where I'd get one anyway."

"I got a couple. Might be able to spare you one. Just a youngster, pret'near six months old now, but he's yappy. He'll make a good watchdog. I didn't have the heart to give him away, but he's thinkin' strong thoughts about his litter mate, and I'm not ready to let her have pups. Not for a while yet, and certainly not from a dog so close in blood."

"I'll take you up on that," Nicholas said. "When can I get him?"

"I left him with Faith Hudson on my way over here. I'll stop by and tell her to deliver him when she gets a chance."

"Faith?" And wasn't that a strange thing to do, Nicholas thought.

"She's a real lady," the sheriff said quietly. "I kinda look out for her. I figured if you were a straight shooter, I'd leave you the dog. If not—" He shrugged idly and grinned. "Well, if you turned out to be a rascal, I wasn't about to give you my pup. So Faith did me a favor today, and here I am."

And that wasn't something he was about to investigate, Nicholas decided quickly.

"Not what you're thinking. She keeps up on my mending and writes letters for me. That sort of thing."

"I wasn't thinking anything derogatory about the lady," Nicholas said, lying with a perfectly straight face. Although he hadn't wanted to consider Faith in that light, he couldn't say he would blame her, should she find the sheriff attractive. A woman alone had to look out for herself in any way she could.

"Need some help with the hay?" Brace asked.

"You know how to handle a pitchfork?" Nicholas asked in return, remembering the blisters he'd tended after long days spent using the scythe, then turning the hay over until it dried in the sun.

"I've been known to get blisters on my hands."

"Well, you're in good company then. Tie your horse on the back and hop on," Nicholas offered, climbing to the wagon seat and lifting the reins. "I've got to unload this before dinner. Maybe you'd like to join us. My wife's a good cook."

"He doesn't seem like a lawman, does he?" Lin ventured, looking toward the window where the trees outside were being whipped by a strong wind. She rose, walking across the room, and lowered the sash partway. "I think it's going to rain by morning."

"Do you know, I can see right through your nightgown when you stand in front of the light that way?" Nicholas asked. His voice held a lazy note, and his position matched it, both hands behind his head as he stretched out on the bed.

"See anything you like?" she asked nicely, turning in a slow circle.

"I'd like it better if I didn't have to squint. You might take the thing off and make it easy on me." He flashed her a smile. "If that moon goes behind a cloud I won't be able to see much of anything."

"The sky is full of them, over to the west," she said,

turning to approach the bed. "You didn't answer my question."

"About Brace? Or seeing something I liked? Or were you wondering if it's going to rain?"

She pounced on him. "You know what I meant. The lawman. I already know it's going to rain." She thought a moment. "He was nice."

"How nice?"

"Probably as nice as Faith. I wouldn't call him pretty, of course. But he was most presentable."

His hands gripped her waist and he rolled with her across the bed, pinning her to the mattress. "He was nice? And *presentable?* And what is that supposed to mean?"

She attempted a shrug, but his weight held her in place, and so she settled for a grimace. "Nothing, you idiot. I just said he was nice, and not bad looking."

"And what am I?"

Her brow lifted and her head turned to the side, just a bit, as if she considered his question at length. "Only the most handsome man I've ever known," she whispered quietly, when she'd made him suffer in silence for almost a full minute.

His grin was quick, his satisfaction apparent. "That's more like it. I like a woman who knows which side her bread's buttered on."

"That's me," she said smartly, and then she sobered, lifting a hand to touch his cheek with a degree of tenderness that caused his heart to beat more rapidly.

"And I like a man who knows his own worth," she told him. "Even if I have to repeat it every so often to pound it into your head, Nicholas. I love you more than life itself. I wasn't playing word games when I told you how handsome you are. You look in the mirror every day, and surely your eyesight is adequate to take note of your striking good looks."

He squirmed at her descriptive language. "I'm an ordinary man, Lin. Dark hair, blue eyes and decent features. Enough to get me by for over thirty years, anyway."

"Enough to have half the women in New York City at your feet, had you chosen that route," she said quietly. "Irene said you weren't a ladies' man, though. You lived a circumspect existence, escorting ladies on occasion, but maintaining a bachelor's home, in a lifestyle above reproach."

"She said all that?"

Lin nodded. "I told you she had a scrapbook filled with clippings and notes she'd taken on your comings and goings."

He bent to touch her lips with a kiss that offered no passion, only tender warmth, seconded by his words. "Thank you. I'd like to have seen it, taken note of what she collected."

"I have it in my trunk, back in Collins Creek," she offered. "One day we'll go over it together. I kept it for Amanda, to begin with. Then, when we came here, I brought it in hopes you might want to see it."

"Are there pictures of Irene?" he asked.

Lin nodded. "A wedding picture, taken when she and Joseph spoke their vows."

"And how about you?" he asked. "Do you have any mementos of your early life? Pictures of your family?" His fingers touched her hair, tangled in the waves, and held her fast for his kiss. It was brief, again brushing her lips as if he could not be long away from the sweetness she offered.

"I need no reminders of my childhood," she said flatly.

"Your whole childhood was unhappy? Or just after your stepfather appeared?"

She hesitated but for a moment and then spoke quickly. "I've mentioned this before, but I probably never will again, Nicholas. When my mother married for the second time after my father died, I got a taste of what hell must surely be like.

"From the time I was but a girl, he expressed an interest in me. My mother denied it. I suppose it was easier for her that way. And perhaps that's one reason why I felt so strongly about Vincent Preston not getting his hands on Amanda."

He stiffened above her. "And why is that?"

"He has the same look."

His words were deceptively quiet, for she felt the tensing of him above her. "And where is your mother's husband now?"

Her hands touched him, flattening against his chest, as though she would reassure him. "They moved away, and I refused to go along." And, for just a moment she felt the same hopeless feeling of loss as when her mother had walked away from her so carelessly on that day over ten years before.

"You never married, Lin. Why? Surely there were opportunities?"

"There was no one who interested me. Not until you."

He kissed her again, and this time the heat of desire touched her with tendrils of warmth that penetrated into that empty place deep within. "I'm glad you waited for me." Simply said, yet with unmistakable emphasis coating each syllable, his declaration touched her and she was lifted from her melancholy as if it might never have been.

"How could you have been so open with me? So ready to grant me…" His words were hesitant as he recalled her willingness to become his wife, that night when he had laid claim to her. Was it only weeks ago? Could he have learned to love so quickly?

"You never reminded me of my stepfather," she said. "Not in any way, shape or form. You were always above-board and honest with me, even when you would have led me down the primrose path, Nicholas.''

A shaft of pain speared through him as he recalled the night he'd first offered for her companionship. ''Will you ever forgive me for that?''

Her smile was quick. ''Forgive? I was a bit flattered, to tell the truth. You were the most beautiful man I'd ever seen in my life, and for some unknown reason, you wanted me.''

''You were tempted, then?''

''You know very well I was,'' she answered, pushing at his chest. ''You bewitched me with your kisses and your flashing smile and sparkling eyes.''

''All of that?'' His brow lifted, her words sweet in his ears.

She nodded. ''All of that.'' And then her hands clasped his face, drawing him to her, her mouth forming over his, her tongue beckoning him, leisurely stroking his lips. As he opened readily to her probing, she sighed.

''You don't put up much of a fight, do you?''

His hands gripped her shoulders, lifting her a bit, her head falling back against the pillow to expose her slender throat to his gaze. He bent to it, tasting the sweet flavor of her skin, only too aware of his arousal that even now was making itself known, nudging impatiently against her belly.

His sigh was deep, as he accepted the pleasure she offered. Moving beneath him, she shifted a bit, lifting one knee, then the other, surrounding him with the warmth and scent of her womanhood. His eyes closed, his words a willing surrender.

''Why should I put up a fight? I've already lost the battle, sweetheart.''

The dog gave a first impression of friendly behavior. Arriving on top of the pale horse, draped over Faith Hudson's lap, he rode with ease, as if it were an everyday event in his short life. White spots on a black coat gave him a dashing appearance, Lin thought as Faith handed him over to Nicholas.

And then he growled, a low sound, deep in his throat, his lip lifting at one corner with a snarl. A quick, single word was uttered in a no-nonsense fashion, solving that problem in short order. Nicholas was not one to step back from man nor beast, and one medium-size mutt of undetermined ancestry appeared to be a very small challenge.

He was lifted by his belly until he looked eye to eye into Nicholas's penetrating gaze. There he hung, seeming baffled by the swift turn of events, as softly spoken yet firm words assured him of his position in the chain of command. Then he was deposited on the ground and Nicholas squatted in front of him.

One paw lifted in a conciliatory gesture, and Nicholas accepted it gravely. "Now that we have that straightened out, let's think of a name for you, pup," he said quietly. His hand touched the dog's head, ruffling the fur a bit, and the creature turned to mush, dropping to the ground and presenting his belly for inspection.

"What shall we call him?" he asked Lin, his smile begging a response from her, even as he scratched at the tender underside of their new acquisition.

"Killer?" she asked sweetly. "Or perhaps Wolf?"

Faith laughed aloud. "You might be surprised at this young fellow. Don't mistake his bowing down to Nicholas as the alpha male in the household as a sign of cowardice. He's only submitting to his human master. This pup will guard you well, if his actions last night are any indication of bravery."

"You had a problem?" Nicholas asked quickly, looking up at the golden-haired woman who still sat astride her horse.

"Someone was moseying around in the woods, I think," she answered. "And tough guy here was snarling at my door, just begging some stranger to barge into the cabin. I don't doubt but what he'd have taken a leg off anyone foolish enough to open the door."

"Have you had such a thing happen before?" Lin asked. "I thought you felt pretty safe alone."

Faith shrugged carelessly. "I do, usually. Maybe it was an animal, or someone who was hunting for small game."

"Perhaps you need the dog more than we do," Lin said bluntly. "I have Nicholas for protection."

"And I have a couple of guns that I'm not afraid to use," Faith said quietly. "I just may ask Sheriff Caulfield to scout up another dog one of these days. I could use the company, anyway."

Amanda stepped closer to Nicholas and the black kitten jumped from her arms, scampering beneath the porch. "Are we really gonna call him Wolf?" she asked dubiously. "I don't think he looks like one, do you?"

The dog rolled over and sat up, one smooth motion that placed him before Amanda's feet. His tongue lolled from one side of his mouth, and he leaned forward to sniff at her shoes.

"I think he likes me," she said confidently, kneeling suddenly to wrap her arms around the animal's neck.

Lin caught her breath, frightened for a moment what the abrupt movement might set off, but the dog only woofed with delight and lapped eagerly with that long tongue against Amanda's cheek. "I don't think Amanda's in any danger."

"I wouldn't think so," Nicholas agreed. "I won't swear to the kitten's safety, though. We'd better introduce them slowly."

"Come in, Faith," Lin invited, remembering her manners.

"I'll take your mare," Nicholas offered, reaching for the reins. "Shall I turn her out in the pasture?"

"I won't be here that long," Faith said quickly. "I've gotten started on a couple of projects, and I shouldn't be gone from home for longer than an hour or so."

"What are you doing?" Lin asked, leading the way into the house.

"I'm sewing a shirt for the sheriff, and I'm trying to figure out how to steal some honey from a dead tree in the woods." She laughed. "Now that I say it aloud, those two things don't seem to go together, do they?"

"Makes sense to me," Lin said with a quick grin. "Shall I make some tea?"

Nicholas watched as the women disappeared inside the kitchen and then turned, leading the mare into the shade beneath a nearby tree. He tied the reins to a low branch, allowing the horse enough leeway to search through the grass for a snack, then ran his hands over the animal's flanks. The ears pricked upward and a soft whuffle emerged from the creature's mouth as the pale head nudged Nicholas, her lips snatching at his pocket.

"You're a beggar, aren't you?" he asked with a laugh. "I'll bet your mistress spoils you rotten." The horse obliged with a low whinny, and Nicholas felt an unaccustomed urge to become better acquainted with the animal. He followed the sleek lines of sides and legs, investigated her teeth with a cursory glance and admired the muscles that formed as she shifted beneath his hands, rippling beneath the glossy coat.

"I'd give my eyeteeth for one just like you," he murmured beneath his breath. "I wonder if Faith has thought of breeding you." And with that idea in mind, he climbed the steps to the porch and opened the kitchen door.

"Something wrong?" Lin asked, as if wary of his sudden appearance.

"No," he said quickly. "I just thought of something interesting, and I wanted to ask Faith about it." He pulled out a chair and sat down, nodding as Lin touched the coffeepot and lifted a brow in his direction. And then his attention switched to their neighbor and he spoke his mind, bluntly, yet with every hope of success.

"Have you ever considered breeding your mare?"

"You're going to buy a stallion?" Lin's eyes were fastened on Nicholas, surprise causing her to ignore Faith's departure. Her voice, of necessity, rose above the pup's barking, as he protested at being left behind by the departing horse and rider.

"I'd like to breed Faith's mare if I can find the right stud," Nicholas said. "I thought you heard me ask her about it."

"I did," she answered. "I heard you ask her if she'd ever considered breeding the mare. But I didn't understand that you were planning on doing it yourself." She looked up at him quizzically. "I thought we were living here on a temporary basis."

"We are," he conceded quickly. "Just until we're in the clear and everything about Amanda's custody is straightened out."

"And where are you planning to do this big breeding procedure?"

He glanced down at her, as if her query confused him. "There's nothing complicated about it, sweetheart. We buy a stud, put the two together in a pasture, or wherever, and then let nature take its course."

"How many times have you done such a thing?"

"I've never gotten married before, but I knew how to go about the business of taking a wife," he answered with a grin. "I'll bet a decent stallion can figure out what to do in no time flat."

And then his look sobered as his gaze tracked Faith's trail toward the woods. "I *am* concerned about her being alone at night, though. I'll warrant the sheriff would be interested to hear that there was something going on out there last night."

"Do you think it was a prowler?" Lin asked, appalled at the idea of Faith being in danger.

"I don't know what to think, but I'm dead certain I'm heading for town in the morning to let Caulfield know about it. And to see if there's another dog available for Faith to keep with her."

The pup slept near the kitchen door, Nicholas unwilling to trust the animal not to follow Faith home should he let him run free outdoors all night. Lin heard the sound of the dog's nails on the kitchen floor once during the night, and then a soft whining as he stood in the doorway of their bedroom just before dawn. She nudged Nicholas.

"Your dog needs to go outside," she whispered.

"*My* dog? When did I claim ownership?"

"When you let him know who was boss around here," she said, pulling the sheet over her head and turning to face the other side of the bed.

He grumbled, a halfhearted sound beneath his breath, but slid quickly into his trousers and headed across the bedroom floor. "Got a problem, dog?" he asked in a low murmur. And then Lin heard the soft opening and closing of the back door as he stepped out onto the porch to keep an eye on the pup.

A sudden flurry of barking brought her to an upright position, and her heartbeat throbbed in her chest as she slid from the bed and hurried to the window. At the edge of the pasture, where a mist hung in layers over the grassy expanse, a figure on horseback appeared, seeming almost to be a part of the eerie half light of dawn. Even as she

watched, the horse turned and stepped into the edge of the
wooded area, and was lost to view.

"Nicholas." She bent to the screened window and called
his name, then held her breath. He walked into view, his
bare feet silent against the dewy grass.

"Yeah." His eyes sought her out, and she breathed a
sigh of relief. "I saw him, too," he said. "Wish to hell I'd
had a gun with me."

"You wouldn't have shot a man just for riding on the
property, would you?" she asked sharply.

"I'd have sure found out in a hurry what sort of business
he had here." His voice was taut with harsh undertones she
was not familiar with, and she caught a glimpse of the man
who had come from the streets of the city. His eyes were
sharp, penetrating, and had lost their warmth, and she shivered, backing from the window.

Then the back door opened and closed, and the dog stood
in the bedroom doorway, shaking himself with a flurry of
muscles, his ears flying outward. Her tension broken by the
exhibit, Lin found herself laughing softly at the creature.
He padded across the floor to where she stood, lying at her
feet in abject humility. Her bare toes tickled his tummy and
he twisted upright, yapping in delight at the attention she
bestowed.

Nicholas appeared then, leaning against the doorjamb,
running long fingers through his hair. "I think we have a
problem," he said, and again she heard a trace of the background he hid so well. His voice was rough, and his gaze
pinned her where she stood. "I'm getting dressed and heading for town. I'm sure he's gone, but I want you in the
house, with the doors locked, while I'm away."

"What about the cow?" she asked. "I'll need to milk
her."

"I'm riding past Faith's place on my way, and I'll send
her here. She can handle the cow and then come in the

house with you and Amanda." He stalked past her to where his clothing was kept in a small dresser against the wall. Clean drawers and stockings in one hand, he opened a second drawer and withdrew trousers and shirt, then stripped from the hastily donned clothing he wore.

"Why don't I make you something to eat first?" she suggested, her mouth dry, her heart pounding with a heavy beat.

"No, I'm leaving in five minutes," he said, denying her offer. "I want your promise, Lin. You won't stick your nose outside the door. And keep the dog inside with you." He sat down on the chair, pulling his stockings on, and then reached for the shirt.

"You'll have that shotgun handy every minute I'm gone, and you'll keep Amanda with you the whole time." He stood upright, buttoning his trousers and tucking in his shirt, then slid into his boots and pulled them on rapidly. His eyes swept over her, taking in every detail from her tousled hair to her bare feet, toes curling into the braided rug.

"Promise me, Lin." It was a demand she could not deny, and she nodded her head obediently. In three strides he was before her, his hands hard and rough as he drew her to her toes and pressed a kiss against her soft mouth. It was demanding, with no trace of tenderness attending his touch; and yet, she felt his possession engulf her as he lowered her to stand before him.

"I promise," she said. And as he turned to leave her, she sobbed his name aloud. "Nicholas?"

He turned, overwhelming her with the force of his brilliant blue eyes, stunning her with the demanding masculine power he exuded. "I'll be back," he promised. "This won't take long. I can't be here to protect you and Amanda. I'm depending on you."

"Yes. All right," she acceded with haste. "Go, Nicholas. Go with God."

Chapter Fifteen

She heard Faith's whistle less than an hour later, and peered from the kitchen window, watching as the golden horse came to a halt in front of the barn. Faith saw her and lifted a hand in greeting, then opened the barn door, leading her mare within. An extra pail was hanging from a nail on the wall and as Lin watched, she saw Faith cross before the open doorway, shiny silver pail dangling from one hand.

It took only fifteen minutes to accomplish the milking, but the moments passed in an agony of silence as Lin watched, her eyes wide and unblinking. Fearful that a hidden assailant might be close, that a gunshot might ring out in the hush of morning, she waited. Aware of Amanda still asleep in the bedroom, conscious of the dog's pacing from room to room, as if he were keeping watch with her, Lin guarded the woman in the barn.

Only when Faith appeared, carrying the pail of milk, did she breath a sigh of relief. With rapid steps, her friend crossed the yard to the porch, and then, as Lin opened the door, she slipped inside the house.

"I've been shaking in my boots," Lin confessed, her voice breaking.

"You? I was terrified that something might happen before I got here," Faith told her, placing the bucket on the floor and clasping Lin close. "Nicholas didn't make any bones about it. He hauled me out of bed—well, not literally—but almost. Told me to get over here without any delay and stay with you."

"Do you always do what a man says?" Lin asked, covering her mouth with one hand as a giddy laugh escaped. The relief of Faith's presence was making her light-headed, she decided.

"No, I don't. Not for a long time." No humor laced the simple reply, and Lin looked up in surprise.

Faith grimaced. "I didn't mean to sound so grim," she said quickly. "I'm just used to being on my own, I suppose. But Nicholas didn't give me any option. Just told me what to do and left. I'll warrant he's in town dragging the sheriff out of bed by now."

"He's worried," Lin said. "And so am I."

"Well, would you like to fill me in on this whole thing? I'm not just being nosy. Normally I wouldn't ask questions, but somehow I've gotten involved in your problems, and I think I deserve to know what I'm looking at."

"Let's have some coffee," Lin said, turning to the stove. "I put a pot on as soon as Nicholas left. It's fit to drink by now." She took cups from the cupboard and filled them, then sliced bread and placed it in the oven to toast while they settled at the table.

"It's a long story," she said. "But I think we've got time enough to spare for you to hear all the details."

The storekeeper was sweeping the wide, wooden walk in front of his store when Nicholas approached, the sheriff at his heels. "Good morning, gentlemen," Mr. Metcalf said cheerfully, although his eyes flitted between his visitors, and his broom strokes became more rapid.

"What do you know about someone asking for information hereabouts?" Brace asked sharply. "I don't want any waffling, Metcalf. Just some straight answers. Did somebody hire you on to ask questions?"

"I only wanted to be friendly," the man said, his voice rising as Nicholas neared. "I wasn't trying to be nosy or anything. Just being neighborly, Sheriff."

Nicholas picked him up by the front of his shirt, and the shopkeeper protested with a squeal. "Looky here! You can't do this to me. I'm a good, upright citizen of this here town, and the folks of Benning, Texas, don't cotton to strangers comin' in here and roughin' up the upstanding folks who live here."

"Dry up, Metcalf." Nicholas's ultimatum resounded in the silence surrounding them. "I want to know, right now, who's paying you to be so neighborly."

"You can't do this," the man whined. "Tell him, Sheriff. Tell him he can't get away with this." He dangled from Nicholas's hands, and his face was crimson with fear and rage combined.

The sheriff folded his arms across his chest and tilted his head to one side. "I'd say from here it looks like he's already got you by the short hairs, Mr. Metcalf. Yessir, I'd say he can do it, all right. If I was you, I'd be singing out everything there was to warble about."

"Put me down," the man demanded. And then was obviously surprised when Nicholas did that very thing. Carefully, he straightened the storekeeper's collar and gripped his shoulders, holding him erect.

"Now, tell me, sir," he said politely. "Who is paying you?"

Mr. Metcalf swallowed, an almost audible reaction to his obvious fear. "Some big fellow from New York City wanted to know if anybody new moved into the area.

He's paying good hard cash for information, and I figured it might as well be me gettin' the reward as anybody else. After all, I see most everything that goes on in this town.''

"Yes, you do," Nicholas agreed calmly. "Now, tell me the gentleman's name."

"Don't know his name. I only know I got a wire from a man I know down near Dallas. He asked me did I want to earn a good bit on the side, and I figured it might's well be me as the next fella."

"And how did you manage to pass along information about me to this New York gentleman?" Nicholas asked politely.

"I just sent a wire that there was a good-lookin' dandy in town, with a wife and a little girl. I told 'em you was living in a place north of town."

"You told them that, did you?" Nicholas asked, and as one brow lifted inquiringly, the shopkeeper broke out in a sweat.

"Well, that's what I said in the wire. But that was a couple'a weeks ago. And then this morning, when another gent came by and wanted to know whereabouts this place of yours was, I said—'' He broke off abruptly and looked past Nicholas, his mouth agape.

"Problem here, Sheriff?" a voice said.

"Not so's you could notice, stranger," Brace told the man.

"This your early morning friend?" Nicholas asked, his thumb crooking over his shoulder.

"Yeah." Mr. Metcalf gulped again, and backed toward the doorway of his store.

Nicholas turned, pivoting on his heel, and faced the man who stood behind him. Tall, well past middle age, and dressed in a dignified manner, the man directed brilliant blue eyes toward Nicholas, and scanned him from top to bottom.

"I'd heard about you," he said, his words seeming to be drawn from his depths. "I wasn't certain before."

"And now?" Nicholas asked, aware only of a fountain of anger bubbling within.

The stranger shrugged, a negligent gesture, and allowed his gaze to collide fully with that of the man who watched him. "Now, I'm certain."

"You've been on my trail, trying to have me killed?" Nicholas asked.

"Now, why would I do that? I only learned from your wire two weeks ago that you were here, and that you claimed to be my son."

"Claimed?" Nicholas shot him a scornful glance, then turned aside. "You find it difficult to believe?"

Horace Grayson shook his head. "No, I don't suppose so. You have the Grayson eyes. You resemble your sister, Irene."

"I didn't expect you to show up here," Nicholas said harshly. "I only asked a favor of you because my wife insisted you could help. That you would because of Irene's daughter."

The reply was slow in coming, and the words were harsh, uttered as if they were dragged from the depths of the man. "My grandchild?"

"Irene left her for me to raise," Nicholas said firmly. "The will is watertight."

The older man lifted his hand in a silent gesture of agreement. "Perhaps. Probably. Joseph Carmichael was a brilliant man. He would have seen to it. But, know this, Mr. Garvey. If I wanted it to come about, I could have the child."

Nicholas eyed him coolly. "You have that much power?"

"If I didn't, you'd be dead right now. Preston's after you."

The sheriff moved, catching Nicholas's eye, and his face was a study in curiosity. "You want to introduce me to this fella, Garvey?" he asked. "I'm getting the message that he isn't the one who wants you dead and buried."

The shopkeeper darted from sight within the store, and the sheriff stepped into the doorway. "Don't be thinking about sending out a wire anytime soon, Metcalf," he called into the dim interior. "You're walkin' a tightrope right now."

Then he turned back to Nicholas and waited expectantly.

"This man is Horace Grayson, Sheriff. Unofficially, he's my father. But, bear in mind, this is the first time I've laid eyes on the man. And he still hasn't claimed me on any level. Only acknowledged that we share the same bloodline."

"I didn't know you were craving a father's love, Garvey." The words were taunting, and Nicholas's hands formed fists at his sides. "I don't owe you anything, boy. I took care of Irene while she lived, and would have tended the child after her parents died. But I won't allow Preston's hands to touch the girl."

"And how can you guarantee that small miracle?"

"Preston is dealing with a judge who owes me plenty. I put him on the bench, and I can take him off if he doesn't cooperate."

Nicholas considered Horace Grayson's words. "I still don't see why you came here. You could have sent me a wire and let me know what you were doing." And then he remembered something, and cursed himself silently for relaxing his guard for even this short time.

"Was that you, out at the edge of the woods this morning just about dawn?"

"This morning? Hardly. I came in on the early train. At

dawn, I was asleep in my railroad car. I only came here because I want to see the child.''

Nicholas turned to the sheriff. ''I'd say we still have a problem to solve then, Brace. The man I saw early on this morning is still out there somewhere, and I've left Lin and Amanda at the ranch.''

''Did you tell Faith to join them?'' Brace asked. ''She can shoot better than most men, and she carries a gun.''

''There are two guns at the house,'' Nicholas said quietly. ''But they're still just two women and a little girl. And we don't know how many men Preston has in his employ.''

''Well, I'm puttin' old Metcalf in a cell till we get back,'' Brace decided. ''I won't take a chance on him sending any more notes to his friend in Dallas.'' He entered the store and walked to the back, returning moments later, empty-handed. ''He must have scooted out the back door,'' he said gruffly. ''I'm heading for the railroad station. See if I can head him off.''

Snatching up a pair of reins from the hitching rail in front of the store, he lifted himself easily into the saddle. ''Tell whoever comes lookin' for this horse that I borrowed it,'' he said with a nod. His heels dug into the animal's sides and dust flew from beneath the horse's shod feet as he dug for purchase in the dusty road.

''Where is your place?'' Horace asked, tugging his vest into place, eyeing the road that led from town. ''Is there a decent conveyance available?''

''The livery stable should have something you can use. It's down at the end of the street. Can't miss it. A big red barn full of horses and rigs.'' Nicholas turned to walk away, crossing the road to where his own mare stood in front of the sheriff's office.

''How will I find you?'' Horace asked harshly.

''Follow my tracks.''

* * *

"Linnie?" The woebegone voice called from the bedroom, and Lin pushed away from the table, her chair clattering to the floor.

"I'm coming, sweetie," she sang out, almost running in her haste to reach the child. "I'm here, Amanda." And indeed she was, crossing the threshold into the little girl's bedroom in mere seconds.

Amanda sat up in the bed, rubbing her eyes and yawning. "I slept a long time, didn't I? I heard a dog barking, and I thought I was dreaming, 'cause it was still almost dark out." And then she blinked and her blue eyes opened wide, fixing on Lin. "We really do have a dog, don't we? And we're gonna call him Wolf, aren't we?"

"We'll call him whatever you like," Lin said, thinking to herself that no dog had ever looked less like the tawny, wild creatures that had haunted the forests in books she'd read as a child. But if Amanda was set on naming the pup, it would be as she said.

"Come on, sweetie. I'll fix you breakfast. Your dog is in the kitchen, sleeping by the door. You can play with him indoors this morning, after you eat."

"Well, I better get dressed, then," Amanda chirped, tossing back the sheet.

"Perhaps Faith will help you dress, out in the kitchen," Lin told her, choosing clothing from the trunk near the window. A growl from the kitchen alerted her and she stiffened, aware of the dog's warning.

A flash of color caught her eye and she stepped closer to the window, the better to see through the pane of glass. Beyond the barn, a chestnut-colored horse was half revealed, an empty saddle and switching tail visible to view. Lin held her breath, her eyes straining to catch any movement, at the same time searching her mind for direction.

Keep that shotgun handy…and Amanda with you. "I'm

trying to do that, Nicholas,'' she murmured, aware that the long gun was in the kitchen, loaded and waiting beside the pantry door.

"What did you say, Linnie?" Amanda wandered to stand beside her, and Lin snatched her from in front of the window.

"I said you must be hungry," she prevaricated quickly, grasping the child's hand and leading her from the bedroom. The pup stood uncertainly in front of the door, barking once when he caught sight of them.

"You slept in this morning, didn't you?" Faith asked Amanda, and then her gaze flew to touch upon Lin's taut features. "Something has the dog riled," she said quietly.

"There's an extra weapon in the pantry, Faith. You might want to make sure it's ready in case you need to use it," Lin said.

"All right." As casually as if she were told to arm herself on a daily basis, Faith rose and went inside the narrow closet that held kitchenware and foodstuffs. A rifle was on the top shelf, out of Amanda's view and reach, a box of shells beside it. From the kitchen, Lin heard the rattle of metal and the sound of bullets being loaded.

"I think we're all set," Faith said, carrying the gun upright and placing it on the floor beneath the kitchen window. Standing to one side, she moved the curtain a bit, revealing a view of the barn and outbuildings. "Nice mare out there," she said quietly. "Not yours?"

"No," Lin said. "I think we have company."

The pup was stiff-legged and alert, his hackles rising as he viewed the door. Faith lifted the rifle from the floor, and levered a bullet, readying the weapon for firing. "Two men," she said quietly. "One in the barn door, the other behind the tree just to the east of the house."

"Anyone you recognize?" And wasn't that foolish, Lin thought, as soon as the words were out of her mouth. These men were sent from back East, hired gunmen, no doubt, not anyone Faith would be familiar with.

"Don't think so," Faith said. "Small arms. Look like regulation army issue to me. Not that I'm any expert. I only know how to aim and fire, when the need arises."

"What's happening?" Amanda asked, her words a whisper, her eyes huge with fear. Kneeling before the sink, her hands clasped in her lap, she looked up at Lin, even as tears streaked her face. "I want my uncle Nicholas," she sobbed.

"So do I, sweetie. But we don't have him right now. We'll have to fend for ourselves."

The pup had taken up barking, a sharp, harsh sound, different from his playful yapping that had only signified his pleasure in their company. Now he combined a growl with a warning bark, and from outdoors a call answered his challenge.

"You, there in the house. We want to see you on the porch."

Faith laughed aloud. "They must think we're fools."

"No, they think we're city folk, used to fearing for our lives from the scum of society."

Faith smiled, a cool rebuttal to that thought. "Well, they've got a surprise coming, I'd say. I didn't spend hours on end firing a gun to give up so easily to a couple of bullies."

"Are you good?"

"Wanna watch me?" Faith asked boldly. She lifted the window, two inches perhaps, then slid the barrel of the rifle through the opening. Kneeling, she directed the gun toward the barn and held it against her shoulder. Even as Lin watched her finger squeezed gently at the trigger, and with an impact that rattled the windowpanes, a shot rang out.

"Well, damn!" From the barn, a voice called out, and in slow motion a man slid down the edge of the doorframe to settle in the dust, leaning against the jamb. One hand still held a revolver, but it lay in the dirt. His other hand was clutching at a wound, high on his right arm, and blood was staining his shirt sleeve.

"They got me," he called out, and from the shelter of the huge tree that shaded the house from the early morning sun, another shot rang out. The windowpane shattered over Faith's head and glass scattered across the kitchen floor.

"Are you cut?" Lin asked quickly, standing in front of Amanda to shield her from any possible harm.

Faith shook her head, shifting to the other side of the window to take aim at the man, almost fully hidden behind the tree. "No," she said shortly, levering another shell into the barrel, "but that jackass is about to discover he's met his match."

Her rifle fired and she uttered a quiet oath, then turned her head toward Lin. "Take the shotgun and go into the parlor. He's gone around the corner of the house. I'm letting the dog out."

"All right." Lin snatched up the gun from beside the door and dragged Amanda with her, leaving her in the small, central hallway. "Stay put, you hear me?" Lin said harshly, and barely noticed the nod the child offered in response.

Next to the solid front door, a window exploded as a bullet shattered one of the panes of glass, and then buried itself in the far wall. "Y'all better come on out of there," a voice called from the front yard. "I'm gonna set the house on fire if you don't get out on the porch right now."

Lin crept across the floor, lest she be seen through the remaining, intact panes of glass and lifted to her knees just beyond the window. From behind one of the tall trees in the front yard, a man was partially exposed, his hand holding a revolver aimed at the house.

How much good the shotgun would do, she had no idea,

for the target exposed did not lend itself to the scattered shot she would produce with the fat shells the gun held. And she would only have two chances to hit him without reloading. The extra shells were in the pantry, where they could do her no good, and she silently cursed her lack of forethought.

And then the man moved, apparently feeling safe given the lack of response from the house. Peering out from behind the tree, he took one step, then another, exposing himself.

Lin held the gun against her shoulder, sighting down the barrel as Nicholas had shown her. She rested it on the empty windowpane, and waited, hoping against hope she would not have to shoot another human being.

The shooter's attention was drawn away by a shout from the back of the house, and then the sound of a barking dog as Wolf dug in with his claws, body low to the ground as he rounded the side of the building.

"Damn dog," the man said, turning his revolver in Wolf's direction and lifting his arm to fire.

Lin hesitated no longer, her index finger squeezing the first trigger. The shot fanned out as it reached the assailant, and she heard his howl of pain, watched as he doubled over, holding his belly with both arms. And then he lifted the gun again as he fell forward, and fired wildly toward the house.

She felt the shock of a bullet, knew a moment of burning pain in her shoulder, and then was catapulted backward from the window.

Nicholas came up the lane at a gallop, his horse shedding foam, the animal's sides heaving with the effort of the prolonged run. Easing up on the reins, he allowed the mare to slow her pace, even as he took note of the broken pane of window glass in the parlor, in the same glance spotting the man who lay crumpled next to a tree, not fifty feet from the house.

From the porch, Wolf barked a welcome, and Nicholas called out the pup's new name, releasing the dog from his guard post. Tearing across the yard, he spared but one short sniff at the prone figure he passed, then dashed to trot proudly beside Nicholas as the mare made her way with caution around the corner of the house.

"Wolf." The single word came from the back, and the pup looked up at Nicholas. Then, torn between the soft voice calling him and the man he had welcomed, he dashed to answer the woman's summons.

"Lin?" Nicholas spoke her name quietly, and even as he uttered the sound, he knew it was not his wife's voice he'd heard.

"Faith?" His horse rounded the corner, and he scanned the yard, suddenly aware of the man who leaned heavily against the barn. His sleeve bright red with bloodstains, he nevertheless attempted to lift the revolver he held, and Nicholas drew his own gun from his belt and aimed it with care.

"If you value your life, you'll drop that weapon," he said. And then, as the man resolutely shifted, still trying to aim the gun, Nicholas fired, only once. But it was enough to halt the movement, the shot entering high on the felon's shoulder. His gun dropped to the dirt, useless, and the man groaned loudly.

"Nicholas?" Faith stepped out onto the porch, rifle in hand. "I didn't want to kill him, but I had my eye on him."

"Where's Lin?" he asked. "Who shot the fella in the front yard?"

"Lin," she answered. "But he put a bullet in her, Nicholas. Come inside."

He slid from the mare and was on the porch in two steps.

Faith held the door wide and he entered, blinking at the dim light. "Where is she?"

"Uncle Nicholas." From the small hallway, Amanda's cry was broken by tears, and she walked toward him. "My Linnie isn't awake, Uncle Nicholas. Come see."

He brushed past her into the parlor, where the sun's rays had penetrated through the side window and now illuminated Lin's body. The shimmering sunlight almost seemed an obscenity, bringing brilliance to her russet hair, and revealing sharply the lines of her face.

"Lin." Dropping to his knees beside her, Nicholas was unaware of Faith in the doorway, uncaring of the dog who sat at Lin's feet, unable to think of anything but the sight before his eyes. A towel was bound in a makeshift fashion to her shoulder, and even as he made to lift it, Faith stopped him with a bloodied hand.

"No, leave it be until I can find bandages and we can get her on the bed. I'd have her there already, but I had to keep watch out back until you returned."

"You find the bandages and I'll carry her into the bedroom," he said roughly. He glanced up then at Faith, and her quick, uneven smile halted his worst fear. "Will she make it?" he asked, even as she nodded with assurance.

"It's gone straight through, and I don't think it even hit the bone," she told him. "There's a lot of blood, but we can stop that, once we get it cleaned up."

"All right," he said, relief washing through him. He lifted the prone woman, held her tightly to his chest and rose to his feet, barely noticing the weight of her slender form. Amanda followed forlornly behind as he carried Lin across the hallway to the back bedroom where they had, just a short time ago, risen from the rumpled sheets.

"There's a lot of blood, Uncle Nicholas," Amanda said in a whisper. "Is my Linnie gonna be all right?" And at

Nicholas's quick nod of assurance, the child stood aside, watching as Lin was placed on the mattress.

"Go get a couple of towels," Nicholas told her briefly. "See if you can help Faith."

"All right," Amanda answered, and her feet flew as she shot across the room and went to the kitchen. "My uncle Nicholas said I should help," he heard her say.

Faith appeared in the doorway, carrying a basin of water, a box tucked beneath her arm. "I found everything you'll need in the pantry, Nicholas. Amanda has the towels and an old sheet we can use as bandage. I'm going back to the kitchen to keep an eye out. I don't trust that there might not be more of those rascals around."

"Well, if you see a distinguished gentleman riding up in a buggy, don't shoot him," Nicholas thought to tell her. "He's on his way. If he didn't get lost. I won't guarantee how good he is at tracking."

"Hmm…" Faith said, flashing him an enquiring look. "That sounds interesting."

And then she nodded at Lin. "Do you know what to do?"

"I'll manage," he said. "I've seen gunshot wounds before."

"And isn't that something I'll want to ask questions about later?" she said, returning to her vigil in the kitchen.

From the bed, he heard the rustle of fabric and he turned to see Lin's knee rising and then falling again, her head turning on the pillow. Then her eyes opened, and she focused on him. "He was going to shoot the dog."

"Wolf never had so wonderful a champion," Nicholas told her, kneeling quickly beside the bed. He bent to kiss her, inhaling her fragrance, blessing the fates that had protected her from a fatal wound. "I love you," he whispered.

Her lips trembled as she attempted a smile. "See, that wasn't so difficult, was it?"

"I'll never be afraid to say it again, love," he told her. And then he straightened and slid from his jacket and tossed it aside, rolled his sleeves to his elbows and rose to seek out the washbasin that shared space with a towel on the small dresser.

"I'll wash up quickly," he told her. "You don't move one little bit, you hear?"

"I always do what you tell me, Nicholas," she said quietly, and he shot her a dubious look, catching the smile that had only wavered but not faded from her face.

Washing hurriedly, he was back at her side, and had torn the dress from her shoulder, releasing the padding from the wound, when he heard a commotion at the back of the house. The sound of Brace calling his name and the whinny of horses announced help had arrived.

"Hold still," he told Lin. "Everything's under control." And then he looked down at the wound he'd exposed, noting the small entry hole, and the blood still oozing from it. "I need to see the back," he told her, and turned her to her side, away from him, the better to examine the wound.

Somewhere, either on the parlor floor, or in the wall across from the window, was resting a spent shell, for it had departed her body, leaving a raw, gaping hole, from which blood flowed at an amazing rate, once he'd lifted the padding Faith had applied. "Well, damn," he muttered, hearing the gasp of pain as he shifted Lin in the bed.

Her head lolled back, her eyes closing and he felt relief wash through him. She'd fainted, and with any luck at all, he'd have her wound cleaned and bandaged before she awoke. "Faith?" he called out and was rewarded by the woman's quick appearance. "I need a hand here," he told her.

"There's a man in the kitchen who looks enough like you to be your father, Nicholas," Faith said quietly. "Is he the one you were expecting?"

He glared at her. "To hell with him. Brace can take care of things. This is more important."

Faith shrugged, bending to wring out the cloth and placing it on the open wound. "I just thought you might like to know that he's very interested in Amanda."

"I'd hope so," he muttered. "He's her grandfather."

Chapter Sixteen

"**D**id I kill him?" Lin asked, wincing as she attempted to sit up in bed. Nicholas had expected the query before, wondering when she would be willing to face the possibility that she had dealt death to another human.

"Not quite," Nicholas told her, easing a pillow behind her back. "You hit him, though, and he's not a happy man."

Her eyes were shadowed, her expression sober as she turned her face up to peer into his. "I didn't want to kill him," she said. "That's why I didn't fire sooner. But I couldn't let him shoot the dog, could I?"

"No, you did just the right thing," Nicholas answered, wisely keeping his thoughts to himself. He almost wished the idiot had died of his wounds, scattered shot penetrating his belly in several places. But the doctor had announced that he had a chance of living to face a judge. And that in itself might be even better. It would be difficult for Lin to face that fact that she had taken a life. Better that the gunman spend his remaining years in a jail cell, if they didn't decide to hang him.

"Can I get up today?" Lin asked, looking down at the

plate on her lap. "I think this would taste better if I sat at the table."

"Do you?" He grinned at her. "That might be arranged. Do you want to comb your hair or wash your face first?"

"Why? Do we have company?" she asked, glancing toward the doorway.

"Well, after three days, I don't know that he's company any longer."

"Someone's been here for three days?" she asked quickly, surprise lighting her features. "Who on earth…?"

"Amanda's grandfather came to visit. He's been here a couple of times to see her, and he's due to show up this morning for breakfast before he heads back to town for the afternoon train going east."

Lin's mouth fell open, but she recovered quickly. "Amanda's grandfather?" Her mind worked at rapid speed, Nicholas thought, and it shouldn't take long for her to figure this one out. "Your father?" she breathed, the words a whisper.

"The man who lent his body for the deed," he corrected her bluntly. "Not a father, actually. Not in the usual sense of the word." Even to his own ears, his words were harsh and unforgiving, and thinking of the cold, implacable man who had faced him in town just three days since, he could not alter his image into anything much more welcoming. And yet—

"He seems to have taken to Amanda, though," Nicholas conceded.

"Well, he's not *taking* her anywhere…is he?" she finished quietly, her eyes filling with quick tears.

Nicholas shook his head. "No. Get that idea out of your head. She's staying with us." And then as he helped her rise from the bed, and walk carefully to the dresser where he'd prepared a basin of warm water for her use, he added a mention of the plan he had formulated.

"However, we'll be traveling, just as soon as you're able to ride in a buggy."

She looked up at him, then reached for the clean cloth he'd provided. He took it from her hand, wrung it out in the water and proceeded to wash her face with a gentle touch. "Where are we going?" she asked, submitting to his ministrations.

"Back to Collins Creek, and from there to New York." The words were brief, but the promise they made was enough to take her breath away, and she leaned heavily against his side.

"When?" she asked, looking up at him in bewilderment.

"When you're able. We have a couple of weeks leeway. The hearing in New York is set for next month, and we need to be there."

"Who said so?"

"Horace Grayson."

"Amanda's grandfather?" she ventured, turning to lean fully against his chest, her legs seeming to lose their strength.

He nodded and held her firmly, his arms surrounding her. "But not until you can travel without harming your convalescence."

"Pooh!" she said, the sound bringing a smile to his lips. "I'm fine already. Just a little weak around the edges."

And indeed, she had begun to heal more rapidly than he'd expected, her healthy body responding to the salves and poultices Faith had prescribed. "I'll want you to rest another week at least," he said, issuing an ultimatum he intended to stick with.

"All right," she acceded gracefully. "May I comb my hair, please?"

He handed her the comb and led her back to the bed. "Sit right there while I get your dressing gown and find your house shoes."

"In the wardrobe," she told him, drawing the comb through the tangled length of her hair. And then she paused and held the ivory instrument out to him. "Could you do this please?"

"Not as strong as you thought, are you?" he asked, carrying the items she would need to the bed, then settling beside her and turning her to face the headboard. "I'll be glad to be your lady's maid, sweetheart. I can even put a braid in place if you like. I've gotten real good at it the past days, working on Amanda's hair."

"Is she all right? I mean, with Mr. Grayson showing up, and all."

"Seems to be. She hasn't asked many questions, just accepted that he wants to sit with her and talk."

"About what?"

"Mostly her mother. And what she's done since she came to Texas with you. He's asked a lot of questions about you, too, Lin."

"Doesn't he think I'm good enough to—"

"Hush." Nicholas tugged at a lock of hair. "Don't even think that. Amanda has sung your praises, one verse after another. He couldn't help but know that you've cared for her as if she were your own." He laughed, thinking aloud.

"You should have seen Grayson when Amanda read to him from the poetry book you both like so well. She had him fooled that she could actually make out the words, until she went on without turning the page once."

He laid aside the comb and set about braiding her hair. "He thinks she's the brightest child he's ever seen." And then he muttered darkly. "Not that he's ever paid any attention to any other child, if his background can be considered."

"This is different," Lin said quietly. "She's Irene's child, and he acknowledged Irene as his own flesh and blood. Maybe aging has changed him."

"Don't count on it." Nicholas put the last twist in her braid and held it between two fingers. "Now what do I do to tie this thing up?"

"Where's my comb?" she asked, and taking it from his outstretched hand, she untangled several strands of her hair from the teeth and wound them with a practiced touch around the tail he'd formed. They clung where she placed them, and he shook his head in wonder.

"I've never seen such a thing."

"Well, you probably haven't paid much attention to a woman's hair before."

His grin was wide and teasing. "Ah, but I have. Yours, especially, love."

"You like it better loose and messy," she accused him, looking over her shoulder at him. "But I'm not about to face a stranger with my hair hanging down my back."

"Agreed," he said quietly. "That sight is for my eyes alone." And then he turned her to himself, careful of the bandage that wrapped her wound. "As is the rest of this beautiful body of yours."

"I'll wear a scar for the rest of my life," she said quietly.

"Ah, but it will be a long life," he told her. "Every day of it spent with me."

"And with me, too," came a small voice from the doorway.

"Amanda." Nicholas turned to open one arm for the child's benefit. "Come take a look at Lin."

"I'm looking already," she said, approaching the bed with hopeful eyes beaming at the two who had made her their own. "Mr. Grayson is here, Uncle Nicholas. And Wolf didn't even bark at him. I think he likes him now."

"Think so?" Nicholas asked, hugging the child, bringing her into the circle, and then lifting her to his lap. "And how about you? Do you like him?"

Amanda nodded quickly. "He's not as nice as you, and

he doesn't hug me or anything, but he talks nice to me, and he asks a lot of questions." She tilted her head to one side and lifted her face, the better to whisper into Nicholas's ear. "He said he'd like me to call him Grandfather, Uncle Nicholas. Do you think I should?"

She looked puzzled as she waited for Nicholas to reply. And then she spoke again. "I don't think I know what a *grandfather* is. Do you?"

"Oh, yeah, I know," Nicholas answered quietly. "We'll need to talk about it."

Settling Amanda back on the floor, he rose and helped Lin to her feet. Then, together, they went to the kitchen, where their visitor waited.

The night was warm and the window was opened, allowing a breeze to waft its way across the room to the bed where they lay. Nicholas had settled her against himself, her wounded shoulder supported by a pillow, her head nestled against his chest.

"Are you comfortable?" he asked, and she nodded, laughing a bit as she spoke.

"If you're asking if my shoulder hurts, you'd better be prepared for howls of agony if you try to do anything very strenuous," she told him, twisting a curling bit of hair on his chest between two fingers.

"I'm not," he said quickly, as if she'd accused him of salacious thoughts. "Not that I wouldn't like to, but I'm not going to do anything that might cause you pain."

"I know," she said, a touch of satisfaction in her words. "I've had you at my beck and call for three whole days. But, since you've been so nice to me and so deserving, I just thought I'd suggest something that might work."

He stilled beside her, his hand, which had been lightly running the length of her side, pausing in its movement, his fingers pressing firmly against her backside. "Like what?" he asked, caution alive in the two words.

"Like, if I were to lie on my back, and you were to very carefully kneel—"

"No," he said quickly, his hand covering her mouth. "I won't take advantage of you, Lin. Not for anything."

She sighed against his fingers, and the tip of her tongue touched them with care. "I wouldn't call it taking advantage if you…if I…" Her voice trailed off, and she swallowed the words she'd almost spoken aloud. "I think I'm teasing you, Nicholas," she said softly. "Just ignore me, please."

"I think I'd enjoy you teasing me," he said. "But there are other things I'd enjoy even more. First I need to know if we're on the same track, here." He waited, and she felt a heated flush sweep up her throat to cover her cheeks.

Pleasure. She wanted badly to be bold enough to speak the word that might best express the joyous thrill that loving Nicholas brought into being. Yet some residue of shyness, left over from her years of innocence, would not allow it to pass her lips. Such a simple word, yet holding such a vast amount of delight in its syllables.

And somehow he knew what she meant, knew her inability to sound out the phrases that would express the glorious heat and passion he ignited with his touch.

"If I were sure to give pleasure?" He bent to her and pressed his lips where his fingers had rested only an instant before. "It would be an honor, Mrs. Garvey," he said gravely.

"Oh, Nicholas—I do love you so much." She whispered the words, and he groaned against her lips and then murmured a reply that soothed her embarrassment and satisfied the cry of her needy heart.

"It pleases me to think that you want me, Lin. I'll always be here when you feel a desire for me, sweet. When you need me," he said quietly. "As you will be for me. As, in another way entirely, we'll both be for our children when they come along."

And as if those words had opened up a new vista for her, she uttered the same, small, enchanting laugh again. "I hope we have a baby soon," she said. And then her voice held a note of eagerness. "Maybe next spring?"

He brushed her hair from her brow. "I'll certainly do my best to make it happen, love. If that's what you want."

"And you? Do you want a child of your own?" she asked.

"Of course. I suppose every man does, deep down inside." And then he hesitated. "I think you know that Amanda will always be special to me. I don't think I could love her more if she were my own."

"I have a confession to make," she whispered. "I used to pretend that she was mine, that I was really her mother. I felt guilty sometimes, but I don't think Irene would have cared, even if she'd known." She lifted her face a bit more and spoke sweetly, as if she instructed him in a basic manner.

"It takes nine months, Nicholas. You shouldn't dilly-dally if we are to—"

His lips halted her words, and he kissed her more deeply, more ardently, impatient now as he considered how he would do this thing she desired. His hand rose to cup her breast and then his fingers were agile, undoing the buttons of her nightgown. "I'll be careful," he promised, easing it from her, drawing her arm from the full sleeve, and then tossing the garment aside.

"Please, Nicholas. Make love to me," she murmured.

He nodded, anticipation rising within him. And even as he rose above her to kneel between her thighs, lifting them to rest atop his own, he repeated the words he'd spoken but minutes ago. "It would be an honor, Mrs. Garvey."

Probably the most difficult part of leaving was the issue of saying goodbye, Lin decided. Oh, she could handle those in town who had been friendly over the past week or so, and the sheriff, who had become a regular visitor. But taking her leave from Faith caused a pain in her heart, one she thought she might not survive so readily.

Nicholas made plans for Faith to move into the farmhouse, since, now that it had been cleaned up and gotten up to snuff, as he said so eloquently, it really stood in need of a caretaker. And then there was the cow, and the empty chicken coop where Faith's clutch of hens would find adequate shelter. It would be doing them a service if she would agree to live in the place. Cleary would appreciate it, he'd told her.

And Faith had agreed, even now was on her way to move in, bag and baggage. Not that there was a whole lot of baggage to deal with. Not if the wagon pulling near the back porch was any indication. Faith, it seemed, lived simply, and had said she was willing to tend the farm and continue with the work Nicholas had begun.

He would leave her the horses and the wagon for her own use, and she in return would take them to town, where they would purchase a buggy and a second mare to draw it on their return journey to Collins Creek. Anything they had brought with them was easily replaced, Nicholas said.

Faith climbed down from the wagon seat, her eyes turning toward the porch where Lin waited. As always, the woman was radiant, her clear skin glowing, her blue eyes shining with humor and affection. She climbed the steps quickly, and her arms surrounded Lin in an embrace that spoke silently of her love.

"I'll miss you," she said, coming right to the point.

"I know." Lin bit her lip, unwilling to blubber aloud. Yet her heart ached for the loss of friendship. Since the death of Irene, she'd known no other woman to fill that emptiness in her life. And knew she would feel the lack of the deep friendship she had allowed to develop between them.

Yet, Nicholas said they must go, and when all was said and done, he must make that decision. He was a man born and raised in the city, a man perhaps destined for larger horizons than a hay field to the west and a small farming community to the south. They would go to New York for this hearing soon, and returning to the city might intrigue him, if he had any reason to miss the excitement of the society he'd left behind.

No matter. Wherever Nicholas was, she would be with him, and with that she would be content.

"You about ready?" he asked, standing beside the wagon, his gaze intent on her.

"I've packed our clothing, most of it anyway. Some I just left behind, things we can do without."

"All right, then," he said with a nod. "I'll unload Faith's belongings, and she can sort them out later. I don't want to let daylight slip away without some miles behind us."

Faith moved quickly down the steps and reached for a valise. "This won't take long, Nicholas. I've learned to travel light." Her laughter sparkled and Nicholas shot her an admiring glance. And then he picked up a basket in each hand and followed her up the steps and into the house, his gaze meeting Lin's as she held the screened door open for him.

Her quick smile and warm look was a reminder of the night just past, and the night before. Nicholas did not spare his attention, and she rejoiced in the quiet message his beautiful eyes offered. *I love you.* As surely as if he spoke it aloud, she felt the comfort of his heart's song radiate to touch her, penetrating deeply, comforting her. And she was content.

"I've often wondered why a trip never seems as long when you're returning home," she mused.

"Probably because we have a light buggy and a quick-footed mare," Nicholas said, grinning down at her. "And this time we know where we're going."

"We knew last time, when we left that evening, didn't we?" she asked.

"I had a map," he admitted. "But we were traveling blind, sweetheart, and in the dark, to boot. And then we wandered all over the place, covering our tracks before we headed in the right direction."

"Well, I'm glad we'll be home to sleep in our own bed tonight."

"We left our mattress at the farmhouse," he reminded her. "I think we'll be making do in the spare room."

"I don't mind," she whispered. "I slept there alone for a while."

"And I wished I were sharing that bed with you, more than one long night."

She tilted her head back and looked up at him, her smile teasing. "Did you, now?"

"From the first day," he admitted with a crooked grin. "I'm afraid I had designs on you from the very beginning."

"I heard from a lady at the emporium that a young woman in town had her sights set on you before I arrived. I think she was warning me off."

"Patience," he muttered. "I sicced Thomas on her. Probably wasn't a nice thing for me to do, but he didn't mind. Even gave him leave to go calling on her in my new buggy."

"He'll be surprised to see you show up at the bank, won't he? I wonder if he's managed all right."

"He's fine," Nicholas said confidently. "I trained him well. And he won't be very surprised. I wired him that we were coming home."

Home. The word had a pleasing lilt to it, Lin thought. But she'd better not get too attached to it. With travel to New York looming ahead, she might have to rearrange her thinking to include life in a big city once more. She'd think in a positive manner, she decided. Whatever Nicholas wanted would suit her just fine.

The town was dark, every light extinguished. The moon was a thin sliver, high in the sky, but the stars lit their way, past the bank and the mercantile, around one side of the town square where empty benches sat, awaiting tomorrow's occupants.

"That's where I play with Sally," Amanda murmured from her spot between Lin and Nicholas.

"I didn't know you were awake, sweetie," Lin said, bending low to peer into the child's face. "We're almost home."

Amanda yawned widely. "I know. I'll bet Katie will be glad to see us, won't she?" And then she jerked upright. "Is my kitty all right?" Bending, she reached to touch the basket at her feet, where the black, half-grown cat slept.

"She's fine," Lin assured her, tucking the girl closer to her side. "Stay awake for a few more minutes, all right? And then you can sleep for the rest of the night in your bed."

"Yes." The word was a soft whisper, and Amanda slumped a bit, as if she could not sit upright. "I'm gonna sleep for a long, long time, Linnie."

"I suspect you will," Lin answered, amused by the vow, knowing that excitement at being home would no doubt prevail once the sun rose in the sky.

"I'll pull the buggy into the yard through the side gate," Nicholas said quietly. "The mare can wait until morning to go to the livery stable. I'll put a halter on her and tie her lead to a tree. There's a bucket in the shed I can fill with water for her."

"I think the grass could probably use some trimming anyway," Lin said.

They opened the back door and entered the kitchen in the dark. And then saw the glow of a lamp shining beneath the door just off the hallway, where Katie's room was located. The knob turned and Katie appeared, holding her lamp high. "Well, land sakes. Would you look at what the wind blew in." Her face glowing with welcome, she held out her free hand to Amanda, and bent to press a kiss on the child's forehead.

"Welcome home," she said quietly. "I had a notion you'd be finding your way back before long. Mr. Cleary said you had things to do, and he figured you'd be showing up right soon."

"Mr. Cleary was right," Nicholas said agreeably. "Now, if you'll take care of these two for me, Katie, I've a horse to tend to out back."

The stairs were long, Lin thought, and her shoulder ached. No matter how well sprung the buggy, it had been a tedious ride, and she was more than ready for a comfortable bed.

"You go along, now," Katie said comfortably. "I'll take care of the little one. Just you get into bed, you hear?"

Lin yawned, stifling the sound with her palm, and nodded her thanks. The bed was wide and the sheets smelled of fresh air. Her chemise would do for a gown, she decided as she pulled her stockings off and wiggled her toes. It was a simple matter to turn to her undamaged shoulder and place her head on the fluffy pillow.

Nicholas found her there, only ten minutes later. She slept soundly, her hands folded beneath her chin, one leg showing from beneath the sheet, its slender lines beckoning him. He stripped quickly, securing the door before he stretched out behind her. One long arm circled her waist, and he pulled her into the cradle of his body.

She grumbled beneath her breath, and he grinned. Her hair was as he liked it, tangled from the wind, unpinned in a careless manner, loose around her shoulders and down her back. She was all his, this woman he'd claimed. And he smiled as he recalled the first night she'd spent in this house. Remembered his solitary stroll across the yard, smoking a cigar as he wondered how he would keep his hands from her.

And now she belonged to him.

Chapter Seventeen

New York City

An oasis in the midst of the city, Central Park served only to add to the spirit of homesick ennui that held Lin in its grasp. At the edge of a duck pond, Amanda held court over a flock of birds who fought noisily over the food she tossed over their backs. Backing from the creatures, she turned to offer a gleeful grin at Lin.

"I think they like me," she said, laughing aloud. She emptied the sack Lin had provided for the ducks' luncheon with a flourish of seeds scattering hither and yon and then scampered to the relative safety of the park bench, drawing her feet high from the few stragglers who followed her flight.

"This is fun," she exclaimed. "I wish Uncle Nicholas was here to see the ducks with us. Don't you?" Looking up at Lin, she was the picture of a well-to-do young lady, albeit only a very youthful version. Celebrating her sixth birthday in New York City would be an occasion to remember, complete with a formal photograph taken at a studio and a late supper at a restaurant Lin had never visited.

Amanda and Lin had both visited a well-known modiste,

where clothing had been made to order. Even now, they were as well-garbed as any fashionable female in the city. And yet…Lin looked upward at the blue sky…it was not enough. Her most fervent wish was to be back in Texas, where that same sky shone a more brilliant blue, where the clouds floated like fleecy cabbages high above, and where the sun burned with a merciless heat during the long days of summer.

"Ah, here you are." Nicholas appeared before them, his smile benevolent as he scanned them. And well he might be pleased, she thought with a trace of rancor. It was because of him that they presented such a delightful appearance. One that matched his own. "I've finished that bit of business, and we're free for the rest of the day. What would my ladies like to do?"

"Would you like to feed the ducks with me, Uncle Nicholas?" Amanda asked, her feet touching the ground as she slid from the bench.

"That would be my fondest wish," he prevaricated, with a sidelong look at Lin, as if he would share his amusement with her.

"When will we be in court?" she asked, as he searched his pockets for money with which to purchase another sack of food for the spoiled creatures in the pond.

He looked distracted for a moment, then pressed coins into Amanda's palm and waved her on her way to where a small stand was tended by an elderly gentleman. They watched together as she skipped down the path and paused to speak to the vendor.

"Tomorrow morning," he said quietly, then turned his attention fully on Lin. "What's wrong, sweetheart?"

"Nothing," she said brightly, aware that he saw beneath her facade of cheerful interest.

"Tired of the city already?" he asked, settling beside her on the bench.

"You may as well stand, Nicholas," she said. "Amanda will be here in a moment and you've committed yourself to the delightful pastime of dodging duck doo-doo."

"Duck doo-doo? Is that closely related to horse droppings?"

"Well, whatever it is, mind you wipe your boots on the grass before we go back to the hotel."

Amanda dashed up, breathless and vibrant. "I'm ready, Uncle Nicholas." She cocked her head and looked up at him. "If you held me, the ducks wouldn't be able to peck at my shoes."

"And so you'd allow them to peck at mine, I suppose," he returned, bending to lift her in his arms.

"You have bigger feet and they won't scare you," she announced, and then looked over his shoulder at Lin. "We'll be right back, Linnie, and then maybe we can go to that place where they have pink ice cream in dishes."

"I told you you were spoiling her," Lin called after them, and received only a flash of white teeth in response as Nicholas turned his head to grin at her.

Indeed, the restaurant they visited had pink ice cream in pretty dishes, but Amanda was allowed a dip only after she had eaten her luncheon. Lin struggled with a plate of delicately flavored seafood and noodles, and felt herself under Nicholas's watchful eye as they walked through the array of tables toward the entrance half an hour later.

"Are you feeling well?" he asked, one hand under her elbow as they crossed the avenue. The smell of horses, blending with the ever present scent of manure, made her stomach churn, as if she were surrounded by a mass of strange and unfamiliar circumstances. And indeed she was.

It had been only a few months since she'd lived here in the city, but in that length of time she'd come to appreciate the wide-open spaces of Texas, had learned to love the slow pace of life and the friendly atmosphere of a small town.

"I'm just a little nauseous," she said in an undertone, thankful for his support as they dodged the leavings of a passing horse and carriage.

"Do you think you're coming down with something?" He sounded more than concerned now, worry roughening his voice, and she hastened to reassure him.

"No, of course not. I'm just feeling lost in the crowd, I think."

They had reached the sidewalk, and Nicholas pressed their way toward the hotel, Amanda skipping beside him, clinging to his other hand. "Maybe a nap would settle your stomach," he suggested, waiting as the doorman held the ornate door for their entrance.

"I want you to feel well in the morning when we appear in court."

"I will," she told him, scraping up a smile for his benefit.

The courtroom was crowded with reporters waiting outside the double doors, their queries tossed about in a jumble of words as Nicholas ushered his charges past their ranks. "Ignore them," he muttered beneath his breath, and then offered a nod to one persistent gentleman who tugged at his sleeve.

"We'll give you a statement after the hearing," he said quietly, and with that the crowd subsided, allowing them passage.

The judge looked threatening, Lin thought, and Amanda was subdued, her feet dangling from the chair she occupied, her eyes wide as she surveyed the small chamber. To their left was a table at which Vincent Preston sat beside another gentleman, both of them dressed in black. Lin met her adversary's gaze and felt the heat of his anger seep into her very pores, so volatile was his expression as he scanned her. And then he transferred his attention to the child be side her.

Amanda was blissfully unaware of the degree to which she was observed, intent only on the judge, flinching visibly when he banged his gavel on the desk, calling the court to order. "He's noisy," she whispered, turning to Lin with a frown.

"I think he scares me," she added in a small voice. "Are you sure I have to talk to him?"

"We don't know for certain," Lin said quietly. "We'll wait and see."

A lengthy petition was read, then commented on by the lawyer who represented Vincent, followed by questions by the judge, who seemed unimpressed by the glowing report of Vincent's suitability to be guardian to his deceased partner's child.

And then it was time for Nicholas to respond. He had chosen not to be represented by a lawyer, and his words were simple and to the point. Stating the wishes of his half sister and her husband, he told how Amanda had been brought to him, how he had provided a home for her, and related the date of his marriage to Lin.

The judge slanted a long look at him as Nicholas took his seat, and then settled his attention on Lin. "Are you Carlinda Donnelly, young woman?"

She rose. "I am, sir."

"And did you marry Mr. Garvey for the express purpose of providing him with a degree of respectability in order for him to be a fit guardian for the child?"

Lin felt a blush rise to cover her cheeks. "No, sir. I did not. I married Mr. Garvey because I love him, and my greatest delight is in living in his home and helping him provide a good life for Amanda."

"Well done," Nicholas whispered, touching her skirt with a discreet tug.

"Are you familiar with Mr. Preston?" the judge inquired.

"Yes, sir, I am."

"And do you consider him to be equally as good a candidate for the child's guardian?"

The attorney sitting beside Vincent rose quickly. "Your honor, I must protest. We know this woman's opinion is slanted."

"Sit down," the judge ordered, looking through his spectacles at the attorney. "I am asking her opinion for my own reasons." He looked again at Lin. "Well?"

"I wouldn't allow any child to be under Mr. Preston's care if it were in my power to stop it from taking place," she said firmly. "If Amanda's parents had wanted such a thing to happen, they would have made provision for it in their wills."

The judge folded his hands and leaned forward, his eyes narrowing. "May I ask you why you feel so strongly, young lady?"

"Mr. Preston has made it his business to send men of low repute to try and take Amanda by force. They were under his orders to bring her to New York, and made no effort to ensure her safekeeping, only handled her roughly. He has tried to have my husband killed in order to have a better chance for custody, and—"

"Your honor! I must object to this woman's scandalous lies. She has nothing on which to base her story." Vincent's attorney was livid with rage.

"Ah, but she has, your honor." From the back of the hearing room, a strong voice demanded attention, and the judge looked at the speaker with respect.

"Mr. Grayson? What do you know about this matter?"

Vincent looked over his shoulder and paled visibly as Horace Grayson walked to the front of the room, halting in front of the judge's high desk. Vincent leaned toward his lawyer and muttered beneath his breath; and beside her, Lin felt Nicholas's tension as if it were a viable entity.

"Mr. Preston has sought to bring bodily harm to Nicholas Garvey and his family. I have proof of this. One ruffian is outside the courtroom as we speak and is willing to testify to that end. Another person has given me a written statement regarding Mr. Preston's plan to bring about an attempt on Garvey's life."

"Your honor," Vincent's attorney said hastily. "This man is prejudiced in this matter. It has come to our attention that Horace Grayson is none other than the father of Nicholas Garvey, a relationship he has avoided acknowledging in the past."

"And what bearing does that have on this issue?" the judge asked mildly.

"He has shown himself not to be trusted," the lawyer blustered, unwilling to look at Mr. Grayson, his hands busily shuffling his papers as he spoke.

"I don't see the connection. However, we will delve into the subject." He turned to Mr. Grayson. "Are you Nicholas Garvey's father?"

Mr. Grayson nodded. "I am his father, yes. I was not aware of his existence for many years, but once I knew who he was, I watched his progress as he rose in the business community in the city. I didn't approach him until he offered an olive branch, so to speak, in my direction, thinking he would not be pleased to have it bandied about that we had a relationship of sorts."

"And how have you come into this case?"

"My son asked for help, and I notified authorities and those who had connections with Mr. Preston to help me with my investigation. I ask at this time that the court press charges against Vincent Preston for the attempted murder of my son and his wife, and the abduction of the child they are raising as their own."

"And you have proof?"

"My lawyer is waiting in the anteroom with a file for your attention."

The gavel banged. "We will recess for an hour in order to give me opportunity to review the facts in this matter. In the meantime, Mr. Vincent is remanded to another room, where he will be under observation until such time as this matter is resolved."

Nicholas lifted Amanda, and with his free arm around Lin's waist, they left the courtroom. Behind them, Vincent was sputtering loudly, his attorney trying without avail to silence his threats against half a dozen people.

"Where are we going?" Lin asked, aware that she was being hustled by two uniformed men before them and two more in their wake, as they left the building. A carriage awaited at the foot of the ornate stairway before the courthouse, and Nicholas bundled his two charges in, just a few feet ahead of the mob of reporters who had followed them closely.

"You told them you'd give them a statement," she reminded Nicholas.

"I lied." He grinned at her. "I think we're home free, sweetheart. Grayson said he'd contact us at the hotel. And while we're waiting, I'll send off some correspondence just to keep things rolling, both here and in Texas."

"And then what?" she asked. "Have you decided what we will do next?" And if he said that this bustling city was his choice of a home? If he missed the noise and the flurry of traffic and the excitement of financial dealings he'd been a part of here, then what would happen?

His head tilted a bit as he considered her. "What are you thinking, Lin? Have you changed your mind about living in Texas?"

She shook her head quickly. And then halted the movement. "I'll do whatever you like, Nicholas. If Collins Creek is your choice, I'll be more than happy to live there. If you decide to stay in the city, I'll be content to be here with you and Amanda."

"Neither of those options appeals to me any longer," he said quietly. "I think we'll discuss this later, when we're in a more secluded spot." His glance at Amanda was significant, and Lin nodded in agreement.

To love, honor and obey. She recalled those words from the ceremony that was actually a blur in her memory. She certainly loved him. He was the most honorable man she'd ever known, and while obedience wasn't her strong suit, she would do whatever Nicholas asked of her. Whatever he had up his sleeve, so long as it involved their being together, she was determined to agree with his plans.

Nicholas stood with his back against the hotel room door, and his hand reached toward the two females across the room. "Ladies," he said solemnly. "I have the verdict of the judge in my hand. Would you like to hear it?"

Lin's heart pounded beneath her breasts, and she touched her cheeks with trembling hands. "Please, Nicholas. Don't make me wait."

He opened the envelope and scanned it quickly. "It says that full custody of the child in question has been granted to Nicholas and Carlinda Garvey. Her financial matters are to be handled jointly by Nicholas Garvey, in whatever area he chooses to call his home outside of the city of New York, and in this city, under the direct supervision of Amanda's grandfather, Horace Grayson. Mr. Grayson has been given the privilege of visitation with the child when it is mutually agreeable to the two gentlemen in question." He paused. "There's a footnote. Vincent Preston is being held for trial."

He looked up at Lin and his smile was a thing of rare beauty. "Does that suit you, sweet?" he asked.

"What does it mean, Uncle Nicholas?" Amanda asked in a small voice.

He bent to lift her in his arms, beckoning Lin to join them. "It means, my little girl, that you are mine. Mine and Lin's to share. We are your legal guardians from this moment on."

"Will you ever get to be my mama and papa, so I can have my own family?"

"Is that what you want?" Nicholas asked her solemnly.

"Oh, yes. I want to call you my papa, and my Linnie can be my mama."

"That suits me just fine," Nicholas said, leaning to whisper in Amanda's ear. "Why don't you call your new mama by that name and see if she answers you."

"Mama?" Amanda allowed the word to roll off her tongue and then repeated it.

"I like the way that sounds," Lin said, fearful of being teary eyed in front of the child, yet unable to hold back the emotion that enveloped her. "I'd like to be your mama," she said, her voice breaking on the words. "I've always thought it would be wonderful to call you my own."

Amanda sighed, snaking one arm around Nicholas's neck, the other encompassing Lin's, drawing them together as a unit. "Do you remember when we all kissed each other one time when we were back home?" she asked. "Could we do it again?"

"I believe that could be arranged," Nicholas said. And so the ceremony was performed, much as it had been on that day only months before, when the kisses had been given and received in the wide foyer of their home in Collins Creek.

"Now it's really true," Amanda said. "When can we go home?"

* * *

"And you, Lin? Are you ready to go home?" They lay in the bed, high in the hotel, listening to the hubbub of nighttime noises from the street below, where carriages and buggies still made their way past the row of hotels and restaurants on this busy avenue. His arms held her in an embrace that still made allowances for her wound, and his loving had included special attention given to the scars she would wear as a reminder of their brush with peril.

"Wherever you are, Nicholas, is home to me," she said quietly, meaning the words from the depths of her heart. She could adapt to any place in the world, so long as Nicholas shared the same home and breathed the same air as she.

"I told you I wasn't content to go back to Collins Creek forever," he reminded her, "and I think I need to let you know my thoughts on that."

"You also said you didn't plan on staying here in the city," she said.

"Is that agreeable with you?"

"Yes, I'll go with you no matter where you take us."

"My thoughts are on a piece of property north of Collins Creek," he told her. "One I thought I might purchase from Cleary. I spoke to him briefly about it, and he seems quite agreeable to selling that thousand acres to me. It seems he and Augusta are happy to stay where they are."

"And you?" she asked. "Where will you be happiest? Are you weary of business and the sounds of the city?"

"I've found little appeal here," he said. "My best times have been in Texas. At the ranch where we began our marriage."

She held her breath. It seemed almost too good to be true. "The ranch? We'd be going back to the ranch?"

"Not exactly," he said, his words slow. "I thought to build a new place for us, down the road a ways from the old house, something a bit larger, more modern, with room for several more occupants, and of course, Katie, should she decide to come with us. What do you think?''

"Could Faith stay on in the old house, then?'' Aware of the hopeful tone of her voice, she held her breath, and was relieved when Nicholas laughed softly.

"Even if I think she's a beautiful woman?'' And then he squeezed her against himself and rocked her in his embrace. "Of course she can. That was part of my plan.''

"Oh, Nicholas,'' she whispered. "I couldn't have thought of anything more perfect.'' And then she pushed at his chest. "You're planning on breeding horses, aren't you? You're wanting to buy a stud to breed with Faith's mare. Just like you planned before.''

"Yes, that's a part of it. But there's more. I want to expand the place, build small homes for hired help, maybe a bunkhouse for extra hands. I have my sights set on ranching. Your city man is ready to shed his suits for denim trousers and settle down.''

"It sounds wonderful, but can we afford all that?'' she asked, thinking of the enormous amount of money that would be involved in such an undertaking.

"Oh, yes, love. Your husband has a number of investments that have paid off well, and the bank in Collins Creek will be making money for years to come. I'll warrant that Thomas would like to be the manager there, and we're not going to be so far away that I can't keep an eye on things if necessary.''

"A new house.'' She closed her eyes, envisioning a wide porch, with a turret on one end, and a room high above where she might look out upon the acres of pasture and the herds of horses he would raise.

"Are you already planning it?'' he asked, his words teasing her gently.

"I'm so happy, Nicholas,'' she said, her arms sliding

around his neck, her face buried in his throat. "You've made all my dreams come true."

"Not all of them, I'm sure," he said. "We have a few more plans to set in motion."

"I want a porch swing," she said. "And a room for our children to play, where they can have their toys and books scattered about and no one will care."

"What children?" he asked idly. "Is there something you need to tell me?"

"Maybe," she said. "We should know for certain within a few weeks if your work has shown results."

Epilogue

"**W**hat do you think?" he asked, standing behind her in order to shield her from the chill wintry wind. His hands pressed firmly against her swollen belly, and she clasped her own over his fingers. Beneath his palm, a tiny foot or elbow nudged him, and Nicholas laughed aloud.

"My son is passing judgment," he said cheerfully. "He likes the house thus far."

"So do I," Lin agreed. "I'll like it better when it's finished though. When do you think we can move in?"

"Not until the weather breaks," he told her. "Another month probably."

"That's after the baby's arrival."

"You said it would be a week or so, yet. Don't you want to stay in Collins Creek for that?"

"Katie will be here," she said, "and Faith will help. She's already offered."

"I want you to have the best medical attention we can get," he said quietly. "You're my very life, Lin. You and Amanda have made me a happy man, and I can only look forward to more of the same, once this rascal makes his appearance. But I won't take any chances with this."

"It may not be a boy, you know. What if it's a girl?" she asked.

"Not a chance, sweetheart," he assured her. "I spoke to him just last night, and he told me he's already planning on learning how to ride in a couple of years."

She laughed aloud. "Is that what you were doing? Talking to your child?"

"My son," he said, correcting her gently.

"You'll wait until I think he's old enough to get on a horse before you put him on the saddle in front of you," she said sharply.

"Until he's out of diapers," he agreed.

"And then some," she muttered, aware that this sham dispute was but another in a long line of such discussions they'd held during the past several months.

"You're cold," he said, feeling a shiver travel the length of her spine. "Let's get you out of the weather."

They climbed into the buggy and he tucked the robes around her, lifting her collar to protect her neck from the wind's bite. Then he picked up the reins and the mare leaned forward, drawing the vehicle into motion.

"We'll stay with Faith tonight, and then head for Collins Creek in the morning," he told her. "I probably shouldn't have brought you here so late in your pregnancy. I don't know how I let you talk me into it."

She smiled, a secret, joyous expression of pure bliss lifting her lips as she felt the drawing of her muscles again. It had begun yesterday, with a backache, and Katie had assured her that she'd be in her bed within a day or two. And so she'd persuaded Nicholas to bring her here—here where the babe had been conceived in the old house, where she'd found happiness beyond her wildest dreams.

It was a short trip to the house, a light snowfall providing a magical setting for the trip. There, Katie, Amanda and

Faith awaited them, and Katie's eyes were sharp as she looked closely at Lin's smile.

"You've done it, haven't you, girl?" she said, the query more closely resembling a statement of fact.

"Done what?" Nicholas asked quickly, looking from one woman to the other, as Faith laughed softly, her hands on Amanda's shoulders.

"I lied," Lin said simply. "I told you there was no chance of the baby being born for a couple of weeks yet."

"You lied." Nicholas looked baffled, and then his brow rose, and his voice followed suit. "You lied? You lied to me? You're going to have the baby? Here?"

"I think so," she said. And then, as a solid contraction caused her to catch her breath and bite at her lip, she nodded emphatically. "I'd say it was a certainty."

It was a boy. He waited until it was almost dark before making his appearance, and Amanda had long since given up staying awake, and was sleeping soundly in the next room. Faith and Katie worked together well, Nicholas decided, coaxing and cajoling their patient. He was given the task of holding her hand and wiping her forehead. That he suffered along with each pain was no surprise to him, for if Lin felt the agony of childbirth on his behalf, he intended to share every groan she uttered.

And so he did. And when the boy, the beautiful, black-haired son Lin offered into his keeping was placed in his arms, he shed tears. Katie and Faith were kind enough to turn aside, as if unable to watch his humble attendance on the child of his heart. But Nicholas felt no loss of pride in his reaction to the babe he held.

"He's more than I dreamed of," he told Lin, settling beside her on the bed. "I think he looks a bit like me, don't you?" His smile was hopeful, and she matched it with one of her own.

"Of course he does," she said practically. "I looked at you every day for a pattern while he was forming inside me. Who else should he resemble?" She watched him, aware of the pride in his expression, the strength in his hands, the love in his eyes. "What shall we call him?" she asked.

"We have a friend in Collins Creek who named his son in my honor, you know," Nicholas said. "Could we return the favor?"

"You want to name him Cleary?" she asked, frowning.

"No, of course not. I'd thought we'd call him Jonathan. It's Cleary's first name."

"Oh, I suppose I knew that, but I'd forgotten." She considered the idea a moment and found it appealing. "What about a middle name?"

Nicholas cleared his throat. "I have an idea for that, too. But it has to be what you want, Lin." He met her gaze and spoke the words slowly. "I'd like to call him Jonathan Grayson Garvey."

"For your father," she breathed, and then she smiled her approval. "I think he'd like that."

"He's made it his business to keep a check on you during the past months, you know. Each wire he's sent, every letter he wrote to Amanda, he asked about you and about the baby. He's planning on traveling here when he hears the news. I'll be sending him a wire when I get a chance to go to town."

"Have you forgiven him then, for his failures?" she asked.

Nicholas was silent. "I can't, Lin. Not yet, though I've tried. It was too long a time of neglect on his part for me to forget so quickly. I think he's a different man than the one who sired me thirty-five years ago, but that remains to be seen. I know he cares about Amanda, and he's diligent in his record keeping as to her legal and financial affairs.

"And most important, it's because of him that Vincent Preston is in prison even now." He met her gaze. "We owe him much, it seems."

"Then we'll call Jonathan by your father's name, too."

"Just like that?" he asked, the query a reminder of other days, when they had come to agreement so readily.

"Just like that. I love you, Nicholas."

"And I love you, Mrs. Garvey," he told her quietly.

"I know. And that fact makes me the happiest woman on the face of the earth."

"And me the most blessed of all men."

* * * * *

researching the cure

The facts you need to know:

- **One woman in nine** in the United Kingdom will develop breast cancer during her lifetime.

- Each year **40,700** women are newly diagnosed with breast cancer and around **12,800** women will die from the disease. However, survival rates are improving, with on average 77 per cent of women still alive five years later.

- **Men can also suffer from breast cancer**, although currently they make up less than one per cent of all new cases of the disease.

Britain has one of the highest breast cancer death rates in the world. Breast Cancer Campaign wants to understand why and do something about it. Statistics cannot begin to describe the impact that breast cancer has on the lives of those women who are affected by it and on their families and friends.

**During the month of October
Harlequin Mills & Boon will donate
10p from the sale of every
Modern Romance™ series book to
help Breast Cancer Campaign
in *researching the cure.***

Breast Cancer Campaign's scientific projects
look at improving diagnosis and treatment
of breast cancer, better understanding how
it develops and ultimately either curing the
disease or preventing it.

Do your part to help

Visit <u>www.breastcancercampaign.org</u>

And make a donation today.

researching the cure

2 Books
and a surprise gift!

We would like to take this opportunity to thank you for reading this Mills & Boon® book by offering you the chance to take TWO more specially selected titles from the Historical Romance™ series absolutely FREE! We're also making this offer to introduce you to the benefits of the Reader Service™—

- ★ **FREE home delivery**
- ★ **FREE gifts and competitions**
- ★ **FREE monthly Newsletter**
- ★ **Exclusive Reader Service offers**
- ★ **Books available before they're in the shops**

Accepting these FREE books and gift places you under no obligation to buy, you may cancel at any time, even after receiving your free shipment. Simply complete your details below and return the entire page to the address below. You don't even need a stamp!

YES! Please send me 2 free Historical Romance books and a surprise gift. I understand that unless you hear from me, I will receive 4 superb new titles every month for just £3.65 each, postage and packing free. I am under no obligation to purchase any books and may cancel my subscription at any time. The free books and gift will be mine to keep in any case.

H5ZEF

Ms/Mrs/Miss/Mr ....Initials......................................

BLOCK CAPITALS PLEASE

Surname...

Address...

....

....Postcode..................................

Send this whole page to:
UK: FREEPOST CN81, Croydon, CR9 3WZ